Robert Thorogood is the creator of the hit BBC One TV series *Death in Paradise*. He also co-created the spin-off shows, *Beyond Paradise* and *Return to Paradise* and has written a series of Death in Paradise novels featuring DI Richard Poole. Robert's first Marlow Murder Club novel, *The Marlow Murder Club*, is now a major TV series starring Samantha Bond as Judith Potts. A second series is on the way.

Robert was born in Colchester, Essex. When he was ten years old, he read his first proper novel – Agatha Christie's *Peril at End House* – and he's been in love with the genre ever since. He now lives in Marlow in Buckinghamshire with his wife, children and two whippets called Wally and Evie.

Follow him on X @robthor

Also by
ROBERT THOROGOOD

The Marlow Murder Club Mysteries
The Marlow Murder Club
Death Comes to Marlow
The Queen of Poisons

The Death in Paradise Mysteries
A Meditation on Murder
The Killing of Polly Carter
Death Knocks Twice
Murder in the Caribbean

MURDER
ON THE
MARL⬤W
BELLE

ROBERT THOROGOOD

ONE PLACE. MANY STORIES

HQ
An imprint of HarperCollins*Publishers* Ltd
1 London Bridge Street
London SE1 9GF

www.harpercollins.co.uk

HarperCollins*Publishers*
Macken House, 39/40 Mayor Street Upper,
Dublin 1, D01 C9W8, Ireland

This edition 2025

3

First published in Great Britain by
HQ, an imprint of HarperCollins*Publishers* Ltd 2025

Copyright © Robert Thorogood 2025

Robert Thorogood asserts the moral right to be identified as the author of this work.
A catalogue record for this book is available from the British Library.

ISBN: HB. 978-0-00-856737-8
TPB: 978-0-00-856744-6

MIX
Paper | Supporting
responsible forestry
FSC
www.fsc.org
FSC™ C007454

This book contains FSC™ certified paper and other controlled sources to ensure responsible forest management.

For more information visit: www.harpercollins.co.uk/green

This book is set in 11/15.5 pt. Bembo by Type-it AS, Norway

Printed and Bound in the UK using 100% Renewable Electricity at CPI Group (UK) Ltd, Croydon, CR0 4YY

For Eileen Breathwick

(1934-2024)

Chapter 1

Once a year, Mrs Judith Potts liked to 'beat the bounds' of her property. It was something her village had done when she'd been growing up on the Isle of Wight, and she'd been delighted when she'd arrived at Oxford University to discover that her college, Somerville, conducted the same ceremony. It involved finding a large stick, and then using it to beat the ground that marked the perimeter of the land that was owned. It was carried out, of course, to check that no neighbours had encroached during the previous year, but, for Judith, it was also an exercise in psychological geography. It was her saying, 'This is my world. Within this area I feel safe.'

She always chose the day of the autumn equinox for the ritual. It was, she felt, the perfect time to check that everything in her life was in order before she hunkered down for the long months of winter.

As she hunted for a branch in the little copse of trees to the side of her house, she marvelled at how very unremarkable the weather was. It wasn't warm, it wasn't cold, there was only the gentlest of breezes tugging at the leaves on the trees, and the sky was a uniform grey. It was mild – that was the word, Judith realised. She hated the word mild. It hadn't even been cold enough for her to put on her woollen cloak.

She loved wearing her cloak, especially on the day she beat the bounds. Wearing it while swishing her stick about the place – ideally in a storm-tossed wind – made her feel like D'Artagnan or Edmond Dantès. The fact that she was a pleasingly plump seventy-nine-year-old woman didn't get in the way of her self-image as a swashbuckling hero.

Some years, Judith looked for something nice and whippy to attack the various weeds and nettlebeds she let grow around her garden, but this year she was delighted to find a thicker branch on the ground. It had a real heft to it, and, as she picked it up, she noted how very gnarled and knotty it was. Yes, she thought, it would do very well indeed. She could do some damage with this.

She took the stick up her little driveway, pausing only briefly to retrieve the cut-glass tumbler of whisky she'd earlier placed on the wonky bird table. Then, with her stick in one hand and a full glass of whisky in the other, she started to tap on the ground around the edge of her land – or as much of it as she could reach. The laurel hedge along the side of her house was now well over three times her height and joyously out of control, she noted with satisfaction. Next, she picked her way over a pile of wrecked pallets that she only remembered existed once a year – on this very day – and, as she did every year, she vowed that she'd get someone around to remove them while also knowing that she wouldn't ever get around to it.

Then, Judith stepped onto the thick grass of her lawn and smiled in satisfaction. It had been over a year since she'd lit a colossal bonfire in her garden, and it was still possible to see evidence of its existence. A large circle of grass in the middle of the lawn was far more lush than the surrounding area. She took a ruminative slug of her whisky and let the stick drag behind her as she made her way towards the river at the bottom of her garden.

She considered how things had changed since she'd let Becks and Suzie into her life and they'd started catching killers together. While she knew she was far happier now than she'd been before, there was still the smallest part of her – barely the size of an aniseed pip – that felt uncomfortable letting them get so close. Showing people her true self made her feel itchy, and she didn't quite know what to do with this feeling of discomfort. The truth was, she enjoyed solving crimes with her friends just as much as she enjoyed closing the door on the world and sitting in bed with rounds of buttered toast and a good crossword.

Judith held her left hand up so she could look at her wedding ring. It was all very well larking about the place catching killers, but only she understood the true meaning of the gold-coloured band. It represented who she really was.

Judith downed a good slurp of whisky, letting the warm glow spread through her and chase away the chill that had crept in. The answer, she told herself, was not to think about the past. Instead, she took her big stick to a particularly lush bed of nettles that bordered the bluebell wood. After a few minutes of hearty decapitations, she felt much better, and was able to continue her journey without any further qualms.

She moved along the riverbank, tapping her stick along the old bricks of her boathouse, and then approached the walled vegetable garden that had a blackberry bush spilling over the top of it with the sort of vigour that would have given the prince from *Sleeping Beauty* pause. She then lost quite a few minutes plucking the gorgeous berries from the canes and interspersing her mouthfuls of blackberries with the last dregs of her whisky. This was more like it, she told herself. Life was for pleasure, and there was nothing more pleasurable than fresh fruit from the vine.

Once she'd had her fill, her lips still stained violet from the berries, Judith carried on around the boundary of her property. Her broken-down Jaguar had made it through another year on its flat tyres, half in and half out of the garage. The wooden seat of the swing she'd played on whenever she'd visited her great-aunt as a child was still hanging from one old rope. And the collapsed wall that separated her land from a nearby stream was still just as collapsed, although she was pleased to see that in the last year a buddleia had taken root at the top of the pile of rubble.

Throwing her stick into the Thames, Judith set off back towards her house, and was surprised to see an old Volvo estate car parked up. She'd not heard anyone arrive. There was also a woman standing by her front door.

'Hello?' Judith called out.

'Oh, there you are,' the woman said, turning to face Judith.

As she approached, Judith could see that the woman was in her mid-sixties, had straight brown hair and was incredibly thin. The jeans she was wearing were like drainpipes and her arms seemed like sticks in her loose white blouse. Judith was briefly put in mind of a praying mantis.

'Can I help you?' Judith asked.

'I hope so,' the woman said. 'I'm Verity Beresford,' she added, and paused, perhaps expecting Judith to know her name. 'I'm sorry to call unannounced, but I'm worried about my husband. He vanished last night and didn't come home. And he's not answering his phone, it's going straight through to voicemail. It's not even ringing.'

Judith felt a little surge of adrenaline.

'Does he often go away like this?' she asked.

'No, never! I mean, actually he goes away every week, but he always lets me know when he'll be out. Him suddenly vanishing like this has never happened before.'

Judith looked at the panicking woman in front of her and knew she could only have one response.

'Why don't you come in?' she said. 'And let's see if we can work out what's happened to him together?'

Judith opened her front door and led Verity into the kitchen, where she clicked on the kettle.

'It's very kind of you to help,' Verity said.

'I'm not sure I'll be any help.'

'But of course you will. You've been the greatest help to the town. When Oliver hadn't returned by this morning, you were the first person I thought of. Although that's not quite true, I rang the police first.'

Judith scoffed, understanding Verity's problem well. As she'd learned when her neighbour Stefan Dunwoody had gone missing a few years before, the police didn't immediately treat the absence of an adult as being in any way suspicious. It had been deeply frustrating for Judith then, and she could see how frustrating it was for Verity now.

'They fobbed you off,' Judith said as she poured scalding water into a large brown teapot.

'You're right,' Verity said. 'They said they couldn't take an interest for forty-eight hours and that most people turned up well within that time frame.'

'But what makes you so sure he won't?'

'I was with him just before he went missing last night. We were on a boat trip on the Thames.'

'How lovely.'

'It was a rather special evening, as it happens. You know the Marlow Amateur Dramatic Society?'

'I'm sorry, I've not been to one of their shows,' Judith said, handing over the cup of tea.

'Oh, don't worry, there's no reason why you should have. Especially if theatre's not your thing. But the society was founded by Oliver – that's my husband – back in the eighties. It's very much been his life's work. Anyway, it was a big celebration last night because Lizzie Jenkins was with us. Do you know her? The film star?'

Judith wasn't aware that she'd ever seen one of Lizzie Jenkins' films, but she knew she was considered something of an *enfant terrible* within the acting industry. She drank too much and broke up too many marriages.

'I only know the name from the papers,' Judith said.

'She's very good. But the thing is, she's originally from Marlow, and she'd been part of MADS – that's what we call the Marlow Amateur Dramatic Society – when she was younger.'

'Lizzie Jenkins is from Marlow?'

'She is,' Verity said proudly, and Judith could see that the woman's panic over her missing husband was in a battle with the thrill of celebrity, and was briefly coming second. 'She's come all the way from Hollywood just to thank Oliver for training her up when she was a teenager. You see, she credits Oliver with being the first person to fire up her enthusiasm for acting.'

'So, you were all out on the boat together?' Judith said to get the conversation back on track.

'Oh – of course – yes, that's right. Lizzie hired this rather grand pleasure cruiser – you know, one of those old things from the 1920s – called the *Marlow Belle*. It was all very glamorous. Not that Lizzie's grand in any way. She'd got the Marlow Bar and Grill to provide the most wonderful spread, and Harrow and Hope had supplied their best sparkling wine. It was all rather special.'

'Where did you go?' Judith asked.

'We went from Marlow to Maidenhead Lock and back again.'

'And your husband was on the boat?'

'Oh yes, he was on the boat. That's something else I should mention. Oliver's rather larger than life – in all respects. He's a big presence, if you know what I mean, and his voice is so loud you always know when he's around. But the thing is, when we got back to Marlow and we were all leaving, I wasn't sure I saw Oliver get off. I mean, he must have been there – I'm pretty sure that Duncan said he saw him head into town ahead of us. Duncan is the technical director of the MADS. I was puzzled that Oliver would slip off like that, but I must admit, I also wasn't paying all that much attention. We'd been drinking sparkling wine for a few hours by this point, and it was so exciting chatting to Lizzie about her life in Hollywood. I must confess I was a bit giddy. Although I was very definitely cross when everyone said their goodbyes and I realised that Oliver had already left. If nothing else, it was rude to Lizzie. She seemed disappointed that he'd gone without saying goodbye. So I went home to find out what was up with him, but he wasn't there.'

'What time was this?'

'I don't know exactly. We got back to Marlow a bit after six. Maybe six thirty? I was home by seven or seven thirty.'

'And when did you last see your husband for definite?'

'That's what I found surprising. I don't remember seeing him at all on the return leg of the boat trip. He gave a speech – toasting Lizzie's success – as we left Marlow. And I remember him as we went down to Maidenhead. We were all milling about, drinking, and chatting, inside the boat and on deck, but I can't recall seeing him after we'd turned around and started to head back.'

'Could he have got off the boat at Maidenhead?'

'I don't see how. We stayed in the middle of the river the whole time, and the boat didn't stop at a jetty or anything like that. He didn't get off.'

'How very curious. Then what about the locks?'

'There's only one lock between Maidenhead and Marlow, and he didn't get off then – I'm sure of it. There's a little reception area at the back of the boat, and we were all on it when we came back through the lock. Thinking about it, I can remember seeing everyone else, but I don't remember seeing Oliver. Not that that's what's puzzling. It's the fact that he didn't come home afterwards. That's what's got me so spooked. I mean, who just disappears like that? And doesn't reply to any of the phone calls and texts and emails I've been sending him through the night.'

'Yes, that is somewhat odd, isn't it? But can I ask, why did you come to me?'

The question seemed to catch Verity by surprise, and she didn't immediately reply.

'You suspect something's happened to him, don't you?' Judith offered. 'Something quite bad.'

'No, of course not,' Verity said.

Judith took a sip of her tea and considered the woman standing in front of her. Verity's nerves seemed real enough, but she couldn't help feeling that there was something a touch staged about their encounter. It was Verity's manner, almost as if she were playing the part of a panicked wife. It would make sense, Judith thought to herself. After all, Verity was into amateur dramatics, wasn't she? Was this another role for her?

A ringtone started trilling from Verity's back pocket. She pulled out her phone and frowned as she looked at the screen.

'Is that him?' Judith asked.

'No,' Verity said, 'it's Sally Boulton.'

'Who's she?'

'An old friend. She played a few small parts in MADS productions back in the day. I wonder what she wants?'

Verity took the call.

'Sally, how are you?' she asked. After listening for a few seconds, she exhaled sharply and started mumbling, 'No, no, no,' over and over. And then the phone fell from her hand and clattered to the floor.

'What is it?' Judith asked.

'It's Oliver. His body's been found.'

And then Judith saw the moment it hit Verity.

'He's dead.'

Chapter 2

Verity's friend Sally had found Oliver's body on a bend in the river, halfway between Marlow and the neighbouring village of Bourne End. Judith knew that the quickest way to get there was along the river, so she helped Verity down her garden, into the boathouse, and onto her punt. Verity didn't resist. It was as if she were sleepwalking, Judith thought, which was entirely understandable, considering the circumstances.

There'd been a storm earlier in the week, so the river was running high and fast, and Judith used her punting pole as a rudder, allowing the weight of the water to push them along. First, they passed the ancient tower of Bisham Abbey before Marlow revealed itself. All Saints' Church was the focal point for the town, its spire reaching high into the sky, and, this morning, the town was particularly full of life. A youth team were getting a rowing boat into the water by the suspension bridge; a group of young men and women were running to and from little cones in Higginson Park; and there were clutches of people strolling along the Thames Path, feeding the ducks, chatting and letting their dogs run pell-mell. Judith couldn't help but contrast their joy with the grief that Verity was carrying. It felt almost mythic to Judith. All around her was vibrant life, but here she was, like Charon, piloting a lonely traveller towards death.

Once the town was behind them, they entered a landscape of fields on one side and, on the other, a wooded hill, that was peppered with pretty houses. Verity remained oblivious and Judith punted in silence.

About ten minutes later, as she steered around a wide bend, she could see a number of people in a clump by the riverbank. They were standing around a dark shape that could well have been a body. It looked as though it had washed up on one of the little beaches that were created by the cows in the fields coming down to the river to drink. As she got closer, Judith steered her punt into a bed of reeds just before the little beach and then thrust her pole deep into the mud to keep the boat from drifting off.

'Are you sure you want to do this?' she asked Verity.

Verity looked up, still uncomprehending, but she nodded.

'OK,' Judith said.

Judith stepped onto land and helped Verity up after her. As they approached the group of people, a friendly faced middle-aged woman wearing a dark-blue gilet and polka-dotted wellies came over.

'I'm so sorry,' the woman said.

This must be Sally Boulton, Judith guessed.

'It's definitely Oliver?' Verity asked.

'We've rung the police – and the ambulance – but I knew I had to call you. I had to be the first person to tell you.'

Verity brushed past her friend and carried on towards the slope that led down to the body. Judith followed.

There was a man lying on his front, half in and half out of the water, his arms at his side, his head turned to face them. Judith could see that he had white hair, looked like he was in his sixties, and had a huge stomach that pushed his lower back and bottom into the air. Verity dropped to her knees by the body, and Judith went to her side and very carefully lowered herself to the mud so she could offer her some support. And inspect the body more closely.

In the distance there was the sound of approaching sirens.

Judith could see that Oliver was wearing beige cotton trousers with a blue-and-white striped shirt that was stained a deep russet around the midriff. By putting her arm around Verity's shoulder, she was able to lean forward and take an even closer look. There was a hole in the cloth on the side of the body and she could see that the skin under it was darker – bruised.

Oliver had been shot.

On closer inspection, Judith could make out a second bloom of washed-out blood that seemed to be centred in the middle of Oliver's shoulder blades. There was another hole in the fabric that looked like it might have come from a bullet. He'd been shot twice, she realised. Which rather ruled out the wounds being self-inflicted. After all, it was very unlikely that someone who'd just shot themself would then be able to shoot themself a second time.

Oliver hadn't done this to himself. He'd been murdered.

Judith flashed a glance at Verity. Had she known that this was what had happened to her husband? And if she had, why would she have wanted to enlist her help to find him?

Judith returned her attention to the body and saw that Oliver was wearing a watch on his left wrist. The hands on the dial were set to just after six o'clock. The fact that the second hand wasn't moving suggested to Judith that Oliver's body had gone into the river shortly after 6 p.m. the night before. Assuming that the watch had stopped when Oliver had gone into the river, of course.

Next she noticed there were deep cuts and bruising on the insides of his wrist and forearm around the watch strap.

'We should get you away from here,' Judith said, turning towards Verity, which allowed her to peer over Oliver's back towards his other arm. His right wrist and forearm were similarly marked. He'd been in a fight of some sort before he died, Judith surmised. Or maybe the wounds had been administered post-mortem? Although, looking back down at the hand nearest to her, she could see there was something embedded in one of the cuts across his palm. It looked like the thinnest slither of dark red wood.

It was amazing what you could discover while comforting a grieving widow, Judith thought to herself. But before she could inspect the body any further, two police cars and an ambulance started bumping across the field and pulled up by the onlookers.

First out of the lead police car was an efficient-looking woman in a smart grey suit, her glossy black hair tied up in a tight ponytail. Her name was Detective Inspector Tanika Malik. She led her officers towards the river at speed, crisply telling her team to secure the scene, move the onlookers on and establish a perimeter, but she slowed to a stop as she saw Judith kneeling by the dead body.

'Not you,' Tanika said in disbelief.

Judith smiled an apology that both women knew wasn't remotely sincere.

Chapter 3

While Tanika and her team worked the scene, Judith made sure that she joined the other witnesses so she wouldn't get in the way. It also allowed her to phone her two friends, Becks Starling and Suzie Harris.

'Bloody hell,' Suzie said as soon as she arrived, taking in the shocking view of the dead body.

'The poor man, just lying there like that,' Becks said once Judith had explained how she'd ended up at the scene.

'Hold on,' Suzie said. 'His wife came to see you because her husband hadn't come home?'

Suzie was a local dog-walker, and she found almost nothing alarming, least of all the revelation that under the polished exteriors of so many people, there lay black hearts capable of committing murder.

'She did,' Judith said.

'Then she's the killer,' Suzie said, her feet planted four square on the ground as she gave her ruling.

'Yes, I was wondering that myself,' Judith said. 'It's all rather coincidental, isn't it? She comes to get help and claims she's upset by her husband's absence. Then, when his body's later found, she can rely on me to say that she was desperately trying to find him, which rather implies she didn't know he was dead.'

'I can't believe you'd think that so quickly,' Becks said, appalled by her friends' cynicism. Becks was the vicar of Marlow's wife, and of the three of them, she found their brushes with murder the most challenging. 'She was worried her husband had disappeared, of course she'd come to you.'

'Are you kidding me?' Suzie said. 'Most women I know, if their husbands didn't come home for the night, they'd be opening the champagne.'

'I do think Suzie has a point,' Judith said. 'At the very least, it's odd that her thoughts turned so quickly to wrongdoing that she felt the need to get me involved.'

'I suppose so,' Becks conceded. 'And the thing is, I knew Oliver Beresford a bit and I could imagine him having any number of enemies. He was something of a force of nature,' she added with a shudder. 'Some would even say tyrannical.'

'Was this through the church?' Judith asked.

'It was. For reasons I don't fully understand, Oliver's always been in charge of the Christmas nativity play. But he's just not suited to it. At one point, he made Joseph cry for forgetting his lines. And, now I think about it, last year he pushed the angel Gabriel off the stage altogether. He didn't mean to – or that's what he said. Apparently he only meant to move him to the correct position, but it was still awful.'

'He sounds horrible,' Suzie said.

'I must say I didn't warm to him. I found him too abrasive.'

'Now that's interesting,' Judith said. 'So we've got an abrasive man who's been shot dead, and a wife who was *very* quick to presume foul play.'

'Maybe you should stay away from her,' Suzie said.

'What's that?' Judith asked.

'Maybe you should try and avoid hanging around a woman who could be a killer.'

'What makes you suddenly so worried about my safety?'

'Me?' Suzie said – but a touch guiltily, as though she'd been caught with her hand in the cookie jar. 'Nothing.'

'You're looking at me funnily.'

'Don't be stupid, Judith. Why would I be looking at you funnily?'

'Because you are. Like there's something you're trying not to say.'

Suzie shrugged as if to say she had no idea what Judith was talking about, and then offered no further explanation. Judith and Becks shared a glance, both of them picking up on their friend's sudden awkwardness.

'Have I told you Chloe's coming home?' Becks said to change the subject.

'She is?' Suzie asked.

Chloe was in her second year at Exeter University reading theology, a fact that both Becks and her husband Colin still couldn't quite believe.

'All the students come home in the middle of term for a reading week.'

'How wonderful,' Judith said.

'She's bringing her boyfriend with her. They're going to spend a week studying together.'

'Yeah,' Suzie said with a grin. 'Right.'

Becks also smiled, although more coyly.

'I'm just happy that she's happy,' she said.

'And how's Sam?' Judith asked.

The previous year, Becks' son Sam had surprised no one by getting what his parents felt had been wilfully eccentric results in his A-levels. An A★, a C and an E. Sam's view was that it was cool that his results spelled 'ACE', and that was all that mattered. In lieu of anyone – the school, Sam, his friends or even his parents – knowing what he could do with such a mixed bag of grades, he'd decided to take a gap year. The fact that he then hadn't applied to any university when the time came around was something he'd tried to finesse by going to Africa with a charitable organisation.

'Sam's doing fine, I think,' Becks said. 'He's in a village in Namibia, building a well that, as far as I can tell, no one in the village has asked for. But I suppose it keeps him out of trouble, so it could be worse.'

'Aye aye,' Suzie muttered as Tanika headed over to join them. 'Talking of trouble . . .'

'It's not my fault this time,' Judith said, wanting to get her defence in first as Tanika stopped in front of the women.

'And yet here you are,' Tanika said. 'Here you all are.'

'I didn't know that a woman would knock on my door this morning. And that we'd find her husband dead only a short while later.'

'And Becks and Suzie?'

'I'm allowed to ask my friends along for moral support when I've had a shock.'

'Are you pretending this was a shock for you?'

'It's always a shock seeing a dead body. Especially when they've been shot. He did die from his bullet wounds, didn't he?'

'Forensics will be able to establish the precise cause of death in due course. Although you're right, he appears to have been shot twice. One bullet went into his side, and another seems to have gone into his heart.'

'Ouch,' Suzie said.

'Indeed. Ouch.'

'How's Verity doing?' Judith asked.

'Not too well,' Tanika conceded.

'Has she told you she's not seen her husband since last night?' Judith asked.

'She has.'

'Do you believe her?'

'At this stage, I'm just trying to collect as much information as possible.'

'She told me she'd been on a boat with the film actor Lizzie Jenkins, until some time after 6 p.m.'

'No way!' Suzie said.

'Is that so surprising?' Judith asked.

'Lizzie Jenkins is a murder suspect?'

'Now let's not get ahead of ourselves, ladies,' Tanika said. 'I'm happy to admit that this is very definitely a possible murder that needs investigating, but we can't presume any of the facts in advance.'

'Do you know who else was on the boat?' Judith asked.

'Verity's putting together a list. I didn't want to press her so soon after the event.'

'Then do you know whose boat it was?' Judith asked.

Tanika could see that an idea had occurred to Judith. She narrowed her eyes. 'Why are you asking?'

'I saw there were splinters of wood in the cuts on Oliver's hand. They were dark red. If the boat they were on has any paintwork on it the same colour, then that might help prove that there was some kind of a tussle on the boat and that's where he died. Before his body was tipped into the river – or fell into it.'

'Yes, I'll admit I was wondering the same thing. And since you're asking, the boat was hired from a man called Lance Goodman.'

Suzie shifted her weight on to one hip.

'Lance Goodman?' she said with a level of sass that could only be described as 'peak'.

'You know him?' Tanika asked.

'Hmm,' Suzie said, as though she was considering whether she knew the answer herself. She didn't say any more on the subject, and the women realised that Suzie wasn't going to offer any further explanations.

'Well, look,' Tanika said, wanting to make her position clear. 'We'll have to take your witness statement, Judith, seeing as you were with the deceased's wife when she found his body. And just so you know, I may yet ask the three of you to help with the case. But it's very important you understand that you don't have the automatic right to be involved.'

'Even though I am already involved?' Judith asked. 'And Becks knows the deceased well.'

'I don't—'

'She couldn't wait to tell us he was a tyrant. And we can all see that Suzie knows Lance Goodman.'

The women looked at Suzie so she could confirm what Judith had said, but she was gazing off into the distance as though she were considering a battlefield that contained the bodies of everyone she'd slain.

They all saw Suzie come to a decision, and then she set off towards the reeds where Judith had jammed her punt.

'Come on,' she said.

'Where are you going?' Tanika asked.

'I don't have to tell you.'

'You're going to talk to Lance, aren't you?'

'I'm a citizen of this country, I can talk to anyone I like.'

'Especially when you're tied up here, processing the scene,' Judith said to Tanika with a twinkle before heading over to join her friend.

Tanika looked at Becks.

'I think they're both brilliant woman,' Becks said. 'But I wish they weren't so . . . What's the word I'm looking for?'

'Mercurial?' Tanika offered.

'That's right. They're mercurial, aren't they? It's all quite exhausting at times.'

'Go on,' Tanika said kindly. 'Go and join them.'

'You don't mind?'

'Oh, I mind, I mind a lot. But I couldn't stop them even if I tried. Any more than you could. And they're right. I have to work the scene here. Having eyes on Lance could be useful.'

'Thanks,' Becks said as she turned and ran to catch up with her friends.

As Tanika watched the three women start to bicker about how they could best get onto Judith's punt, she couldn't help but smile. The women were often infuriating, always refused to follow orders, and seemed to cause as many problems as they solved, but she knew that when it came to catching killers, no one was better. If anyone could work out how Oliver Beresford had wound up with two bullets in him, it would be Judith, Suzie and Becks.

Chapter 4

Lance Goodman's boatyard had been in his family for over a hundred years, and it didn't look as though much had changed in that time. In fact, it wouldn't have been out of place in a Wild West movie, with its weather-stained clapboard buildings, rotting jetty and piles of broken equipment, tatty ropes and old boats. And just to the side, there was a little river that fed into the Thames, in which some truly ancient boats were sitting, semi-submerged.

The only exception was a gleaming cruiser that was proudly moored in front of the main workshop. The *Marlow Belle* was a gorgeous wooden vessel that was polished to a bright sheen, with an enclosed driving position at the front, brass-rimmed portholes down the side, and a large viewing area at the back. Unlike everything else that was nearby, it looked in perfect condition.

As Judith tied up her punt and helped her friends onto the jetty, she saw the *Marlow Belle* and was put in mind of the sort of boats that might have ferried impecunious Brits from Portsmouth to Dinard in France in the 1920s. Its lines and design were so elegant, it was so obviously built for pleasure – although she also couldn't help noticing that the deck at the back was only a foot or so above the water and was painted a deep red.

Judith leaned over from the jetty so she could better see the deck, but Suzie grabbed at her arm.

'What are you doing?' Judith asked.

'Sorry, sorry,' Suzie said. 'I thought you were about to fall into the water.'

'Why on earth would you think that?'

'You looked like you were about to go over.'

'I don't understand you today, Suzie Harris. First you're saying I can't consort with murderers, and now you're suggesting I can't look at a boat without falling into the Thames.'

Suzie had the good grace to look embarrassed, and Becks did what she always did when local squalls picked up – she tried to pour oil on troubled waters.

'Do you think that's the boat they used?' she asked.

Before Judith could answer, a door slammed nearby and they saw a man emerge from a dark green canal boat that was moored in the inlet to the side of the main building. He was holding a large silver-backed insulation board in his hands and, as he approached, Judith noted that he wasn't very tall – perhaps only as tall as her – but he made up for it in muscle. In fact, as the man put the insulation down and she could see his figure under his tight T-shirt, he appeared to be made entirely of muscle.

He let out a groan when he saw the women waiting for him.

'That's Lance Goodman,' Suzie said, just as disappointed with him as he seemed to be with them.

Lance picked up a rag, wiped his hands and headed over. As he got nearer, Judith could see that he was in his fifties, hadn't shaved for a couple of days and he had a suspicious air about him, as though he was already expecting three middle-aged women to give him trouble. But then, from the way Suzie was looking, Judith could see that trouble was indeed brewing.

'Suzie,' he said by way of opening.

'Lance,' Suzie replied.

Despite his suspicious demeanour, Judith could see that Lance had sparkling eyes of the clearest blue. And thick eyelashes. Up close, he was actually rather attractive, she realised. Like a pocket Paul Newman.

'My name's Judith Potts,' she said.

'And I'm Becks Starling,' Becks said. 'Do you mind us asking you a few questions about last night?'

Lance looked at the women, nonplussed.

'What do you want to know?' he asked.

'Well, for starters, did you really have Lizzie Jenkins with you? You met her?'

'Might have done. Why are you asking?'

'Oliver Beresford's body has just washed up,' Judith said. 'Someone shot him. Twice.'

Lance didn't say anything; didn't react at all.

'Doesn't that surprise you?'

Lance looked at Suzie.

'This is a joke, right?'

'No way,' Suzie said.

'It's got nothing to do with me,' Lance said, flashing a glance at the pleasure cruiser that was moored to the jetty.

'Ah yes, I guessed as much,' Judith said. 'That's the boat you took them out on.'

After a moment's reflection, Lance nodded.

'It's something of a beauty,' Judith offered.

'She was a wreck when I got her. Used to do the route from here to Abingdon in Oxford and down to Chelsea in London. And she was one of the Little Ships at Dunkirk. When I found her, I couldn't let her die. I've spent the last two years doing her up.'

'She's splendid,' Judith said.

'Why are you so interested?'

'That's a very good question,' Judith conceded. 'We'd like to know what happened last night, in an official capacity. You see, we're with the police.'

'We're not—' Becks interjected.

Judith dug her elbow into her friend's ribs and finished the sentence for her: '—going to take up much of your time.'

Lance looked at the women and gathered his thoughts.

'He's really dead?'

'He's really dead,' Suzie said.

'That's crazy. Someone like him.'

'How do you mean "someone like him"?' Becks asked.

'He wasn't the sort of guy you'd think would ever die. You know? I've seen him around town, and he's always talking at the top of his voice. And dressing like a bloody lord – going down the high street in his stupid waistcoats. One time I think I saw him with a hat with a feather sticking out of it. It wasn't a good look, a man his size.'

'He was something of a popinjay?' Judith asked.

'No idea what one of those is, but he was vain, I'll tell you that much. He wanted the world to look at him the whole time.'

'You didn't like him?'

'I don't think I'd ever spoken to him before a couple of weeks ago. I don't have any opinion one way or another. I'm only saying he's well known around Marlow. Like you,' Lance added, looking at Judith.

'I am?' Judith asked, surprised as always that she had any kind of a reputation in the town.

'So you'd not spoken to him before a few weeks ago?' Suzie asked.

'That's right. He rang me out of the blue. Said he had a top secret request. He wanted to hire the *Marlow Belle* – that's her name,' Lance added proudly, indicating the cruiser.

'He said it was a secret?' Judith asked.

'He wanted me to sign a form saying I wouldn't tell anyone he was hiring the boat. I told him where to go with that. If he wanted me to keep my trap shut, all he had to do was ask and I'd give him my word. My word has always been my bond.'

Suzie laughed. Lance scowled at her, but didn't say anything.

'I don't understand,' Becks said. 'Why did it have to be a secret?'

'I found out why last night. First up, Oliver and his friends spent the afternoon getting the boat ready. Fresh food, wine in ice buckets, a projector and screen in the main cabin. They wanted to show old video footage of the Marlow Amateur Dramatic Society. God help me, but that's who they were. Actor types. I got why they were so excited when the film star, Lizzie Jenkins, arrived.'

'I still can't believe she's here in Marlow,' Becks said. 'What's she like?'

Lance smiled at the memory.

'The first thing she did was neck a glass of champagne. By the time she'd introduced herself to everyone, she was on her third glass and had lit up her second fag. I liked her. Nothing puts you at ease like meeting someone who's not in control.'

'You didn't think she was in control?' Becks asked.

'Maybe that's overselling it, but she didn't stand on ceremony, let's put it like that. We set off around three, got to Cookham Lock about fifty minutes later. Then it was plain sailing straight through to Maidenhead.'

'What did everyone do on the journey?'

'I couldn't see much. The *Marlow Belle*'s driving position is at the front of the boat,' Lance said, pointing at the glassed-off area. 'But they were loud enough. Laughing, chatting, popping champagne, and in and out of each other's cabins.'

'Your boat has cabins?' Judith said, impressed.

'It was built for more than just day trips. Oliver wanted everyone to have the full experience, so everyone had their own cabin.'

'Not that they needed them on such a short journey,' Suzie said.

'He'd hired the boat, it didn't bother me.'

'So they all got on?' Judith said.

'I reckon so.'

'What happened once you reached Maidenhead?'

'Not much. When we were almost at the lock, I turned the boat around. The drive back took around an hour and a half, and we docked at about 6.30. Everyone got off and then I brought the boat back here, and that's it.'

'Can I ask where on the river the boat was at 6 p.m.?' Judith asked.

'OK,' Lance said, trying to gather his thoughts. 'We cleared Cookham Lock at 5.30, 5.40, I reckon. So, by six o'clock I guess we were about halfway between Cookham and Marlow.'

'Thank you,' Judith said. 'And how was Oliver last night?'

'He was just like I expected him to be. He thought he was the centre of attention, and he was kind of patronising. Especially with Lizzie. Everyone else was walking on eggshells around her – including me. It's not every day you get a real-life Hollywood star in Marlow. But he talked down to her – like he was the big actor or director or whatever he is and she was a nobody.'

'Can you give examples?'

Lance paused, thinking, then said, 'He made this speech before we set off, about how Lizzie had learned to act with the Marlow Amateur Dramatic Society, and she had a lot to thank them for.'

'How was she when he was saying this?'

'She didn't seem bothered. I think it amused her. In her own way, she's pretty classy. Despite the drinking and smoking, that's the word I'd use to describe her. Classy. She gives off this air that she's seen everything and nothing can surprise her, or impress her.'

'Who else was on the boat?' Becks asked.

'Let me think. There was Oliver and Lizzie, like I said. And Oliver's wife, Verity.'

'Yes, I've met her,' Judith said. 'What did you think of her?'

'She seemed nice enough, I suppose. Can't say I paid much attention. Then there was Duncan Wood,' Lance added with a chuckle.

'Who's he?' Becks asked.

'A nice guy. Lives on a houseboat, so I've known him a few years – we river folk look out for each other – and he does odd jobs around the town. You know, he'll rewire your house, or build a wall, or move in when you're on holiday and cat-sit for you. Now who else was there . . . ? The last person on board was a guy I wasn't expecting to see. His name's Toby Vincent. Works at Platt's garage. I don't know what he was doing on a boat with a bunch of actors.'

'You know him?'

'Not exactly, but we had a chat about the boat's engine. It's been playing up a bit, and he had a few ideas about what might be wrong with it. He seemed like a good bloke.'

'Who else was there?'

'That was it. There were five of them. Oliver and his wife, Verity. Lizzie. And Duncan and Toby.'

'And you,' Judith added. 'You were the sixth person.'

'I suppose so. Yeah.'

'And you're sure there was no one else on board?'

'Of course.'

'No one could have snuck on beforehand?'

'When they all arrived, I gave them a tour of the boat. It was her maiden voyage last night, I wanted to show her off. They poked into every nook and cranny. There were no stowaways.'

'Could anyone have got onto the boat once you'd set off?'

'No way. We didn't stop, and the boat never moored.'

'What about Cookham Lock?' Becks asked. 'You must have tied up when you went through it and back again.'

'You're right there, but that's when I'm at my most vigilant. I can't have any damage to my boat, she's my pride and joy.'

'Did anyone get on or off?'

'Not me, not anyone. It's too dangerous with all that water sloshing about.'

'Fascinating,' Judith said. 'Because it rather suggests we have only five possible suspects.'

'You don't seriously think he died on my boat?'

'I'm sure the police will be able to find out one way or another.

Did you hear a gunshot at all? Two, in fact – I imagine in reasonably quick succession.'

'This is nuts! I didn't hear any gunshots . . .'

As Lance spoke, his brow furrowed.

'What is it?' Becks asked.

'You know how I said Toby and me talked about the engine? I've been having trouble with my crankshaft.'

'Ha!' Suzie exploded. 'Ain't that the truth.'

Everyone looked at Suzie, but it was clear she wasn't about to explain what she meant.

'On the boat,' Lance said testily. 'It caused a bit of a problem last night, Oliver wasn't happy about it. Kicked off about it, saying he hadn't paid all that money to have a boat that sounded like it was falling apart. The bloody cheek! He didn't pay for the boat, it was Lizzie's money. And when I spoke to her, she said she had no problem with the odd clanking noise from the engine, it only added to the charm. See what I mean about her being classy?'

'"Clanking noise"?' Judith asked.

'I'll be honest, the boat wasn't quite ready for her first outing, but money's money, so I decided she'd have to do the best she could. And anyway, it wasn't all that bad. Every five minutes or so – OK, maybe a bit less – there'd be a loud bang from the engine.'

'One loud bang at a time, or more?'

'It could be one bang or a few bangs – it was all pretty random. It sounded like someone was hitting the engine block with a hammer. Then it would run smoothly again. Most of the journey it worked fine.'

'And how loud would you say these bangs were? As loud as a gunshot?'

'No way,' Lance said, before considering the question more carefully. 'Although they weren't that far off, I suppose.'

'So it might have been possible for someone on the boat to have mistaken a gunshot as one of the bangs from the engine?'

'It's possible, but I don't think it's what happened.'

'Tell me, do you own a gun?'

'What? No.'

'Are you sure?'

'I just said, didn't I?'

The women could see that Lance's patience was wearing thin.

'One last question,' Judith said. 'Did you by any chance see Oliver get off the boat on your return to Marlow?'

Lance searched his memory.

'You know what? I remember seeing everyone disembarking – I was bloody glad I was done for the night – but, now you mention it, I don't remember seeing Oliver. I'm not saying he didn't leave then, but I don't remember seeing him get off.'

'Hmm. So that's you and Verity both saying you didn't see Oliver get off the boat at the end of the cruise.'

Everyone turned at the sound of a vehicle approaching, and a police car pulled up in the yard. Tanika got out.

'Well met, Tanika!' Judith cried as the police officer approached them. 'This is DS Tanika Malik,' she added, for Lance's benefit.

'Good morning, Mr Goodman,' Tanika said. 'As I'm sure you're now aware, we're investigating the death of Oliver Beresford. I believe he was last seen on one of your boats.'

'He was. I took members of the Marlow Amateur Dramatic Society out for a boat trip yesterday evening.'

'It was that one,' Judith added helpfully, indicating the *Marlow Belle*.

'Thank you, Judith. I have to inform you,' Tanika continued, turning back to Lance, 'that your boat is a possible crime scene. We'll need to search it – and we'll also need to take a witness statement from you.'

'Of course,' Lance said. 'You don't have to worry about me. I'll do whatever I can to help with your enquiries.'

Judith looked at Lance and realised that his manner had changed as soon as Tanika had arrived. He looked worried; nervous, even. Why was that? Was it because he was in the presence of a police officer, or was it for some other reason? And there was something else Judith wanted to know. What on earth was going on between Lance and Suzie?

Chapter 5

As Tanika started to organise her team, Judith suggested to her friends that they withdraw to her punt. Pushing off, she let the current catch them and once again used the pole as a rudder as they carried on downstream.

'Aren't we going back to your house?' Becks asked.

'I don't think so,' Judith said. 'Not when we've another key witness to interview.'

'Who's that?'

'The lock-keeper at Cookham. I want to know if Lance's story stacks up. And the journey will give Suzie time to tell us all about her and Lance.'

'Tell you what?' Suzie said, pretending the question was a surprise to her.

'The way you were with him, and all your references to his crankshaft not working. You and he were an item, weren't you?'

Suzie looked from Judith to Becks, and then from Becks back to Judith. Her shoulders slumped.

'It's possible we might have been,' she mumbled.

'I knew it!' Judith said.

'A hundred years ago, mind, and only for the briefest second.'

'How delightful!'

'What? That I went out with someone who's now a suspect in a murder case?'

'Not at all. But you can't deny it's useful that you know one of the suspects so well.'

'I know him too well, that's the problem,' Suzie said.

'Tell us about him,' Becks said.

'What's there to say? He's a typical bloke. Not unkind, but not kind either. Says he'll take an interest in you, then doesn't. He'd rather have been with his mates down the pub than out with me. That became clear soon enough. Even if he bought me flowers to apologise when he let me down. But he never meant any of it. That's why I ended things.'

'Would you say he's honest?'

'If you mean, could he kill someone, I'd say no. At least, not unless he was provoked. You know, if another bloke went for him, I could imagine him killing in self-defence. But if Oliver's death was in any way planned in advance, there's no way Lance could have done it. That's not how his brain works. Not normally. Although, if you're asking, is he truthful . . . ? I'm not sure I know.'

As Suzie spoke, the punt rounded a corner and the women saw that a police forensics tent had been erected over Oliver's body. Officers were still collecting evidence and working nearby. The women fell silent as they passed. Then, as the river curved around a wide bend, they found themselves surrounded by the tall-masted dinghies from the sailing club, their sails cracking in the breeze. Calling 'Sorry! Excuse me!' at every near collision, Judith was able to steer her punt through the boats and past the riverside Bounty pub until she finally reached Cookham Lock.

She moored her punt and then she and her friends walked up the path that led to the lock-keeper's red-brick house. She saw a man in a dark waistcoat and peaked cap on the far side of the lock pressing a button on a board.

'Good day,' Judith greeted the man as they approached.

'Morning!' he replied cheerily as he pressed another button. The ancient wooden gates of the lock started to open and he beckoned to a longboat to come forward.

'I thought you had to do all this by hand,' Judith said.

'Not these days,' the man replied with a smile. 'You wouldn't get many takers for the job if you had to do this with winches, I can tell you.'

'Judith Potts,' Judith said, deciding to introduce himself.

'Andy Ford,' the lock-keeper said, pulling out a vape. 'Mind if I vape?'

'Of course not. Could we ask a few questions?'

'Sure. What about?'

Judith explained how Oliver Beresford had been shot the night before, and had almost certainly been on Lance Goodman's boat at the time. At the mention of Lance's name, Andy frowned.

'What's up?' Suzie asked.

'Lance was involved?' Andy asked.

'We don't know for sure,' Judith said. 'But his boat was.'

'Oh, OK – sorry. You see, I know him a bit and I can't believe he'd hurt anyone.'

'Did you see Oliver last night?' Judith asked. 'He was in his sixties, with white hair, and very much larger than life.'

'Let me think . . . I was kind of distracted. It's not every day you see Hollywood royalty here.'

'You mean Lizzie Jenkins?' Becks asked.

'Yeah – her. She was on the back of the boat with a few other people as I worked the lock. She spoke to me,' he added, his cheeks flushing with pride.

'What did she say?'

'She thanked me for what I was doing.'

'So you remember seeing her. Was Oliver one of the people talking to her?'

'Well, let's see. There was one other woman on the boat with Lizzie Jenkins. She was a bit older – in her sixties, I reckon. Thin as a stick.'

'That would have been Verity.'

'And Duncan Wood, he was there. Do you know him? He's a card. Oh – and a guy in his forties with a buzz cut. A big unit. You know. He was wearing a Hawaiian shirt covered in pineapples. Looked a bit out of place, if you ask me.'

'I imagine that's Toby Vincent,' Judith said. 'The man who works at Platt's garage.'

'But no – since you're asking, I don't remember seeing any larger-than-life older guy with white hair.'

'Are you sure?' Becks asked. 'It could be very important.'

'He wasn't in the main group of people at the stern of the boat. But he could have been below deck. They only spent a few minutes in my lock before I waved them on their way.'

'Very well,' Judith said. 'Did you notice anyone get on or off the boat at all?'

'No way. It's basically why I'm employed by the Environment Agency – to make sure all safety measures are followed, and we can't have people coming and going while the lock is in use. No one got on or off – I'd swear my life on it.'

The bell of an old-fashioned phone started ringing from inside Andy's house and he headed over to his front door.

'Sorry – office phone. Could be important.'

Judith and her friends were still within earshot as he opened the door, plucked up an old Bakelite handset and put it to his ear.

'This is Andy Ford at Cookham Lock,' he announced in his most official-sounding voice. 'I'm sorry?' he said, then listened intently. 'Yes, I've just heard the news,' he replied, then frowned as the caller continued. 'No, I'm sorry, that won't be possible. I can't leave my post.' There was another pause as he listened, and then Andy cut in, 'No, I'm sorry, I know you're the police, but I'm not allowed to leave my post when I'm in the middle of my shift.' Again he listened to the officer on the end of the line, but it was obvious from Andy's upright bearing that he wasn't going to back down. 'I'm here until 7 p.m.,' he said. 'You can come and take my witness statement any time you like.'

Andy hung up the call, and Judith could see that he was particularly pleased with how he'd handled himself.

'I take it that was DS Malik,' she said.

He nodded. 'She seemed a bit officious, if you ask me.'

'But you can't possibly be interviewed, you're needed here.'

'That's it exactly,' Andy agreed. 'She wanted me to join the other witnesses to talk about what happened.'

'She doesn't understand how important your job is. Although – where was it that she said the witnesses were meeting?'

'The Little Theatre.'

Judith knew that the Little Theatre was where the Marlow Amateur Dramatic Society put on their productions.

'Yes, that makes sense – the Little Theatre. We won't take up any more of your time,' Judith said, already heading to the road that led away from the lock.

Becks and Suzie were slow to catch up with their friend.

'Where are you going?' Becks asked.

'If Tanika's going to interview the suspects,' Judith said, 'then we need to be there.'

'But what about the punt, we can't leave it here.'

'It will be fine tied up, we can come back and get it later. We haven't a second to waste – there's a taxi firm in the village, we can take a cab back to Marlow.'

'Don't you think Tanika will object if we all turn up to her interview?' Suzie asked.

'She'll have no choice if that's what we do.'

'There's no way she'll let us attend.'

'Although she might let you,' Becks said to Judith. 'It's like you said earlier. Verity came to see you this morning. You were with her when she discovered the body. You're a key witness.'

'You know what?' Judith said, delighted with her friend's logic. 'I think that's *exactly* what I am.'

Chapter 6

The pride and joy of the Marlow Amateur Dramatic Society was its theatre. The building had always been owned by the council, but a wealthy benefactor had installed a theatre in it in the 1920s. The auditorium was snug rather than grand – which is how it had got the name the Little Theatre – and for decades it had taken in touring shows and variety acts, but it always put on a Christmas pantomime written and performed by the people of Marlow. When the touring acts dried up at the beginning of the 1980s, the theatre fell dark, which was when Oliver Beresford founded the Marlow Amateur Dramatic Society and convinced the council to lease the building to the society for a peppercorn rent.

As Tanika arrived outside the theatre, she decided to wait thirty seconds to see what happened, and wasn't disappointed when a taxi arrived and Judith got out. Once she'd paid the driver, she headed over with a big grin on her face.

"'Ill met by moonlight, proud Titania"!' Judith called out, which made very little sense to Tanika.

'I had a hunch that if I arranged to meet the witnesses, you'd somehow be here.'

'Of course I am. I'm as much a key witness as anyone who was on that boat. It was me who Verity came to see this morning, and I was with her when she discovered the body,' Judith continued, with a sniff of grief that both she and Tanika knew was fake. 'It's possible I'll have some insight about Verity – how she was this morning, or how she's behaving now – that could prove vital. We both know the professional thing to do is to let me come with you.'

Tanika knew that her first duty was to the victim, Oliver Beresford. She had to do everything within her power to catch his killer, and she could see some sense in what Judith was suggesting.

'Come on, then,' she said.

When they arrived at the entrance, Judith had the good grace to open the door for the police officer so she could enter first. Inside, there was a red-painted lobby lined with dozens of framed posters and photos of past productions, and a little window for selling tickets to one side. Pushing through a set of double doors, the two women made their way into the auditorium. Stacks of chairs were propped up against the wall, and the raised stage ahead of them had ancient red velvet curtains hanging at the sides. In the sunlight coming through the high windows, the whole room looked tatty and dusty, but Judith loved it.

'The swish of the curtain!' she said to herself as she took in the room. Her eyes were immediately drawn to the four people waiting on chairs arranged in a semicircle in the centre of the room.

She couldn't help but notice Lizzie Jenkins first. It wasn't because of what she was wearing – she was dressed in Doc Marten boots, a pair of green corduroy trousers and a fitted white shirt. And it wasn't because of her physical presence. She was in her early fifties, Judith guessed, and was what her great-aunt would have called 'a tiny slip of a thing', but there was a vitality about her that made her the only person Judith wanted to look at in the room.

She was smoking a cigarette, using her left hand as an ashtray.

'You must be Lizzie Jenkins,' Tanika said.

'I am,' Lizzie said in a breathy voice that seemed to resonate with kindness, empathy and deep tragedy all at once.

Yes, Judith thought. She could well understand why the woman was such a star.

Judith could see Verity Beresford sitting at the end of the row. She was staring blankly ahead of her. Judith recognised the look. The poor woman was in shock.

The man next to her had his arm around her shoulders in support. He was wearing blue jeans and a dark blue V-necked T-shirt that showed off his tattooed biceps. He hid his receding hairline behind a number one buzz cut, and there was an air of menace about him – almost of danger, Judith thought. This must be Toby Vincent, she decided – the mechanic who worked at the local garage.

The last of the four witnesses was a man in his sixties who had a thick bush of curly blond hair that fell to his shoulders, half-moon spectacles, and a look of quiet amusement about him. This must be Duncan Wood, she guessed. He was wearing dark jeans, old trainers and a faded black T-shirt that had the word METALLICA written across the front of it in a jagged font.

As Tanika introduced herself to the group, Judith kept her eyes on the witnesses. Verity remained a little confused, nodding slowly in agreement with what Tanika was saying, but not quite following. Toby listened intently, but there was a watchfulness about him that put Judith in mind of Stanley Kowalski from *A Streetcar Named Desire*. She realised she'd maybe misjudged him; he had a brooding presence that would go over well on stage. As for Duncan, he seemed to hold himself separate from the others, and Judith was put in mind of a teacher who feels they need to demonstrate their status by remaining aloof. Above all, what she thought when she looked at him was that he wasn't very well. His skin was sallow, and he had bags under his eyes.

When Tanika asked about everyone's movements the night before, Judith's attention sharpened.

'I've been thinking about this,' Duncan said with a warm Oxfordshire burr to his voice. 'Just because Oliver's body was found in the river, that doesn't mean he died on the boat.'

'You should know that we've searched Mr Goodman's boat and found two bullet casings on the deck area at the back.'

The witnesses looked at each other, stunned by the news, and Judith caught Tanika's eye. The police officer nodded once in acknowledgement that what she'd said was true.

'We've also found traces of blood,' she continued.

'That doesn't mean it came from Oliver,' Duncan said, but it was obvious that he was no longer sure.

'And splinters we found in the palm of Mr Beresford's hand appear to be a match for the wood on the decking. I'm sorry to say that it very much looks as though he was shot last night on the back deck of the *Marlow Belle*.'

'No way,' Toby said, a challenge in his voice. 'If that was what happened, we'd have heard the gun going off, but none of us heard anything.'

'So you've talked among yourselves about this?' Tanika asked.

'It's all we've talked about.'

'Although there's the small matter of the crankshaft,' Duncan said. 'It kept clanking all through the journey. Toby, you tried to fix it, didn't you.'

'The bearings weren't aligned properly,' Toby said. 'It was running off-true. There was nothing I could do. Not without stripping it.'

'Yes,' Tanika agreed, 'Mr Goodman mentioned that the boat was having engine trouble. He said there were intermittent bangs throughout the journey.'

'It wasn't that often,' Toby said. 'More like a popping noise from time to time. Nothing like a gunshot, if you ask me.'

'You know about firearms?' Tanika asked.

'No way, I'm just a mechanic. But every machine's got its own sound. Its own voice, if you like. A gun being fired's going to sound completely different from a crankshaft that's not properly centred.'

'Can I ask, do any of you own any kind of firearm?'

'Of course not,' Toby said, affronted by the question.

'No,' Verity said, engaging in the conversation for the first time. 'I don't even know anyone who owns a gun.'

'Mr Wood?' Tanika asked.

'Me neither,' Duncan said.

'Then what about you, Ms Jenkins?' Tanika asked Lizzie, who seemed to wake from her reverie at the question.

'What's that?' she asked.

'Do you own a gun?'

Lizzie had smoked her cigarette down to the filter and she very carefully balanced it vertically on the floor so it would burn out without causing any damage. Only once she'd done this to her satisfaction did she sit back and look Tanika in the eye.

'I do in America, but that's where I left it. In Los Angeles. Which is where I was until yesterday morning.'

'You only arrived in the country yesterday?'

'Oxford Airport, landing shortly before midday.'

'There's no international airport in Oxford,' Judith said.

'I'm sorry, who are you?' Lizzie asked.

'Judith Potts,' Judith said.

'You weren't on the boat yesterday.'

'But I was with Verity this morning when we found Mr Beresford. Can you tell us how you managed to land in the UK at Oxford?'

'Sure. There's a private air field.'

'Oh,' Judith said, finally realising that Lizzie had flown all the way to the UK from Los Angeles in a private jet.

'Thank you, Judith,' Tanika said in a tone that made it clear she didn't want her asking any more questions. 'I know this is hard for everyone, but could you help me understand how Mr Beresford was last night?'

'How do you mean?' Duncan asked.

'What sort of mood was he in?'

'He was his usual self. Full of beans and bumption. I've known him since we were kids and he's not changed in all that time.'

'So, he was happy?'

'Very,' Duncan said confidently.

'He didn't seem worried at all?'

'The opposite, if you ask me,' Toby offered. 'He was up for it – it's like Duncan's saying. He was like he always is, but even more so. You know? Even more loud, telling even more jokes

– giving speeches, making toasts – but we were all pretty excited. It's not every day you get to meet an Oscar winner.'

'This isn't about me,' Lizzie said, in a way that suggested she thought it actually was all about her.

'Then, can I ask,' Tanika said, 'when was the last time you all saw Mr Beresford?'

The question didn't immediately elicit a response.

'Or, to put it another way,' Judith said helpfully, 'where were you all at 6 p.m.?'

'What's that?' Toby asked sharply.

'Is that time significant to you?'

Toby blinked a couple of times, and then he turned to look at Lizzie. He seemed to be weighing up his options.

'Why do you mention 6 p.m.?' he asked Judith again.

'I'll do you a deal,' Tanika said, wanting to wrest back control of the interview. 'You tell us what's interesting about 6 p.m., and then I'll tell you why Mrs Potts asked.'

'OK,' he said. 'It's simple enough, I was in my cabin.'

'Yes, Lance told us you all had cabins,' Judith said.

'Oliver said that, since we were hiring such a big boat, we had to use all the facilities. It seemed rather stupid to me – not that my cabin wasn't nice. There was a single bed and chair, and a little fold-down desk. But who was going to spend time inside the boat when there was a party going on outside?'

'And yet that's where you were at 6 p.m.?' Judith asked.

'That's right. I was there at 6 p.m. because that's where I was told to go. In a message. It was pushed through my letterbox yesterday afternoon. Hold on – I think I've still got it on me. I wore these trousers last night.'

Toby reached into his back pocket and pulled out a crumpled piece of card. He handed it to Judith.

A message was printed on it, although she could see that the signature was handwritten.

Go to your cabin at 6 p.m. I have a secret I need to share with you.

Lizzie Jenkins

P.S. don't tell anyone, this is a matter of life and death.

Judith read the message out loud and when she announced who had signed it, Lizzie shot up from her chair as though she'd had an electric shock.

'That's not from me!' she said. 'Hand it over,' she added.

'Judith, don't,' Tanika said as she got some evidence bags out of her handbag. 'I'll need to take that note in as evidence.'

'But I didn't write it!' Lizzie said.

'It says here that you did,' Judith said as she handed the card to Tanika.

Once it was inside the evidence bag, Tanika held it up for Lizzie to look at more closely.

'Is that your signature?'

'It looks like it,' Lizzie said, confused. 'It must have been forged – you have to believe me. Why would I arrange to meet a man I've never met before in his cabin?' she added, not entirely kindly.

'Are you really saying it wasn't from you?' Toby asked, equally mystified.

'Yup. That's a forgery. Someone has been impersonating me. So which one of you was it?'

'It wasn't just him,' Duncan said as he reached into the pocket of his jeans. He pulled out a cream-coloured piece of card. 'I got the same message. Left in my mailbox yesterday.'

Duncan held his note up and they could all see that it was the exact same message as Toby's. It was also signed by Lizzie.

'No, this is impossible,' Lizzie said. 'What's going on?'

'So, like Toby,' Duncan said, with a quick glance at the mechanic, 'I was in my cabin waiting for a movie star to knock on the door at 6 p.m.'

'But so was I,' Verity said, as confused as everyone else.

'Not you as well?' Lizzie asked, throwing her arms up in the air.

Verity reached into her handbag and pulled out a third cream-coloured piece of card. It had the same message on it.

'All three of you received the same note and were in your cabins at 6 p.m.?' Tanika asked.

Verity, Toby and Duncan confirmed that they were all in their cabins at 6 p.m.

'And where were you, Lizzie?' Judith asked.

'Me?' Lizzie said, and everyone could see how thrown she was by the question.

'Yes, you. At 6 p.m., when everyone else was in their cabins, where were you?'

'Well . . .' she said, her eyes looking for support among the other witnesses but only receiving blank stares in return. 'I was in my cabin as well, wasn't I? Same as everyone else.'

'You were?' Tanika asked.

'That's right,' she said, finally finding some confidence.

'Even though you didn't get a note?'

'How could she get one?' Toby asked. 'Why would she write a note to herself?'

'But I didn't write any kind of note!'

'It's your signature at the bottom.'

'I sign things all the time. Anyone could have got hold of a copy of my signature and printed it underneath the message. The first I knew about these cards was thirty seconds ago.'

'Very well,' Judith said. 'Let's take what you're saying at face value. You were in your cabin on your own at 6 p.m. when Oliver Beresford was shot on the back deck of the boat. As for everyone else, they were also on their own in their cabins – but only because they received notes that purported to be from you.'

'How many times do I have to say this, I didn't write them!'

'Does it even matter where we were?' Toby asked.

'Oh it matters very much,' Judith said. 'You see, the evidence is pointing towards Oliver dying at about 6 p.m. Which, thanks to those notes you received, was also the time when you were all separated from each other. None of you have an alibi.'

'Seriously, why would any of us need an alibi?'

'Don't you get it?' Duncan said. 'She's saying one of us wasn't in our cabin, but was instead on the back of the boat shooting Oliver dead – isn't that right?'

'Yes,' Judith said. 'I'm sorry to say, it very much looks to me as though one of you – or Lance Goodman, the boat captain – is the killer.'

Chapter 7

There was uproar in the room following Judith's accusation, all the witnesses horrified by the suggestion that one of them might have been involved in Oliver's death in any way. Tanika calmed everyone down by reminding them that Judith wasn't in fact a police officer and therefore her opinion was just that – an opinion.

'I don't understand how those cards came about,' Lizzie said. 'Seeing as I didn't write them,' she added pointedly, for Judith's benefit.

'Can I ask when they were first found?' Tanika asked. 'Mr Vincent?'

'I don't know when mine was delivered,' Toby said. 'It was waiting with the rest of my post when I got back from work yesterday afternoon.'

'Mr Wood?'

Duncan's brow creased as he tried to remember.

'I was out and about in the morning, but I returned to my boat for lunch. I live on a houseboat,' he added, by way of explanation. 'And the letter wasn't there, you're right. So it wasn't delivered in the morning. I had a couple of drinks at lunchtime, repaired to my bedroom for a doze and – that's right, the letter was on my doormat when I woke up.'

'What time was that?'

'I don't know – maybe 3 p.m.? Maybe a bit before that.'

'So it wasn't part of your normal post?' Judith said.

'It must have been hand-delivered – not that I saw who delivered it.'

'Then what about you, Mrs Beresford?' Tanika asked Verity.

'I remember the letter being delivered,' Verity said as she searched her memory. 'It was about 2 p.m. I'd already collected the post that morning, and I was upstairs getting my outfit ready for the boat trip when I heard something come through the letterbox. I went downstairs and there was an envelope with my name printed on it. And that note inside.'

'Why does it matter what time the notes arrived?' Lizzie asked.

'I imagine the detective inspector is trying to work out if it was possible for you to have delivered them,' Judith said.

'But I was at the airport!'

'You said you arrived shortly before midday – which would have given you enough time to deliver the letters.'

'Are you serious! I didn't know who I was going to be meeting on the boat. Oliver was in charge of all that. I didn't know their names, and I had no idea where they lived. And why would I want to kill Oliver bloody Beresford? I haven't seen him in decades – I've been in the States for the last thirty years. Do you seriously believe I landed at Oxford Airport in the morning and delivered those letters in the afternoon so it would be just me and him on the back of the boat at 6 p.m.? And then – what? – I shot him dead?'

'I know it sounds a little far-fetched,' Judith offered.

'Far-fetched? It's deranged! But if you're looking for someone who could have pulled the trigger, I reckon you don't have to look any further than that one there,' Lizzie said with a nod at Verity.

'What?' Verity said, shocked.

'It's obvious you and your husband didn't get on,' Lizzie said, yanking out her packet of cigarettes and lighting up.

'That's not true.'

'You can't fool me. I've made it my life's work to study people, and you hated your husband. I could tell from the way you held yourself around him. How you went quiet every time he came near. Come on,' she said, turning to include Toby and Duncan, 'you must have noticed too. You've known Verity and Oliver for years.'

'How dare you!' Verity spat at Lizzie. 'You don't know me. You don't know *anything* about my relationship with Oliver.'

No one dared break the silence that followed, although Judith couldn't help noticing that neither Duncan nor Toby leapt to Verity's defence. But there was something else as well, Judith realised. The accusation had been designed to throw suspicion on Verity and take the spotlight off Lizzie. Judith remembered what Lance had said about Lizzie seeming 'not in control', but Judith wasn't sure she agreed. She suspected that Lizzie knew exactly what she was doing.

The door banged open and a woman in her seventies strode into the room wearing a dress that was covered in a pattern of brightly coloured flowers, her arm trailing behind her in a way that showed off the fabric to full effect.

'I've only just heard the news!' she announced in a husky voice as she went over to Verity and threw her arms around her. 'Are you all right?' she asked, before throwing her hand to her chest. '"O that this too too solid flesh would melt"!'

'Excuse me?' Tanika said.

The woman turned her attention to Tanika.

'Yes,' she said, as if this one word answered all the questions that had ever been asked by humanity. 'I came.'

'No, I'm sorry, I don't know who you are.'

The woman twitched.

'You don't know who I am?'

'Nor do I,' Judith added.

'Detective Inspector,' Verity said in an attempt to avoid the sudden demise of the new arrival from shock, 'this is Mrs Eddingham. A stalwart of the MADS.'

'First you're the young ingénue,' Mrs Eddingham said, not entirely approvingly, 'and then you're the mother, the matron, the matriarch. I never thought there was a stage beyond that – the stalwart. Even so, Verity, I knew I had to come as soon as I heard the news.'

'How did you know Mrs Beresford would be here?' Tanika asked.

'Well, I went to Verity's house, and when she didn't answer, I guessed there'd only be one place she could be. And she'd have her friends with her. I wasn't wrong,' she added with a look of warmth at the others in the room, although Judith noticed that her glance particularly lingered on Lizzie.

'This is a police interview,' Tanika said.

'And I have information for the police.'

'Sorry – can we start again? How are you connected to Oliver Beresford?'

'I've been the leading lady of the MADS since its inception. It's possible you've heard of me. Mary Eddingham? I did a revue show with Kenny Williams and Sheila Hancock at the Wyndham's in 1976. In the West End,' she added.

'I'm sorry,' Tanika said, 'I wasn't born then.'

'Then perhaps,' Mrs Eddingham said without missing a beat, 'you've read reports of my Lady Bracknell, performed in this very theatre' – she pronounced the word thee-ate-her – 'in 2018? Or my portrayal of "the Scottish Lady" in "the Scottish Play" two years earlier? It was fascinating, pulling off the great aristocratic female roles back to back.'

'What happened in 2017?' Judith asked.

'I'm sorry?'

'Only, it's not back to back if you had a year off in between.'

'As it happens, I had sciatica in 2017 – we don't need to mention that. Oliver was forced to put on *Long Day's Journey into Night* – with not a single female role to be found among its cast. You see, when it came to the MADS, I was the star Oliver sailed by.'

'Then why weren't you on the boat last night?'

'I'm sorry?' Mrs Eddingham said, her smile freezing on her lips.

'Why weren't you on the boat?'

'Well, that's a very good question,' Mrs Eddingham said, fixing Lizzie with a beady stare. 'Why wasn't I invited?'

'I'm sorry . . . Mrs Eddingham,' Lizzie said. 'I didn't know you were still . . .' Lizzie only belatedly realised how impolite it would be to suggest that she thought Mrs Eddingham had died. 'Acting,' she said to finish her sentence and save her blushes.

'You know each other?' Judith asked.

'Oh yes,' Mrs Eddingham said. 'I was here the first day that young Lizzie walked into this hallowed hall. What was it?' she added, pretending to rack her memory. 'A Ray Cooney farce, I think. *Don't Dress for Dinner* – you played the floozy,' she added with a smile that could have dissolved stone.

'I'm sorry you weren't invited,' Lizzie said. 'I told Oliver I wanted to throw a party for you all, and he was the one who chose only to invite the committee rather than a wider membership.'

'How strange,' Mrs Eddingham said. 'I'm on the committee.'

'That's not strictly true,' Duncan said.

'I'm an honorary lifelong member.'

'You should have been there,' Verity said. 'And I'm sorry Oliver didn't invite you. We only found out who was on the guest list when we arrived at the boat.'

'Thank you,' Mrs Eddingham said, glad to have been offered this concession.

'That must have been irksome,' Judith said. 'Not being invited.'

'What was it Noël Coward said?' Mrs Eddingham asked airily. 'I'm sure you'll be able to tell us.'

'When anyone treated him poorly, he'd tell himself, "Rise above it". That's the mantra I live my life by. "Rise above it".'

'Just to check,' Tanika pressed on. 'Where were you last night? In particular at about 6 p.m.?'

'Me?' Mrs Eddingham said, delighted. Being questioned by the police was exactly what she wanted.

'Last night, let me see . . . I think I was on my own – yes, that's right, I'd found the original TV production of *A Voyage Round My Father* on YouTube. It's old-fashioned, of course, but Larry Olivier as John Mortimer's blind father is simply sensational. You can *see* how he can't see.'

'You can see how he can't see?' Tanika asked.

'If you acted, you'd understand.'

'But are you saying you were on your own?'

'I live on my own, it's hardly surprising I'd be on my own. But if you want me to prove it, I can tell you every single scene from the teleplay. We open on Larry Olivier in a train in a business suit—'

'I'm sure there's no need for that,' Tanika said.

'But I'm not only here to offer support to Verity, I've also got something I think you need to know. You see, it's simply impossible that anyone connected to the MADS could have hurt Oliver. He lived for the theatre, and we lived for him. But I also know that you were on Lance Goodman's boat last night. And I happen to know that Lance and Oliver had a bust-up a few weeks ago. I popped into the Old Ship pub before closing time – I sometimes have a little crème de menthe when I'm "weary with toil" and need to "haste me to my bed" – Shakespeare,' Mrs Eddingham added, for the benefit of the room. 'But I saw Oliver and Lance in a corner booth arguing, so I ducked into an alcove so they didn't see me.'

'You spied on them?' Judith chipped in.

'Certainly not! I didn't want Oliver to feel embarrassed if he saw me. I couldn't make out everything they were saying, but the disagreement seemed to be about the terms for hiring a boat for the event last night. And the thing is, I heard Oliver say to Lance, "If you want me to keep your secret, you'll hire us the boat and make sure it's ready in time."'

'What did Lance say to that?' Tanika asked.

'I couldn't hear his reply,' Mrs Eddingham said. 'He leaned forward and whispered something to Oliver. But he wasn't happy, I can tell you that much.'

'Then what happened?'

'Oh, I left them alone, went to the bar and had my crème de menthe. It was only today, after I heard the terrible news, that I realised I had information and simply had to tell the police.'

'Are you prepared to give a witness statement?'

'I'd be delighted to,' Mrs Eddingham said with relish.

As Tanika began explaining to the others that she'd also need to take their formal witness statements, she noticed Judith get up from her chair and slip out of the room. Telling the witnesses she wouldn't be long, she followed Judith out and caught up with her in the lobby.

'Don't even think about going to talk to Lance Goodman,' she said.

'What's that?' Judith asked innocently.

'We both know that's where you're planning on heading. Please, Judith, you can't talk to him.'

There was an edge of desperation in Tanika's voice that caught Judith by surprise.

'What is it?'

'I hoped I wouldn't have to tell you this, but I got into a bit of trouble after we caught Geoffrey Lushington's killer last year. There was a complaint from one of my team – Brendan Perry. He's a detective sergeant.'

Judith snorted. 'I remember him well. A man without talent, I thought.'

'The point is, I'm on probation while an investigation into my conduct is ongoing.'

'Are you serious?'

'I've got to make sure I do everything by the book.'

'But you keep catching killers, don't you?'

'No one's denying I get results. But it's my methods that are causing problems.'

'You mean enlisting me, Becks and Suzie? Surely all that matters is that murderers get put behind bars.'

'Shanti needs me. As does my dad. And Shamil, for that matter. I can't mess up at work. My life would fall apart.'

'I'm so sorry you're having to deal with this.'

'I'll sort it out. Don't worry.'

'Are you saying we can't help you? As civilian advisers?'

'It would be much better if you didn't, for the time being at least.'

'But you let us talk to Lance earlier.'

'I wasn't thinking, and I realised I'd done the wrong thing as soon as you left. We can't do things the way we've done them in the past, Judith. If I put a foot wrong, I could be suspended.'

'That would be terrible. Not just for you, but for Oliver Beresford. You're his best chance of getting his killer caught. Very well, I'll do as you ask. Seeing as it's so important.'

'Thank you. Although, to check, is this one of the times you're lying to me?'

'No,' Judith said, with all the sincerity she could muster. 'I promise you I won't try to help you in any way.'

'Thank you.'

They were interrupted by the sound of a commotion in the auditorium. They hurried back, arriving in time to hear Mrs Eddingham declare, 'The show must go on!'

'It's in bad taste,' Toby said.

'What show?' Tanika said.

'Our next production,' Mrs Eddingham said, as though Tanika should have already been aware of the answer. '*The Importance of Being Earnest* has been in rehearsals for the last three months and it's due to open in two weeks' time.'

'Oh,' Judith said.

'Which we now can't do,' Duncan said. 'Not without Oliver – he was playing Lady Bracknell.'

'He was?' Tanika asked.

'Following in the steps of Sir David Suchet,' Mrs Eddingham explained. 'Not that I entirely approved. I've always felt that to have a man playing Lady Bracknell misses the essential femininity in the role.'

'This whole conversation is ghoulish,' Verity said.

'We can't let our audience down – we've already sold ninety per cent of our tickets.'

'Of course!' Judith said, realising what the argument was about. 'You want to play Lady Bracknell.'

'It's the most logical solution to our problem,' Mrs Eddingham replied. 'After all, people are still talking about the last time I played her. And I first played the part for the MADS in 1987, and you know what they say, third time's the charm. I know the lines, I "get" the character, I'm the right age, I've the right stature and experience and talent. I should play her.'

'But who will play your part of Miss Prism?' Verity asked.

'Does that matter?' Mrs Eddingham asked. 'We both know it's a nothing part. Oliver was testing our friendship as it was by casting me as Miss Prism.'

'I'll do it,' Judith said, before she could stop herself.

Everyone turned to look at her.

'What's that?' Tanika asked.

Judith had never enjoyed performing on stage, but she knew that being in the next production would be the perfect way to get to know the suspects better.

'If you can no longer play the part, I'll do it. I'll play Miss Prism.'

'Well, isn't that wonderful!' Mrs Eddingham said, clapping her hands together. 'I mean, of course, it's a sad day,' she added as she remembered why she'd got her big break. 'A day of real loss. But Oliver would be the first to say the show must go on. Duncan will be in touch with a rehearsal schedule,' she told Judith. 'Won't you, Duncan?'

Judith smiled, but inside she could already feel a rising sense of panic. Had she really just agreed to make her theatrical debut with the Marlow Amateur Dramatic Society?

Chapter 8

Judith rang Suzie and Becks and was pleased to learn that they'd gone for a walk while she'd been in the Little Theatre. It was easy for them all to meet up at Judith's punt as it was still tied up at Cookham Lock. Once they were all together and she'd cast off, Judith filled them in on her encounter with the Marlow Amateur Dramatic Society and the fact that Mrs Eddingham saw Lance and Oliver arguing a few weeks before.

'Which is why I'm suggesting we pop in on Lance on the way back to my house,' she said. 'And ask him a few pointed questions.'

'I'm well up for a few pointed questions directed at him,' Suzie said.

'How did you and he meet?' Becks asked.

'What is there to say? We have a friend in common, and a few years back she thought we'd be good together, so she helped fix up a blind date. And it went OK. Not like I'd set the bar high at all. You can't at our age, can you? But he was attractive — in his own way. He'd at least cleaned himself up and made an effort. There was a directness about him that I liked. And there's no getting away from the fact that people who actually do things with their hands – who are capable – are kind of attractive. So we started dating, and it was good for a while. I knew he wasn't "the one" – I'm not sure I was even looking for that. But it was nice to have company, and he was good company.'

Suzie drifted off into her memories.

'What happened?' Becks asked.

'It was little things at first. He didn't follow rules. He'd park in a disabled spot at the supermarket. He had no problem drink-driving. There was one time he left Hunt's with an expensive screwdriver – by mistake, he said – and he didn't take it back. I even worried if he'd nicked it on purpose.'

'He's a crook?'

Suzie shook her head. 'It's more like the bit of him that should have cared about right and wrong wasn't there. If something benefited him, then that was all that mattered. Don't get me wrong, I know I sometimes sail pretty close to the wind, but I always know the difference between right and wrong. It caused massive arguments. And the more we argued, the less he bothered with the relationship. He became unreliable. Flaky. I realised he's basically your typical man, only in it for himself. When it ended, things got messy. That's the other thing about him. When he's backed into a corner, he comes out fighting.'

'How very interesting,' Judith said, thinking how this new information impacted on the case.

'That must have been so hard on you,' Becks said, thinking of her friend.

'Of course. And that as well,' Judith added hurriedly, realising she'd alighted on the wrong part of Suzie's story.

She then went on to explain how Toby, Verity and Duncan had all received letters from Lizzie telling them to go to their cabins at 6 p.m.

'What!' Suzie said, amazed. 'Then forget Lance – or Verity, for that matter – she's the killer!'

'It's certainly hard to explain otherwise.'

'If you want everyone out of the way so you can commit murder, you don't send letters that get them out of the way and sign them in your own name, do you?' said Becks.

'Unless you're particularly stupid,' Suzie said.

'I got the impression that Lizzie's anything but stupid,' Judith said. 'In fact, I think she's very clever indeed. Or cunning, at least.'

'So who delivered those letters?' Becks asked.

'The killer did,' Suzie announced. 'It must have been. Although, you're right, Becks, it would be a bit dim of Lizzie, if she's the killer.'

The women fell into a ruminative silence, and Judith smiled to herself.

'There's one other thing,' she said. 'I've agreed to be in the Marlow Amateur Dramatic Society's next production.'

'But that's wonderful!' Becks said.

'I'm not sure I'd agree with you there,' Judith said. 'But it will give me a chance to snoop around.'

'What's the part?'

'A character called Miss Prism in *The Importance of Being Earnest*. She's the chaperone to one of the lead characters. A very boring older woman.'

'Ha! As if you could ever be boring.'

'When is the first performance?' Becks asked.

'In a couple of weeks' time.'

'And you think you can learn the part in that time?'

'Funnily enough, when we did *The Importance of Being Earnest* at school, I was cast as Miss Prism then. So it's a part I already know.'

Judith pushed her pole into the mud to give the punt another kick of forward momentum. As she did, she spotted something colourful caught in the river up ahead.

'What's that?' she asked, pointing at a bush that was half growing out of the riverbank and half out of the river.

'What's what?' Suzie asked.

'There's something caught on a branch over there. It looks like an item of clothing.'

It was true. A piece of fabric was lodged in the water among the branches.

Judith steered the punt over to the bush and Suzie grabbed hold of the overhanging branches to keep them in position.

The fabric was a purple-and-green tartan.

'Those look like suffragette colours to me,' Judith said as she leaned out of the punt and retrieved the fabric.

'Careful, Judith!' Suzie called out, grabbing her friend's arm.

'What on earth are you doing?' Judith said, irritated.

'Saving your life. You could have fallen in and been swept away.'

'I swim in the river every day, I wouldn't have been swept away. And what on earth makes you think I'd fall in?'

'I want you to be safe, that's all.'

'No, there's something up with you, Suzie Harris,' Judith said.

'Me?' Suzie said, guilt written across her face.

'But now's not the time,' Judith said, examining the item.

'I think we'd better not touch it too much,' Becks said as she took it from Judith, laid it on a seat of the punt and then got out her phone and opened an internet browser.

'Why?' Suzie asked.

'I think I've seen this scarf before.'

'But how come it's here?' Suzie asked. 'We punted past this spot earlier and didn't see anything.'

'The water level of the river's been going down ever since the storm a few days ago,' Judith said. 'That might explain why the scarf's only now revealed itself.'

'I think I'm right!' Becks said, holding up her phone so her friends could see.

On the screen, Judith and Suzie could see that Becks had navigated to the 'Who We Are' page of the Marlow Amateur Dramatic Society website. There was a head-and-shoulders photo of Verity Beresford smiling for the camera, announcing that she was the society's secretary. Around her neck she was wearing a silk scarf with identical purple-and-green stripes.

'This is Verity's scarf,' Judith said, looking at the fabric in the punt.

'I remember her wearing it when she came to one of the rehearsals for the nativity play,' Becks said. 'And then I noticed it again when Suzie and I were going through the MADS' website on our walk. It wouldn't have stuck in my mind if it hadn't been a suffragette scarf. You don't get many people in Marlow aligning themselves with protest groups, even if they're historic ones.'

'And now that same scarf is in the water,' Suzie said. 'The day after her husband was shot on the river.'

'We *think* it's the same scarf,' Judith corrected.

'It'll be easy to find out. We're Tanika's civilian advisers – we can give it to her, then she can get her team to do a forensics test on it.'

'Ah,' Judith said. 'We may have a bit of a problem there.'

Chapter 9

Judith explained to her friends how Tanika had been put on probation and couldn't hire them to work on the case.

'I don't understand,' Becks said. 'If you're saying we can't help her, then why are we going to talk to Lance?'

'It's quite simple,' Judith said matter-of-factly. 'Tanika said we couldn't help her officially or unofficially, and I promised that we wouldn't do either of those things. But we're still citizens. We can still talk to people.'

'Oh, I get it,' Suzie said appreciatively. 'We aren't helping the police, we're helping ourselves. By fishing scarves out of the river, for example.'

'I know it goes against the spirit of what Tanika said, but I'm not putting down my crime-fighting cape just because an inadequate man is threatened by a successful woman. And I'm sure she'll agree with us when she sees how useful we are,' Judith added as Lance's boatyard came into view.

The women could see Lance on the back deck of the *Marlow Belle*, cleaning it with a hose and brush.

'Making sure you've cleaned off the evidence?' Suzie called out as they approached.

Lance turned off his hose and looked at the women.

'What are you doing back here?' he asked.

'Exercising our rights as British citizens to go where we like, when we like. And we've got something we'd like to ask you.'

'No, I'm done with it,' Lance said, stepping onto the jetty from the low deck. 'First the police pull my pride and joy apart looking for God knows what – not that they found anything, I can tell you. And then I'm questioned like I'm guilty of something.'

'Then why are you cleaning your boat?'

'A guy was killed on it, and then it got covered in that powder the police used to collect fingerprints. I'm getting her shipshape again. Starting over.'

'I thought that's what you could never do,' Suzie said, folding her arms. 'Start over.'

'I wonder if the pair of you would be better off admitting the fact you used to be together,' Becks offered.

'Together?' Lance said with a snort. 'It never felt like that at the time.'

'You can say that again,' Suzie said, her jaw jutting. 'You were never around.'

'I'm not doing this again.'

'That's fine by me. Neither am I.'

Suzie and Lance stared daggers at each other.

'This has started well,' Judith said with a sigh. 'Would this be a good time to ask about your secret?'

'What?' Lance said, panic slamming into his eyes.

'How interesting,' she said.

'I don't have to talk to you,' Lance said, and then he turned from the women and started to walk towards the main workshop.

'Oliver Beresford knew all about it, didn't he?' Judith called after him.

Lance stopped in his tracks.

'That's right,' Suzie said. '*That* secret.'

Lance turned slowly.

'You and Oliver Beresford were overheard in the Old Ship,' Becks said.

'Hold on,' Lance said, as he worked out what the women were insinuating. 'You're talking about that stupid old bat, aren't you? She's about a hundred years old and thinks she's Queen of Marlow. God knows what her name is, but Oliver didn't like her.'

'You mean Mrs Eddingham,' Judith said.

'That's right – that's who he said it was.'

'Why don't you tell us what happened?' Becks asked.

'Sure. Whatever – it's nothing. This was the night he hired the *Marlow Belle*. We met in the Old Ship. I got why he was being all cloak-and-dagger when he told me that a movie star he knew was looking to hire a boat to go up the Thames, and it had to be the *Marlow Belle*. I was surprised he even knew about my boat, I'd only just listed it on my website for hire, but for later in the summer. It wasn't quite ready.'

'The crankshaft wasn't working,' Suzie said.

'That's right,' Lance said levelly. 'The crankshaft wasn't working. But Oliver said it didn't matter. The movie star wanted a cruiser with half a dozen cabins below deck.'

'He said that, did he?'

'Sure. There had to be cabins, and a party deck. Oh – and there was one other thing. He said that the movie star also wanted to know where the driving position on the boat was. So I said it was in a cabin at the front of the boat. It was a weird question, if you ask me, but Oliver said that privacy was important to this movie star. If she hired the boat, she wanted the skipper – i.e. me – to stay out of the way in the driving cabin as much as possible.'

'What did you say to that?' Judith asked.

'For the sort of money I knew I'd be able to charge, I said I'd be happy to do the whole thing in my underpants if it made her happy.'

'So, to clarify, you're saying it was the movie star who wanted you to stay in the driving cabin?' Judith asked.

'That's what Oliver told me. The point is, there we were, talking in our booth, and suddenly Oliver leans across and says some old woman is eavesdropping on us, and how she's the bane of his life.'

'He didn't like her?'

'He said he'd been trying to get rid of her for decades. Apparently she's too grand to come to rehearsals or learn her lines. And she looks down on everyone else in the cast. The only revenge he could get was to keep her at arm's length – which was why she wasn't coming on the boat. In fact, he said over his dead body was she going on the boat with any movie star.'

'Hold on,' Suzie said. 'He said "over his dead body" was Mrs Eddingham going on the boat?'

'It's a turn of phrase,' Lance said. 'The point is, Oliver said he wanted to spike the woman – give her something fake to gossip about. That's how he dealt with her. Giving her rubbish to get in a spin over. You know, saying he was going to end their amateur dramatic club, that sort of thing. So he pretended to have an argument with me. You know, with him saying

I had some big secret and he was blackmailing me to get cheap access to my boat.'

'You were play-acting?' Judith asked.

'It wasn't my idea – it's the way he was. You know, melodramatic and whatever. It was him who did all the talking, I just played along. But that's what happened. It was a joke, that's all. And it worked, didn't it? That woman got the wrong end of the stick. Meaning, Oliver had the last laugh, didn't he?'

Judith looked at Lance long and hard. His story didn't sound remotely plausible, and yet, wasn't it the case that sometimes in life, the most implausible things were true? After all, if Lance was involved in Oliver's murder, wouldn't he have come up with a better explanation for the argument?

Although, what Mrs Eddingham did or didn't overhear wasn't necessarily the important revelation, was it? If Lance was to be believed, Lizzie had wanted a boat that had cabins below deck and a driving position that would keep the boat captain hidden away as well. When this was added to the fact that everyone on the boat had received letters from Lizzie telling them to go to their cabins at 6 p.m. – the very time, according to Oliver's waterlogged wristwatch, that he went into the water – Judith could see that the case against Lizzie was increasingly compelling.

That said, Lizzie had been right about one thing. It didn't seem credible that the first thing she'd do after landing in the UK would be to kill someone she hadn't seen for decades.

'Did you get a note from Lizzie?' she asked.

'How do you mean?'

'A printed note, telling you to go to your cabin at 6 p.m.'

Lance paused, and then shook his head.

'No,' he said.

'Are you sure?'

'Look, I've been racking my brains trying to work out what I might have seen that was in any way suspicious, and the thing is, I didn't see anything. It's like I said. I was in the driving cabin most of the time. Doubly so when the engine started playing up. But from what I saw, everyone was excited, all mobbing Lizzie, wanting to hear her stories. There was no tension, no weird looks – no nothing. None of the people on the boat had a problem with Oliver. So I got to thinking, what else did I know about him? Precious little, if you ask me. We'd never met before. But there is one thing. A couple of months ago, I was at the GP's surgery. It was a routine check-up for me, but Oliver was there too. And I saw him leave the doctor's room with a look on his face. He was white as a sheet and he had to go and sit down.'

'Do you know what the problem was?'

'There's only one thing that makes a man our age go weak at the knees. He'd just had a diagnosis. If you ask me, it was something bad.'

'That's all a bit convenient,' Suzie said.

'What's that supposed to mean?' Lance asked.

'Only that we come here saying we have a witness who said Oliver threatened to reveal your secret if you didn't do as he said, and now you're trying to distract us by saying that Oliver was ill.'

'I know what I saw. You ask his wife – that Verity woman. She'll know.'

They all looked up as a police car pulled into the boatyard.

'The police!' Suzie said.

The women turned and ran for the jetty – Judith calling out behind her, 'Sorry, got to go!' As soon as they'd all clambered into her punt, she cast off and started punting upstream.

Glancing over her shoulder, Judith could see Tanika approaching Lance. She breathed a sigh of relief. They'd got away without being seen.

'I'm not very happy about this,' Becks said as Judith punted them back to her house.

'We've done nothing wrong,' Judith said.

'You know we've done wrong, Judith, or we wouldn't have run away. Even though we've found possibly important evidence,' Becks added, indicating the bag that contained the suffragette scarf they'd fished out of the river.

'Very well,' Judith said, 'then I suggest we go and see Tanika with the scarf and have it out with her. She can't possibly solve the case without us. Our involvement doesn't have to be official, but we have to be involved. We'll get her to agree with us, and Brendan be damned.'

'Maybe Tanika's right,' Suzie said. 'And we should sit this one out.'

'Are you serious?' Judith asked.

'I'm only saying, what if it's better we don't get involved?'

'OK, you've got to tell us what's going on.'

'Judith's right,' Becks said. 'This isn't like you at all.'

'I don't know what you're going on about,' Suzie said, although it was clear to her friends that she knew exactly what they meant.

Judith said, 'We can play the game of you pretending you have no idea what we're talking about, or you can tell us the truth. Why are you being so lily-livered?'

Suzie thought about trying to keep up the pretence, but then she put her head in her hands and let out a cow-like moan.

'What is it?' Becks asked.

'I don't know why I did it,' she said to the floor of the punt.

Becks and Suzie exchanged a glance. What on earth had Suzie done?

'It's all my own stupid fault. It was a moment of weakness.'

'Go on,' Becks said.

When Suzie raised her head, she looked haunted.

'OK, but you'll be particularly angry, Becks.'

'I won't,' Becks said. 'I promise you.'

'I did a tarot reading.'

'Why on earth would you do that?' Becks yelped.

'I told you you'd get all judgy.'

'But why would you open yourself up to spirits you can't possibly control – or understand, for that matter.'

'Don't tell me you believe in tarot cards?' Judith asked Becks.

'Not exactly,' Becks said. 'But we all know spirits exist – in some way or other – and I don't think you should risk trying to communicate with them.'

'Not you as well,' Judith said with a sigh. 'Spirits – and ghouls and ghosts – don't exist. Surely we can all agree on that? Which means that tarot has about as much to say about the future as playing the card game Happy Families.'

'I'm not so sure,' Becks said. 'The magic in tarot goes back a long way. Well before organised religion.'

'Becks is right,' Suzie said. 'Think about it. There's got to be a reason why people don't do tarot.'

'There is,' Judith said. 'It doesn't work.'

'That's not true,' Suzie said. 'It's because it's too spooky. Too accurate.'

'Why were you doing tarot in the first place?' Becks asked.

'Oh, I don't know, I was feeling out of sorts the other night. I'd done my radio show a couple of days before.' Suzie presented a Sunday-night show on Marlow FM where listeners were encouraged to phone in with stories of their pets' antics. 'And I had a clear day ahead of me – with no dogs to look after. And my daughters weren't around for a chat. You know? It's like I said – I felt on edge. So I decided to have a tidy up and I found my old tarot cards in a drawer. Before I knew what I was doing, I was shuffling the deck and laying down three cards.'

'What did you get?' Becks asked.

'Queen of Swords. Wheel of Fortune.'

'And Death?' Judith guessed.

'How did you know?' Suzie asked, wide-eyed.

'It would hardly be worth all this palaver if you hadn't.'

'But that's the thing, the third card I pulled was Death.'

'That's bad,' Becks said.

'Listen to the pair of you!' Judith said. 'Are you now going to say that just because you pulled the Death card out of the deck, Oliver Beresford died?'

'No – no way,' Suzie said. 'Those cards couldn't have had anything to do with a man. The Queen of Swords represents female energy. And it specifically refers to mature feminine energy. As for the Wheel of Fortune, that can mean Fate, Destiny or Change.'

'So what was their message?' Becks asked.

'Well, when you do a three card spread, the order you draw the cards matters. The first is the Situation, the second is the Action, and the third is the Outcome. So Queen of Swords was the situation, which means we're talking about an older woman. As for the action, that's obvious – it's the destiny of our older woman, and that destiny is the third card, Death.'

'You're saying your life is at risk?' Becks asked, horrified.

'No – not mine. You see, there are four queen cards and the Queen of Swords refers specifically to the intellect – which isn't where I'm at, we can all agree on that. But it is where Judith is.'

Becks and Suzie turned and looked at Judith, worry etched on their faces.

'You think my life is in danger?' Judith scoffed.

'It doesn't have to mean a literal death,' Suzie said. 'It can also mean a time of great challenge or change. But I can tell you, it's not good news.'

'Which is why you've been keeping a beady eye on me?'

'The cards don't lie.'

'The cards don't say anything!'

'We don't know what the cards say for sure,' Becks clarified.

'It's superstitious twaddle,' Judith snorted. 'Cards are cards, they can't tell the future in any way. So let's go and talk to Tanika. And stop worrying, I've got a few years left in me, thank you very much.'

Judith thrust her punt pole deep into the Thames mud and pushed forward, pleased that she'd closed down the subject of her upcoming demise for good.

Days later, she'd reflect that she'd been a fool not to heed the cards' warning. Her life was indeed in the deepest peril. She just didn't know it yet.

Chapter 10

Maidenhead Police Station was a 1980s red-brick building that, for the purposes of quick access, had been built between a series of roundabouts and a multi-storey car park on the outskirts of the town. Years of car fumes and rain had made it look almost wilfully drab, and the inside of the building wasn't any less tired.

As Tanika stood at the whiteboard in the incident room, she tried to focus on the case, but was struggling to shift her feeling of low-level panic. She didn't respond well to being undermined by her team, and Detective Sergeant Brendan Perry lodging a complaint about how she'd handled the Geoffrey Lushington case was the definition of being undermined.

Her boss was too smart to start any kind of internal inquiry he didn't already know the outcome to, but she knew that if she took even one misstep now, DS Perry would run straight to him to trigger a formal investigation. It was all about following correct procedure, she told herself for the hundredth time. Her job was to collate the facts of the case and then make the right decision, as per correct procedure.

Tanika had ordered the diving team to look for evidence on the riverbed of the Thames in the 500 metres or so either side of where the *Marlow Belle* was most likely to have been at 6 p.m. In particular, she was hoping they'd find the gun that had been used to shoot Oliver Beresford. They'd found no pistol on the boat when they'd searched it, and it seemed entirely possible that the killer had thrown it into the water after committing murder. Officers had also taken in all of the victim's electronic devices and correspondence so that they could scour his life for any clues that would reveal who might have wanted him dead. She'd also appeared on the local news, appealing for potential witnesses. She was surprised that no one had been on the banks of the river at the time of the murder, but there was still time for someone to come forward.

DS Perry called over from his desk. He was going to seed and had stubble that might have once made him look rugged, but now it just gave him an air of dishevelment.

'Boss?' There was a critical tone to his voice.

'Yes, Brendan?' she said with a forced smile.

'Mrs Potts is in reception.'

'What's she doing here?' Tanika said, before realising how weak that made her sound.

'She says she's got a piece of evidence – to do with the Beresford case. She needs to hand it in.'

'I told her she couldn't be involved,' Tanika said as she headed for the door, her cheeks burning with embarrassment.

She clattered down the stairs to reception and discovered that the duty officer had put Judith and her friends in an interview room. With a sense of mounting irritation, Tanika pushed through the intervening doors and entered.

'What on earth are you all doing here?' she demanded.

'I'm so sorry,' Becks said, knowing how badly they were transgressing. 'I tried to stop them from coming.'

'But we had no choice,' Suzie said.

'Suzie's right,' Judith said. 'Because we've found what could be a key piece of evidence.'

She pulled a dog poo bag from her handbag and plopped it onto the table.

'What on earth is that?' Tanika asked.

Judith explained that the bag contained a silk scarf that they believed might have belonged to Verity Beresford.

'And you found it when you were punting on the river?' Tanika asked.

'It was all completely by accident,' Judith said. 'It's a piece of great good fortune that it was us who found it and recognised its possible significance,' she added as she rooted in her handbag and pulled out a little tin. Popping the lid, she offered it to Tanika. 'Travel sweet?'

'My career's on the line,' Tanika said.

'So that's no to a travel sweet?'

'And the superintendent's already spoken to me since Mr Beresford's death. One slip and he'll take me off the case is what he says, but what he really means is that I can't have the three of you helping me.'

'Why not?' Suzie asked. 'We work well together – the four of us.'

'If you recall, the last time we all worked together, I allowed the fire brigade to be called to a very large fire that you, Judith, had started on purpose.'

'We caught the killer, didn't we?' Judith said indignantly.

'While using up a lot of the resources of a sister service. It didn't go down well.'

'It didn't go down well with Brendan, you mean,' Judith said. 'He's never liked us. And it's obvious that he struggles with having a woman as his boss.'

'It's not that simple,' Tanika said. 'He works hard, but he's going through a tough patch right now. He took his inspector's exams earlier this year and failed.'

'So he's taking it out on you, because you passed yours,' Suzie said.

'Even so, I can't include you in any way. My every move on this case is being put under the microscope. I did try to tell you this before, Judith.'

'And we've not tried to get involved,' Judith lied. 'It was merely a lucky coincidence, us finding this scarf. We only saw it because we went back to Cookham Lock to get my punt.'

'And you're perfectly capable of solving your crimes without us,' Becks said.

'Hear, hear to that,' Suzie said.

'Thank you.'

'So we've done our civic duty in dropping off that scarf,' Judith said, 'and we'll be on our way. You won't hear from us again. Although, seeing as we're not coming back, perhaps before we go you could share with us any aspects of the case that are puzzling you. Since we're all together. Maybe we can help you one last time before we leave.'

Tanika looked over at the door to the interview room to check that it was shut, and then she looked at the mirror of the two-way glass.

'There is one thing,' she said, leaning forward in a conspiratorial whisper. 'And it's the sort of puzzle you're so good at solving, Judith.'

Judith fluffed herself up like a mother hen.

'Go on, then. I'm all ears.'

'It's those cards that everyone on the boat received telling them to be in their cabins at 6 p.m. We've had forensics go over them, and the only fingerprints they've been able to lift belong to the individual who received each card. So, the only prints on Duncan Wood's card belong to Duncan Wood, the only prints on Toby Vincent's card belong to him, and the only prints on Verity Beresford's card belong to her.'

'Well, there's no mystery there,' Judith said. 'Whoever put the letters through their doors must have made sure they didn't get their fingerprints on them. It's yet more proof that this was a well-planned murder.'

'So are we back to saying Lizzie Jenkins is the killer?' Suzie asked.

'It's not that simple,' Tanika said. 'She was telling the truth when she said she hadn't signed the notes. The signature had been downloaded from her Wikipedia page. Whoever made the invites put it at the bottom to make it look as though she'd signed them when she hadn't. So there's no way of proving that the notes were sent by her. Which is where the puzzle comes in. You see, we found a mystery when we carried out a full search of Mr Beresford's body—'

'What about the post-mortem?' Judith interrupted. 'Did he die from those bullet wounds?'

'He did.'

'So he was killed on the boat?'

'He was killed on the boat.'

'Is there any way he could have shot himself?'

'We found no gunshot residue on either of his hands from

firing the gun. And it wouldn't have had time to wash off in the water – he wasn't in it long enough. He didn't fire the gun at any time. What's more, the first bullet was fired into his stomach from very close range—'

'How do you know that it was the first shot?' Suzie asked.

'Because that first shot only wounded him. And the burn marks on the skin, and the limited spread of gunshot residue, make it clear it was fired from point-blank range. The muzzle was held up to his body. But the second shot, the killing shot, was fired from a distance of about four or five feet. The spread of gunshot residue on his clothes around that entrance wound is that much bigger.'

'And nobody has arms five feet long,' Judith said.

'Got it in one. Mr Beresford didn't shoot himself. It was some-one else. And you should know, the second bullet pierced the left ventricle of his heart. According to the pathologist, Mr Beresford would have died almost instantly – which is consistent with the evidence from his lungs. He swallowed almost no river water. He was already dead by the time he went in.'

'So the first shot was from up close, the second from a distance,' Judith said, wanting to make sure she'd got the order of events correct. 'And he was dead before he hit the water?'

'That's what the pathologist is saying.'

'Yes, that would make sense of the splinters of wood in the palms of his hands. There was a struggle of some sort, wasn't there? Either before the first shot was fired, or maybe after the first shot – which only wounded him – and the second, which was the killing shot.'

'We've found pre-mortem bruises on his legs and arms that would be consistent with that interpretation.'

'Have you found the murder weapon?' Becks asked.

'I've got police divers scouring the riverbed. It wasn't found on the boat, so my working theory is that the killer threw it into the river after the murder.'

'When did he die?' Suzie asked.

'At about 6 p.m. – as his wristwatch suggested. But let me get back to the puzzle I need your help with.'

'Of course,' Judith said. 'But can I ask? Did the post-mortem reveal that Oliver had cancer when he died?'

Tanika looked sharply at her friend.

'As it happens, he had liver cancer. How did you know?'

'How far along was it?' Becks asked, trying to deflect attention from Judith.

'One of my team spoke to his doctor. She said it was discovered very late and Mr Beresford had refused treatment. She added that it wasn't an unreasonable position to take. When they discovered it, it was already stage four.'

'That's terrible,' Judith said. 'Thank you for answering our questions. Now back to your mystery. How can we help you?'

'It's something I can't make head nor tail of. When we searched Oliver Beresford's body, we found an invite in his pocket. It was exactly the same invite as those received by all of the other passengers – complete with Lizzie's signature downloaded from the internet – telling him to go to his cabin at 6 p.m.'

'So he was supposed to be in his cabin?' Becks asked.

'That's the most obvious explanation.'

'Were you able to lift any fingerprints from his card?' Suzie asked.

'Yup. The only prints on it belonged to Mr Beresford.'

'As was the case with all of the other invitations,' Becks said.

'So what does that mean?' Judith asked. 'Everyone on the boat received one of those cards, apart from Lizzie and Lance?'

'That's how it looks.'

'Then why did those two not receive a card?' Becks asked.

'That's not what I want to know,' Judith said. 'Because if Oliver was supposed to be in his cabin at 6 p.m., why wasn't he? Why was he on the back of the boat getting shot?'

'That's what I can't work out,' Tanika said.

'And there's something else,' Judith said. 'An aspect of this case we've not addressed yet. There are so many ways of killing someone – and plenty of ways of shooting someone dead – but this murder was staged so elaborately. Hiring a boat with cabins below deck. Sending fake invitations to get people out of the way – even to the murder victim, which, I agree, seems to make no sense. But the point is, the murderer must have felt that this was the best and perhaps only way of killing Oliver Beresford. How on earth could this have been a logical way of killing him?'

The women looked at each other. None of them had any answers.

Chapter 11

Over the following days, Becks was pleased to see that Judith had been telling the truth when she'd said that she wouldn't try to play any further part in the investigation. Becks had even rung her friend a couple of times to check that she wasn't secretly sleuthing, and Judith had been home to answer her landline every time.

After the third call, Judith snapped at her that she wished her friends would leave her alone – which seemed an overreaction to Becks, until Judith explained that Suzie was also pestering her to make sure she wasn't doing anything risky. Suzie remained convinced that Judith's life was in danger following her tarot reading, and nothing Judith said could change her mind.

As far as Becks was concerned, the pause in the investigation couldn't have been better timed, because it allowed her to focus on Chloe's return for her mid-term break from university with her new boyfriend, Hugo.

'He's terrific, isn't he?' Colin said to Becks as they got ready for bed one night.

'Hmm?' Becks said, barely looking up from her book. 'Oh yes, he's lovely.'

'You don't sound enthusiastic.'

She lowered her book. 'No, you're right. He's delightful. Did you see how he was the first person to get up from the table and offer to clear away? And he laughed at your jokes and even asked questions.'

'He's a well-brought-up lad.'

Hugo's family owned a large house, land 'as far as the eye could see' in Lincolnshire, and he'd been educated at one of the most expensive all-boys boarding schools in the UK. He was studying Classics at Exeter and was, by some distance, better educated, more attractive and charming than Chloe, Becks or Colin.

'He is,' Becks agreed. But she had a sense there was something not quite right about Hugo – not that she could put her finger on it. She worried that her unease was mostly caused by his name. Who even calls themself Hugo any more?

The following day, Becks was in the kitchen organising the rota for cleaning the church when Chloe burst in, bright-eyed and fizzing with excitement, Hugo at her side.

'We've got news,' she said.

'Oh God, you're pregnant,' Becks said in horror.

'No, Mum, I'm not pregnant.'

'Thank God for that – not that it would be a bad thing, but it would very definitely be a surprise. Considering I'm sitting here trying to work out how often the brass eagle lectern in All Saints' needs polishing.'

'But it's still big news,' Chloe said. 'Isn't it, Hugo?'

'Hey,' he said, holding up his hands to demonstrate his impartiality in the matter. 'This is between you and your parents.'

'I'm dropping out,' Chloe said. 'Or rather, we're dropping out.'

'I'm sorry?'

'I mean, who needs a degree in theology?'

'Well, I know that's how it might—'

'And it's been work, work, work for years for us. GCSEs, A-levels, and then straight to university three months later.'

'I know, darling, it's why your father and I thought you might have liked to take—'

'I agree with you!' Chloe said, cutting in. 'I didn't before, but I was talking to Hugo about how you said I should have had a gap year before I went off to uni, and he said that if that's what I wanted to do, we should drop out and follow our hearts.'

'You suggested my daughter drop out?' Becks asked Hugo.

'Chloe's not quite remembering it right, Mrs Starling. Although I did say that if she wasn't enjoying uni then why was she at uni.'

'I thought you were enjoying your course?'

'I am,' Chloe said. 'Or I was, I suppose. But it's a big world out there. I've spent my life with you and Dad, and I might have left home, but I've just gone down to a different junction of the M4. I want more. To go to Thailand, Vietnam – to head east and not even know where we're going, to make a real start on the rest of my life. And the thing is, Hugo's got this great idea that we can do charity work while we're out there, and raise money beforehand to fund the whole thing.'

'Are you sure this is what you want to do?' Becks asked.

Chloe took a breath to steady herself and then said, 'Yes.'

Becks looked at her beautiful daughter, her skin glowing with youthful excitement, and all she could feel was love.

'Then you should go for it.'

'Thank you!' Chloe said. 'I knew you'd get it.'

Chloe and Hugo stayed and babbled on for a little while longer about what their plans could be, but Becks wasn't listening. There was an image in her head that she couldn't seem to shake. It had struck her when she'd asked her daughter if she was sure she wanted to go travelling. Becks had been giving Chloe her full attention, but she couldn't help noticing the change in Hugo's manner as they waited on Chloe's reply. There had been a look in his eyes that Becks thought was calculating – almost cold. And then, as soon as Chloe gave her answer, Hugo's countenance had cleared and they were all laughing together. And then Colin had come in and agreed with his daughter's change of plans – not least, Becks knew, because Chloe's degree in theology had meant she'd been winning more than her fair share of theological discussions in a way that Colin had found challenging.

Colin was now talking excitedly about how his position in the community – both within Marlow and the wider cluster of parishes – could help them raise funds for their trip.

'As long as it's for charity, of course,' he added.

'Of course, Dad,' Chloe said. 'You know I wouldn't take a penny unless we were going to do good with it.'

'How about we find the right charitable organisation to work for,' Hugo said, 'and run it past you first, Mr Starling? You can decide if it's something your parishioners can get behind.'

'I think that's an excellent idea,' Colin said.

Seeing all the buzz of excitement and chatter in the house, Becks decided that she'd keep her concerns about Hugo to herself. After all, Chloe was happy, and that was all that mattered, wasn't it?

★

Judith, meanwhile, had been horrified to discover that she was expected to have almost daily rehearsals for the upcoming production of *The Importance of Being Earnest*. Miss Prism wasn't a big part – she was only in the second and third acts – but Judith hadn't counted on how seriously the rehearsal process was taken by the Marlow Amateur Dramatic Society. In her first scene, Miss Prism mostly interacted with the character of Cecily, who was being played by a young woman called Kay. Judith wasn't sure that Kay was a very good actor, but she was enthusiastic, unfailingly polite, and her parents ran the Two Brewers pub, so the cast were always treated like royalty when they went for a quick, post-rehearsal pint. Judith had yet to join the cast on any of their pub trips, and knew she never would, but she enjoyed how much Kay believed that one day she might.

Her second scene was with Dr Chasuble, the character to whom Miss Prism was romantically attracted. The part was being played by Toby Vincent, and Judith found the process of working with him fascinating. He never did the same thing twice. Each time they rehearsed, his movements changed. According to him, it would keep things 'fluid', which wasn't Judith's style at all. In the end, she took to standing still while Toby ranged around the stage picking up various props, pausing in odd places and then finding ways of saying lines that were nothing less than startling. It was all very impressive, Judith supposed, even if it wasn't exactly what she thought the scene needed.

As for Toby himself, there was an intensity to his work that Judith found a little unsettling. His focus during rehearsals was total, and he tended to refer to himself in the third person when he was in the role of Dr Chasuble. Judith had the impression that he was a man who'd not quite achieved what he'd wanted to in life so far, and was desperate to make up for lost time. She wasn't surprised to learn from the other cast members that Toby had recently applied to the most prestigious drama school in the country – the Royal Academy of Dramatic Arts – and been offered a place.

While she stood watching him during rehearsals, Judith found herself wondering if Toby were capable of committing murder and came to the conclusion that he very definitely was. His intensity of concentration felt so very close to pent-up fury. But it was equally clear to her that Toby was the last person who'd have wanted Oliver Beresford dead. He hero-worshipped him. During a coffee break, he'd told Judith that, before he joined the Marlow Amateur Dramatic Society, no one had thought he had anything useful to offer. His grades at school had been average, he'd not been good at sport – or anything, really, as he'd put it. He'd fallen into working as a mechanic because he had a mate at Platt's garage who got him a job there when he was sixteen. He'd been happy for years. Or thought he'd been happy. But then Oliver had changed all that when he'd showed him that there was a wider world out there. A world where he had something special to offer. It had been Oliver who'd suggested he apply to drama school, and Toby said he'd be eternally grateful to the older man for giving him a second chance at life.

As for the third act, it contained Miss Prism's big confrontation with Lady Bracknell, as inhabited by Mrs Eddingham. Judith found these rehearsals a struggle, if only because it was so hard to tell where Mrs Eddingham stopped and Lady Bracknell began. Judith wouldn't have minded being bossed around by Mrs Eddingham so much if she'd known any of her lines and didn't blame her lack of memory on everyone but herself.

At the end of a particularly taxing rehearsal with her, Judith came across a glum-looking Duncan in the wings.

'You know, she's always been like this,' he said, coughing wetly into his hand. Not for the first time, Judith noted that Duncan seemed to be perpetually ill.

He went on to explain that Mrs Eddingham's behaviour was why Oliver had sidelined her – and that the only way of managing her was to tell her precisely what she had to do and when, and then hope that she'd learn at least some of her lines. In the meantime, he said that desperate times called for desperate measures. Judith had no idea what Duncan meant by that, because he'd succumbed to another coughing fit and she didn't wait around to find out. However, all became clear the next time she attended a rehearsal and discovered that Verity was now the show's director.

And what a revelation she was, Judith noted. The moment she walked into the building, she exuded a quiet authority. She was direct in her instructions, but she also listened to what the actors had to say.

As Kay later confided in Judith, it was like night from day, compared to Oliver's directing style. Apparently, he'd been loud, temperamental and made it obvious who his favourites were among the cast. Kay had been one of them, which Judith thought she'd have liked, but it had only made her feel embarrassed that everything she did was met with approval, and everything others did or suggested was liable to be shot down.

It turned out Verity had an encyclopaedic knowledge of Oscar Wilde and the history of the various performances of the play, and everyone's energy levels seemed to lift when she was in the rehearsal room.

Judith was fascinated by her transformation, if only because the one thing Verity didn't seem to be doing in any way was grieving for her dead husband. During one rehearsal when Toby was resisting her efforts to get him to do what she wanted by saying Oliver always let him make his choices 'in the moment', Verity responded, 'But Oliver's not here now, is he?' Judith thought she'd even detected a hint of glee in her voice. Maybe Lizzie Jenkins had been right when she'd said Verity had hated her husband.

Spending so much time with the people who'd known Oliver best meant that Judith had plenty of opportunities to think about his murder. And she could feel an itch building up inside her. Or rather, not quite an itch; it was more like the feeling of anticipation she'd get when a sneeze was about to overtake her. She knew what was about to happen and there was nothing she could do to stop it: she was going to talk to Verity about Oliver. And as with the build-up to a sneeze, the feeling was one of excitement as well as dread.

The opportunity presented itself at the end of a particularly long rehearsal. Judith went outside to find Suzie and Becks waiting for her. She'd forgotten that they'd agreed to go for afternoon tea together.

'How were rehearsals?' Suzie asked as Judith headed over to her friends.

'Somewhat challenging,' Judith said, and no sooner had she spoken than the heavens opened up.

'Quick, into the van,' Suzie said, scrabbling round to the driver's side while Becks and Judith piled into the back to escape the downpour.

'Where did that come from?' Becks said, looking up at the sky. 'Rain wasn't forecast today.'

As Becks and Suzie discussed the extent to which they should or shouldn't have been surprised by the deluge, Judith spotted Verity coming out of the building. She put her coat over her head and started to walk at speed through the rain. Judith smiled and opened the passenger door as she passed.

'Verity!' she called out. 'Can we give you a lift to wherever you're going?'

'That would be so kind of you, Judith. I was hoping Duncan would give me a lift home, but he says he's staying behind to do some rewiring.'

'Then hop in,' Judith said, and squashed up against Becks to make room.

As Verity climbed in and removed the coat from her head, she didn't notice – although Becks and Suzie most certainly did – that Judith was smiling like the fox who'd just invited the gingerbread man to climb onto his nose.

Chapter 12

As Suzie drove and Judith asked questions about the play, Suzie and Becks realised that their friend was trying to put Verity at ease and gain her confidence. It was almost indecent, Becks thought, as Verity happily talked about costume fittings and viewings of the model set.

Verity and Oliver's house was down a track that ended at a red-brick cottage with roses around the porch and a little garden that led down to the river. By the time they arrived, the storm had blown through and a watery sun was peeking out from behind the clouds.

'What a beautiful spot,' Becks said as Suzie pulled up by the front door.

'Yes, this place has always been my pride and joy,' Verity said as she climbed out of the van. 'Anyway, thank you for the lift. And good work today, Judith, your performance is really coming on.'

With a smile, Verity closed the door to the van and approached her house – Becks keeping a beady eye on Judith.

'You can't,' Becks said.

'Can't what?' Judith replied in all innocence.

'You promised Tanika—' Becks said, but it was too late. Judith pushed the door open and started to follow Verity to the house.

'Oh, Verity?' she called out, and Verity stopped and waited until Judith had caught up with her. She was soon followed by Suzie, and then a very reluctant Becks.

'I'm sorry to ask,' Judith said, 'but you seem so very cheery.'

'I know,' Verity said. 'I should be in mourning, but I've wanted to get my hands on a production for years. Decades almost – but Oliver always had to be the director. And I've always had a soft spot for Wilde. Who wouldn't?'

'It must have been difficult living with someone who wouldn't share.'

'Yes, not that I'd ever want to speak ill of the dead, of course, but it could be difficult.'

'But Lizzie Jenkins was more right than wrong, wasn't she? The first time we all met, she suggested that you and Oliver didn't get on.'

'That was none of her business.'

'I quite agree,' Becks said, wanting to mend any bridges that Judith was burning. 'Which is why I'm sure you slapped her down. Anyone would.'

'Yeah, but she couldn't have been that far wrong,' Suzie said. 'You and Oliver must have had a tricky time together. He was a man. Of course you did.'

'Everything we've learned about him suggests he was a difficult man,' Judith said. 'At the very least he was self-centred, and that couldn't have been easy to live with.'

Verity looked at the three women and all she saw was sympathy and support. She took a deep breath and said, 'You've no idea how bad it was.'

There was such a depth of feeling to Verity's words that Judith found herself reaching down and twisting the gold ring on her wedding finger. She knew well enough what it was like being in a bad marriage.

Verity could see Judith's sadness.

'You're married?' she asked.

'I was,' Judith said. 'A long time ago.'

'You left him, or did he leave you?'

Judith's husband had died during a storm and she didn't want to have to excavate the story.

Seeing how uncomfortable Judith was, Becks said, 'Did things change between you and Oliver when he got his diagnosis?'

'You know about that?'

'Why don't you tell us about it in your own words?'

Verity took quite a while to gather her thoughts.

'Have you any idea what it's like,' she said, 'when the man you live with – and yes, I'll admit it, he made my life a living hell with all of his bragging and "big me" acting – comes home one day and says he has cancer, and it's terminal? I didn't know what to think. Of course I was shocked. And horrified. But I also realised that this was my way out. It's terrible when you say it out loud, isn't it?'

'You're only being truthful,' Becks said.

'And how things had got in our relationship wasn't entirely Oliver's fault. He was like that when I met him. It's just, over the years, I began to see that there was nothing else there. All the "big me" posturing that had drawn me to him when we first got together was just that – posturing. All his fancy clothes and props? It was like the Wizard of Oz. Only, when I finally got to see behind the curtain, I found a man who was – and I'm sorry to say this – a bit of a monster. And his cancer diagnosis made his many bad traits even worse. It didn't help that he'd been told the cancer might have been caused by the asbestos he was exposed to when he was a young surveyor working in condemned buildings.'

'He was a building surveyor?'

'That's how he earned his money – not that he'd ever talk about it. Whenever he met anyone new, he'd tell them he was a theatre director, which I always found a bit pathetic. But yes, his doctor believed that the years he'd spent working around asbestos were at least partly to blame for his cancer diagnosis all these years later.'

'I'm so sorry,' Becks said.

'There's only one person I feel sorry for, and that's my younger self. I wanted to be an actress – so very badly – and I saw him as my way to a career. He convinced me he'd be my entrée into the profession. And he's terribly convincing – that's the other thing you need to know about Oliver. He wasn't tricking me – or any of the other young people he'd spun his golden lies to – he genuinely believed what he was saying. He was a fantasist.'

'That sounds very challenging,' Becks said. 'How did you cope?'

'The same way any woman copes when she finds she's made a terrible mistake. By leading increasingly separate lives. I dropped the acting. It was something of a blessing, truth be told. I think, despite all of my efforts, I wasn't actually very good. But the MADS rehearsed most weekends, and Oliver's work always took him away every Wednesday, Thursday and Friday, so I only had to share a house with him Sunday night through to Wednesday morning. And I made sure I joined a weekly bridge club on Mondays and ushered at the Wycombe Swan Theatre on Tuesdays, which meant it was possible to go a whole week – sometimes even longer – without spending any time with him. It was an arrangement that suited him as much as me.'

'I see,' Judith said. 'And where was he working when he went away?'

'He was surveying buildings around the country. I have no idea where – the last few years, I'd stopped asking. I wasn't interested as long as he was gone three days every week. So, in our own way, we rubbed along. I'm sure there are couples who've fared worse.' She let out a sigh. 'He was a Peter Pan figure. He thought he was immortal. He got his diagnosis so late because he'd refused to go to the doctors when he started feeling ill a year ago. Even though I'd told him to. And because he left it so late, they didn't catch it in time.'

'How long did he have?'

'The doctor said it could be six months, maybe a year – but it was unlikely to be much longer. And here we are, with Oliver having had the last laugh. It wasn't the cancer that did for him in the end, it was a bullet. Macabre though it may sound, he'd have appreciated the drama of it all. And a quick bullet is preferable to a slow, lingering death. Is it possible he did this to himself?'

'You think he'd have been capable of taking his own life?'

'Before the diagnosis, I'd have said definitely not. But he'd been making cryptic comments about how he wanted to go out with a bang, not a whimper – you know that phrase? It seems slightly indelicate to mention it now – considering what happened. But it's why I went to see you, Judith, when he didn't come home after the boat trip. He'd been strange for weeks. And then, when he vanished from the boat like that – and then didn't answer his phone, or his texts or emails – I worried that he'd done something stupid.'

'He didn't do this to himself,' Becks said. 'We spoke to the DI who's running the case and she told us there was no gunshot residue on Oliver's hands. And the gun was fired from too great a distance from his body – at least for the second bullet.'

'They can tell that?' Verity asked, surprised.

'So if it wasn't him, do you have any idea who pulled the trigger?' Judith asked.

Verity paused, weighing up how best to answer the question.

'I refuse to believe it was Toby. He adored Oliver, I'm sure you've seen that, Judith? As for Duncan, he and Oliver used to get into stupid little fights over the trivial things, but they've been friends since they were at school together – they were almost like a married couple,' she added with a weary smile. 'One of those couples who're always sniping at each other but they're inseparable. I don't think the boat driver, Lance, even knew Oliver. And I know I didn't kill him – so that leaves only Lizzie Jenkins who could have done it.'

'You think she shot him?'

'I don't know why she'd want to do such a thing. Then again, there was an odd vibe between her and Oliver that night – I couldn't quite put my finger on it.'

'Lance said a similar thing,' Becks said. 'He said Oliver was trying to lord it over Lizzie.'

'Yes, that was part of it. Oliver was being superior with her – it was embarrassing to watch. But Lizzie put up with it. It was almost as if she were keeping a secret to herself.'

'How do you mean?'

'It's hard to explain, but it's like she was happy to have him be as superior as he liked, because all the while she was playing him. If that makes any sense.'

'Maybe the secret she was keeping was that she planned to kill him,' Suzie suggested.

'It's possible, I suppose. I can't help noticing that it was her who organised the boat trip in the first place, and sent us those cards that made us go to our cabins at 6 p.m. And there's something else I find odd. She seems to have vanished.'

'How do you mean?' Judith asked.

'I got her contact details from Oliver's desk diary. And I've rung her and texted her a few times – I'm trying to organise the funeral and I need to know if she'll attend – but she's not responded, not even once. I spoke to your friend, DI Malik, and she said that Lizzie's still in the country. She's not allowed to leave while the investigation's ongoing. So why would she be ghosting me if she's not guilty?'

'That's interesting,' Judith agreed, as she realised she was going to have to make a decision. Her chat with Verity had so far been the sort of thing that anyone wanting to understand what had happened to Oliver might have engaged in. But Judith and her friends had found Verity's suffragette scarf in the river and had handed it in to the police. She was just weighing up whether she dared mention it, when her eye was drawn to movement in the field on the other side of the river. Someone was cycling along the Thames Path. Looking more closely, she could see that it was Duncan Wood. He came to a halt alongside a canal boat moored on the riverbank opposite Verity's house, got off his bike and climbed aboard.

'What's Duncan doing there?'

'Duncan?' Verity said. 'He lives there.'

'Opposite your house?' Suzie asked.

'It's part of the petty disagreement he had with Oliver,' Verity said. 'Stupid men. Look, I need to get on – I've got to prepare for tomorrow's rehearsals. But I'm glad we've had this chat, Judith. Believe it or not, it's helped me organise my thoughts. So, if you're asking me whether I'm pleased Oliver's gone . . . Between us four? I'm not – that would be horrible – but I am relieved, I'll admit that much. I've had to put my life on hold for too long. As to whether I'd kill him – of course I wouldn't. After all, I knew that cancer would be taking his life soon enough. Why on earth would I risk going to prison for murder when I could let Mother Nature do the dirty work for me?'

With a sad smile, Verity headed into her house. Judith and her friends returned to Suzie's van, keeping their own counsel until they were inside.

'Her last point's pretty compelling,' Becks said. 'Seeing as she knew about the cancer, she can't be the killer.'

'Yes,' Judith agreed. 'Although it raises an interesting question, doesn't it? I wonder who else knew about Oliver's cancer diagnosis?'

'You think whoever shot him can't have known?' Suzie asked.

'It seems a reasonable working theory.'

'Lance knew about it – or guessed,' Becks said. 'And Verity knew. So that puts them both in the clear.'

'Which leaves Duncan, Toby and Lizzie, who maybe didn't know about his cancer and therefore could be our killer,' Suzie said.

'I'll tell you what I want to know,' Judith said. 'What was this petty disagreement Verity mentioned between Duncan and Oliver?'

'Yeah, it would be good to get to the bottom of that,' Suzie agreed.

'I know!' Judith said, pretending to have an idea. 'How about we drive around to the car park by the Spade Oak pub? We can get to Duncan's houseboat on foot from there. And I know you're going to say we shouldn't investigate, Becks, but this is far too important a matter for such niceties. Besides, we only promised Tanika that we wouldn't interfere in *her* investigation, which we aren't. I didn't even ask Verity how her suffragette scarf ended up in the river the day after the murder – I was the model of restraint. We're not asking for privileged information or access, we're just talking to some of the people who were there on the night.'

'Is there any point me saying what I think?' Becks asked.

'And remember,' Judith said, proving Becks' point by ignoring it, 'I'm now friends with these people through the MADS. There are any number of reasons why I might want to go and have a chat with Duncan. Travel sweet, anyone?' Judith said, pulling her tin of sweets out of her handbag and popping the lid.

With a grin, Suzie plucked a hard sweet from the icing sugar. Becks knew she'd lost the argument. Her fingers hovered over the tin as she tried to decide which colour she wanted, but then she realised she didn't want one after all.

'Actually, I'd better not,' she said, as Suzie crunched down on her sweet and got into her van with her friends.

As the van left Verity's driveway and turned onto the track that led back to the road, Judith noticed a woman to the side of the little road. Something about her jarred with Judith. It seemed so incongruous that someone would be standing there on their own. Where had the woman come from and where was she going?

As the van passed, the woman seemed to turn her face away – although Judith just had time to take in her straight, shoulder-length dark hair, and her bright red puffa jacket. Intrigued, she kept her eyes on the woman for as long as she could.

From her position in the front of the van, Suzie saw in her rear-view mirror that Judith had twisted around in her seat, and she tried to see what it was that had caught her friend's attention. As she did so, she saw the woman step into the middle of the track so she could get a better view of Suzie's departing van.

Suzie slammed on the brakes.

'Whoa,' she said, her eyes fixed on the reflection of the red puffa-jacketed woman in her rear-view mirror.

'What is it?' Becks asked.

'Did anyone feel as though someone just walked across their grave?' she asked with a whole-body shiver, before turning to look at Judith. 'Are you OK?'

'What are you talking about?' Judith asked, baffled.

'That woman back there. It's like she was mesmerising you.'

'I was only looking at her.'

'No, it's more than that. You couldn't take your eyes off her.'

'I'm looking at you!'

'And she couldn't take her eyes off you,' Suzie said, bulldozing through Judith's objection. 'And we both know why she's so fixated on you.'

'We do?' Becks asked.

'She'll have second sight, you mark my words. She knows something bad's going to happen to Judith.'

'I do think you should stop talking nonsense like this,' Judith harrumphed.

'Sorry,' Becks said, 'what woman is this?'

'There's a woman in the road back there,' Suzie said, turning to Becks. 'In a bright red jacket, watching Judith.'

'She isn't watching me,' Judith said.

'She is — look!' Suzie said.

The three friends turned and peered through the back window of the van.

The woman in the red puffa jacket had vanished.

Chapter 13

'What woman?' Becks asked, looking back along the track.

'She was there a second ago,' Suzie said as she looked at Judith in mounting horror. 'And then she vanished into thin air!'

'She didn't vanish,' Judith huffed.

'Then where is she?' Suzie said, and then the truth of the situation dawned on her. 'What if—' she said, only for Judith to interrupt her.

'Don't say it, Suzie.'

'You can't stop me from speaking.'

'But you could at least try to make some sense.'

'What are you going to say?' Becks asked.

'Well, it's all tied into the prophecy.'

'There's no prophecy!' Judith said.

'And now we've got spectral figures on the side of the road.'

'There was nothing spectral about her! She was wearing a big, red jacket.'

'Are you saying she was a ghost?' Becks said, her eyes widening.

'Or wraith – or something,' Suzie said.

'Becks,' Judith said, turning to her friend. 'Please tell me you don't believe her.'

Becks looked back through the window at the deserted road.

'There was a woman there?'

'She watched us pass,' Suzie said with a shiver. 'It was uncanny.'

'And now she's not there . . . ? I don't know, Judith. I don't see where she could have gone. Not unless she's hiding in the bushes or something, and why would she be doing that?'

'I'm sure you'll come up with a reason why we can't go back and look,' Judith said, fed up with the pair of them.

'What?' Suzie said, outraged. 'That was a warning – a woman in a red coat, meaning danger. Meaning blood. We need to get away as quickly as we can.'

Without waiting for a reply, she put the van in gear and drove off.

As they returned to Marlow and crossed the suspension bridge that spanned the River Thames, Judith found herself twisting the wedding band on her ring finger. It was something she did when she felt uneasy. Of course she didn't believe in tarot predictions, but there was no denying it. The woman in the red coat had spooked her.

★

Once they left the van in the car park behind the Spade Oak pub and followed the path to the river, the women could see Duncan's houseboat moored up ahead of them, with Verity's house visible on the opposite bank.

'It's funny how Duncan's only a hundred yards from Verity's house,' Becks said. 'And yet it's taken us nearly twenty minutes to get here.'

Judith knocked on the side of the boat. Duncan's face appeared at a porthole, and when he saw it was Judith, he frowned.

'Permission to come on board?' Judith asked with a smile that brooked no disagreement.

'OK,' Duncan said, and then ducked away from the porthole.

Judith, Becks and Suzie stepped up the short plank that led to the back of the boat. They then picked their way down the steps into an Aladdin's cave of old computer equipment that was piled up by the cooker, half-dismantled lighting boards in a mess by the window, and all the remaining surfaces were covered in theatrical memorabilia and old costumes and props.

'Oh,' Becks said, her nose twitching at the dust in the air.

Smelling the mould and dust, and seeing the chaos of Duncan's life all around him – with unfinished plates of food and cups of tea balanced precariously on piles of junk – Judith began to understand why he was so pale and pasty all the time. He clearly had an extremely unhealthy lifestyle. But she could also see that Duncan was on edge. Was it because he didn't want anyone to see the mess his home was in, or was there some other reason?

Judith made the introductions and explained that her visit wasn't connected to the production of *The Importance of Being Earnest*.

'Or, at least, not directly,' she explained. 'It's about the night Oliver died.'

'I've already spoken to the police,' Duncan said, 'and that, as far as I'm concerned, is the end of the matter.'

Duncan squared his shoulders and stood tall. It was clear that this was all he was prepared to say on the subject.

'Oh gosh, who's this?' Becks asked, indicating a framed photo on the sideboard in an attempt to thaw Duncan. The photo

showed a man in uniform standing by a dark green truck in front
of a barren landscape of scraggy grass and rocks.

'That's my uncle Ray,' Duncan said as he came over and picked
up the photo.

'He was in the army?'

'Royal Engineers.'

'Is that where you got your love of fixing equipment?'

'You could say that,' Duncan said. 'It certainly wasn't my dad.'

'Where's this photo taken?' Judith asked.

'Outside Port Stanley in the Falklands.'

'He served in the Falklands War?'

'Look, what are the three of you doing here?'

'Us?' Judith asked innocently.

'I know your game. You only joined the MADS to keep an
eye on us. Your reputation precedes you.'

'As what?'

'As someone who catches killers. It's what the three of you
do. So what are you doing on my boat?'

'We're famous?' Suzie asked eagerly.

'Not now, Suzie,' Judith said. 'But you're right, there is a loose
end I was hoping to tie up. You see, Verity says you've been
feuding with Oliver.'

'Verity?' Duncan said, irritated. 'She said that, did she?'

'She did,' Becks said.

'Very well then, I don't deny it,' Duncan said as he started to
collect up all the old plates and mugs that were lying around.
'But it's not a big deal. I've known Oliver since we were at school
together, when he was this shy kid. Then one day some bigger
boys beat him up for wearing a waistcoat under his school jacket.
Must have been our second year, something like that, so it wasn't

a big deal. But Oliver made a choice from that moment on. He could retreat or he could attack, and he's been attacking ever since. Wearing more and more outlandish outfits, using flowery language. It's like he thought he was Oscar Wilde – which I can tell you, he wasn't.'

Duncan carried the crockery over to the sink and put it in a bowl before turning on the hot tap. He then started to do the washing-up.

'You found him irritating?' Suzie asked.

'Like I said, we'd been friends since we were at school, and he was brilliant in his own way. We both loved doing theatre together. Me behind the scenes, him in front. When it comes to putting on a show, nothing would ever get done if you didn't have these larger-than-life figures cracking the whip.'

'Which doesn't exactly answer my question,' Suzie said.

'Yes, I found him irritating – but only from time to time. Exasperated, that's more how I felt. He drove me nuts. He drove everyone nuts.'

'So what was this feud about?'

'It's stupid. It goes back to the time I lent him a book by Kenneth Tynan. It was his reviews of shows in the 1960s and 1970s. It wasn't that valuable in itself, but when I asked Oliver for it back, he said I'd never given it to him. Which was crackers. We both knew I had. But we were in the middle of rehearsals for *Bedroom Farce* by Alan Ayckbourn. The whole company was there, and he wanted to make me look stupid – and defy me to call him out as a liar, which I didn't. I should have done, but I was so weirded out that he'd straight up lie like that, I didn't say anything.

'So he got his moment in the spotlight. Making me look like an idiot. It got under my skin. Then, after the show opened, on the night the *Marlow Free Press* were in, I spilt some water on the plug for the lighting desk during Oliver's big scene and tripped the fuses to the whole building. It was pathetic, I'll admit it, but he'd made me look stupid in front of the company. As far as I was concerned, now it was his turn to look stupid in front of a much bigger audience.

'What I didn't realise was how badly it would knock his confidence. When I finally got the electrics for the building turned back on, he gave a pretty bad performance – which wasn't what I'd wanted at all. The papers said he was over the hill. The *Marlow Free Press* even said it was time for younger blood to take over the MADS. I think it was Toby's first show playing the lead, and he'd been the star of the piece – which the papers were very happy to point out. Toby was the future and Oliver was the past, that was the gist of it.'

'This was some time ago, then,' Judith said. 'How come your feud's still ongoing?'

Duncan pulled the plug out of the sink and watched the water gurgle out before replying.

'That's where it gets petty. I used to be moored on a stretch of land by the rugby club. You're not supposed to stay there longer than one night at a time, but I was known in the town – and nobody cared anyway. If I wasn't moored there, there'd have been a different boat every day with who knew what going on. It was an arrangement that suited everyone. But, after I'd messed up the lights, Oliver decided to get revenge by complaining to the council. They served me with a notice to move on – they had to, once there'd been a formal complaint – which was irritating as hell. But the thing is, I knew Oliver had been behind it, so I decided to get my own back. The land on this side of the river is owned by a farmer. He normally charges five pounds a night, but he's done me a deal. I can moor here for two hundred quid a year, which means that instead of Oliver having his pristine view of the river – that he's worked so hard to get – I'm parked slap bang opposite his house. And who can blame me if, every now and then, I like to play my rock music nice and loud? It's not my fault he doesn't appreciate the genius of Led Zeppelin.'

'That *is* petty,' Becks said.

'I'm the first to admit it,' Duncan said, picking up a filthy tea towel and drying his hands on it.

'And all of that came about because he forgot that you'd lent him a book of reviews?' Suzie asked.

'You know this has nothing to do with his death,' Duncan said. 'We were still friends. This was just something on the side – something that was going on in the background. We never even argued about it, or even acknowledged it. I don't think anyone other than Verity was aware of it. And anyway, I got to park my houseboat here. I won.'

'Unless he'd escalated it again,' Judith said.

'What's that?'

'Had Oliver done something to you recently that meant you had to kill him?'

'What?' Duncan said, repelled by the question. 'How can you even say that? I said I found him exasperating, not that he made me want to kill him. If you're looking for someone who might have wanted him dead, you don't need to look any further than Verity. She and Oliver had stand-up rows with crockery being thrown – the whole shebang. I'd sometimes watch through the windows as they moved from room to room going for each other.'

'Verity said he was a difficult man to live with,' Becks said.

'It was never Oliver who started the rows – that's one of the things about him, he never started an argument. He'd make up any old bollocks rather than have a confrontation. It was always Verity who'd kick off. Don't let her fool you. She used to be an actress. And it's true what they say. Once an actress, always an actress.'

'What do you mean by that?' Becks asked.

'She flies off the handle – and there's been no excuse these last few months. She should have been giving Oliver an easier time.'

'Why?' Suzie asked.

'I suppose it doesn't matter if I tell you now. Oliver had cancer – terminal cancer.'

'How do you know that?' Judith asked.

'How could I not know? They've been going at it hammer and tongs on the other side of the river. I hear everything – and I can tell you, when Verity gets going, she doesn't take prisoners. More than once I've heard her say that Oliver's cancer was his punishment for what he'd done.'

'What had he done?' Becks asked.

'I've no idea, but I heard her say it to him at least half a dozen times. Oliver's cancer was God's punishment for what he'd done. That's what she used to say.'

Judith and her friends looked at each other. What on earth had Oliver done that made Verity believe terminal cancer was a suitable punishment?

Chapter 14

Thanking Duncan for his help, the women left his houseboat and headed back to the van. As they crossed the field, they tried to make sense of what they'd learned.

'Well, for starters,' Becks said, 'that houseboat is filthy.'

Judith and Suzie smiled at their friend's ever-reliable panic at any kind of mess.

'And that story of shorting the lights to punish Oliver shows he was pretty vindictive,' Judith said. 'Oliver may have embarrassed Duncan in front of some actors, but that's an extreme response.'

'As is moving his boat to block his view,' Suzie said.

'You're right. It feels to me like Duncan was the person driving that feud far more than Oliver.'

'And he couldn't wait to stick the knife into Verity, could he?'

'That's what I couldn't understand,' Judith said. 'I've seen him in rehearsals, and he's always quiet. He keeps himself to himself. I've never picked up anything to suggest that he dislikes Verity. He's happy to be bossed around by her. I wonder what that's about?'

'Maybe he's trying to divert our attention to someone else? Anyone other than him.'

'Although, he was right about having won,' Judith said. 'He had the upper hand in their feud.'

'Assuming he was telling the truth.'

'Either way, I think it's time we spoke to Toby Vincent, don't you?'

'Sure,' Suzie said. 'But why?'

'I want to find out if he knew that Oliver had cancer.'

★

The women found Toby in the workshop of Platt's garage, fixing up an old BMW.

'Hi, Judith,' he said as the women approached.

'Can we ask you a quick question?' Judith asked.

'Sure. So long as I can keep on working . . . ?' Toby said as he went over to a toolkit and picked out a long screwdriver. As he returned to the car and set about replacing the side mirror, Judith realised that she still couldn't square a blue-collar worker like Toby being such good friends with a man like Oliver Beresford.

'Is this the elephant in the room?' Toby asked with a smile in his voice. 'Cos I can see it in your eyes when we're rehearsing, but you're too polite to say.'

'And what elephant would that be?' Judith asked.

'What am I doing prancing around on the stage?'

'Well, I wouldn't call it an elephant, but it has crossed my mind to wonder.'

'Don't worry, I think it too, most of the time. And the MADS are forever talking about their motivation, and how they feel – it's just people with too much money and time on their hands if you ask me. No offence to the present company,' he added as he opened the car door and started checking the fuses in the glove compartment.

'How did you get involved?'

'It was the panto a few years back. *Puss in Boots*. Platt's was sponsoring it and us mechanics had to come on and do a dance in tutus.'

'I remember that!' Suzie said. 'I mean, I didn't see it – my kids are too old to go to the panto – but everyone talked about that dance. You brought the house down.'

'Oliver pulled me aside afterwards and said I had something about me, and he was thinking of doing a farce for the next production – *Don't Dress for Dinner*. There was a part he reckoned I'd be good for – a comedy burglar. Of course, I leapt at the chance.' Toby stopped tinkering with the car, his eyes lighting up as he continued: 'There's this feeling I get when I walk out on stage, under those lights. It's like you know what everyone's thinking as they look at you. You can see every speck of dust in the air . . . I loved it and I wanted more. And hey – guess what? – when I did that farce, I had the audience in stitches. Who knew? Me! Oliver always said it's because I played the truth of what I was saying and never the joke – which I get now, but I didn't back then.'

'He was something of a mentor to you?' Becks asked.

'"Something" of a mentor? I date my life from the day I met him. Before, I didn't amount to much at school or at work. I mean, don't get me wrong, I've always muddled along OK, but I'd never done anything special. So yeah, there's Before Oliver and there's After Oliver, and it's day from night. He was such a big influence. When we first got to know each other, he hated how I'd smoke weed at the weekends. Never during the week – not near all this machinery – but I wasn't up to much when I wasn't here, so I'd get mashed. When Oliver found out, he was spitting mad. Said I was addling my brain and wasting my life smoking spliffs. And he's so insistent, you know? He got through to me and I cleaned up my act.'

'Which is why you're packing all this in and heading off to RADA,' Judith said.

Toby blushed as he busied himself with the car.

'Yeah,' he said. 'He reckoned I should aim for the stars. I didn't believe him to start with. But he thought I was that good. Still, it's a big deal to up sticks and move to London – to leave Marlow and my friends and family. And my job. Jesus! Who'd want to start being a student at my age? But Oliver wouldn't let me back out. He even paid for all my auditions and got his friend to help me choose my Shakespeare monologue. I still didn't think it was a good idea, but the thing is, Oliver had had a few health issues, and he didn't want to waste time.'

Judith caught Suzie and Beck's eyes at the mention of 'health issues'.

'I guessed he was kind of living out his dreams of fame and fortune through me,' Toby continued. 'But there was this tiny voice in my head that kept going, "What if he's right? What if I *am* good enough?" I can't tell you how much I wanted it. That's why I wrote to Lizzie Jenkins.'

'She came to the UK because you wrote to her?' Suzie asked.

Toby leaned over to look at the warning lights on the dashboard. He wasn't happy with what he saw and returned his attention to the wires and fuses of the glove compartment.

'That's right,' he agreed. 'Because there's no way I could afford three years living in London. So Oliver told me I had to write to anyone famous or rich – or preferably both – that I could lay claim to and ask them to help fund me. I was dead against it at first, but he showed me on the internet how this was standard practice. When you go to drama school, you ask for help from rich actors, and then, if you ever become a rich actor, you help pay for others to go.

'Mind you, I didn't expect the response I got from Lizzie. She wasn't even on my list until Oliver told me that she was from Marlow and had cut her teeth with the MADS. I couldn't believe it! I'd acted on the same stage as Lizzie Jenkins. So I wrote to her and she said she didn't want to just help fund me if I got into drama school, she wanted to come over to see us all. She'd not been back to Marlow in decades and she figured it was time. That's why she hired that boat – she wanted to throw a party for us.'

'Yes, can I ask about that?' Judith said. 'There must be hundreds of people in the town who've done productions with the Marlow Amateur Dramatic Society, why were there so few of you on the boat?'

'I'm not sure,' Toby said with a shrug. 'Oliver said that Lizzie only wanted to take the committee out. I was voted on to the committee last year. As the acting representative. It put Mrs Eddingham's nose out of joint, I can tell you. She'd held that post for years. Decades, even.'

'Going back to what you said earlier, what did you mean, Oliver had health issues?'

Toby kept his attention focused on the BMW.

'Sorry, I shouldn't have said that,' he said.

'I understand you wanting to protect your friend's privacy,' Becks said, 'but it could be very important. What were his health issues?'

'I don't think I'm going to say, if you don't mind.'

'If it helps at all, we know about his diagnosis.'

Toby looked up at the women. His expression was unreadable. 'You know?' he asked.

'We know about his cancer,' Judith said.

Toby sighed.

'He told me when we were rehearsing my Shakespeare piece for the audition. It was Enobabus' speech about Queen Cleopatra.'

'Ah,' Judith said. '"The barge she sat in, like a burnish'd throne".'

'That's the one – it's pretty good, isn't it? And not so popular that it's been done a thousand times before. Anyway, he got onto immortality, and how that's what Shakespeare had given all the subjects of his plays, because his plays will never die. He was so sad about it that I asked him if he was all right and that's when he told me he had liver cancer. Terminal. He had months to live. It still gives me the shivers, thinking about it. It's why he was so keen for me to get into RADA, he said. He wanted to do as much good as possible in the last few months he had. He wanted to leave a legacy.'

'Isn't the Marlow Amateur Dramatic Society his legacy?' Suzie asked.

'That's what I told him, but he said it wasn't enough. I think it's why he jumped at the chance of getting Lizzie over from the States. He had so many weaknesses,' Toby said with a sad smile, 'but the biggest was how famous he wanted to be. Don't get me wrong, he was the first to admit how shallow he was. He used to laugh at himself a lot, don't let anyone tell you any different. He knew how preposterous he was with his outfits and booming pronouncements.'

'You liked him,' Suzie said.

'Sometimes I feel like I was the only one who did.'

'Verity and he didn't get on, did they?' Judith said.

'I never got to the bottom of their relationship,' Toby said. 'But Lizzie Jenkins was right when she said she picked up on the tension between them. It was simmering under the surface the whole time, like static electricity.'

'Why?' Becks asked.

'That's a hard one. I think Oliver was a bloke's bloke when it came down to it. When it was him and me, he dropped the "I'm a big cheese" act. He told me he found it tiring, but he'd started being this flamboyant guy all those years ago and he couldn't change. Basically, when you stripped everything away, he was a great guy.'

'And Verity didn't see any of that?' Suzie asked.

'God knows what goes on in relationships. You never know for sure, do you? But she was just as capable as Oliver of starting a disagreement. On balance, I'd say she started more arguments than he did. Tetchy – that's how Verity was around him. Not that she was like that with the rest of us – she couldn't have been nicer. But I'd almost say Oliver was the victim in that marriage.'

Judith tried to work out what she thought about this particular revelation. It chimed with what Duncan had told them, but she found it hard to imagine a personality as large as Oliver Beresford ever being the victim in a relationship.

'Duncan Wood said Verity believed Oliver's cancer was punishment for something he'd done,' Becks said.

'Ouch!' Toby said. 'That's exactly what I mean about how she could be with him. That's harsh.'

'I don't suppose you know what she was referring to?'

'Punishment? No. I didn't see him do anything bad. And I wouldn't trust what Duncan says about Oliver anyway. There was a weird rivalry between those two. It was like Duncan had a problem with Oliver, but wouldn't ever confront him or get it out in the open. That's Duncan all over. He's a bit like a spider, scuttling about the place and plotting.'

'In what way?' Becks asked.

'He's never direct, you know? So if there was a problem with a production – like Oliver wouldn't let him have the set he wanted or whatever – he wouldn't confront Oliver, he'd speak to the other members of the cast. Or their partners. Try to get them to do his dirty work for him.'

'He's devious?' Suzie asked.

'It can come across like that sometimes.'

'If that's what he's like, do you think he could have been behind those fake invites that told you all to go to your cabins at 6 p.m.?'

'Well, I know I didn't send them. And it's way too sneaky for Verity – she's one of the most direct people I know. You've seen her in rehearsals, Judith, she doesn't mess about, does she? But I reckon Duncan's exactly the sort of person who'd come up with a scheme like that.'

'Could he have killed Oliver?'

'That's what I've been trying to think, but I just don't see it. The thing is, I know that Duncan had problems with Oliver, but he's kind of a coward. I don't think he'd have the courage to kill anyone. Unless it was a spur-of-the-moment thing, you know? And there's no way this murder was spur-of-the-moment.'

'That's right,' Judith said. 'Whoever planned it was obviously pretty capable.'

Toby was about to agree when he realised what Judith was implying.

'You think I did it? Are you crazy? It's because of Oliver I'm going to be getting out of this back-end town. Besides, I'm about the only person in Marlow who thought Oliver was a good bloke. No, you're barking up the wrong tree if you think I was involved. Now, if you don't mind, I've got to get the electrics on this car fixed before I can break for lunch. I'll see you at rehearsals, Judith.' And with that, Toby turned his back on the women.

The three friends, knowing when they weren't wanted, made their exit.

'Now that's very interesting,' Judith said as they stepped out of the workshop into the sunshine.

'That Toby hero-worshipped Oliver?' Becks asked.

'There is that, of course, but it's not what I had in mind.'

'I know,' Suzie said. 'The fact that Duncan's a spider scuttling about the place.'

'That, too, was illuminating, but it wasn't my main conclusion. Because I now know we can't put it off any longer.'

'We can't put what off?' Suzie said.

'That's "full house" as far as I can see. Lance Goodman, Verity Beresford, Duncan Wood and Toby Vincent all knew long before Oliver was shot dead that he not only had cancer, but that it was terminal.'

'Oh, I get it,' Suzie said. 'There was only one person on that boat who didn't know he was going to die anyway – Lizzie Jenkins.'

'But she can't be the killer!' Becks said. 'She'd not seen Oliver Beresford in years. In decades. And you said it yourself, Judith, this whole murder was premeditated. That whole business of the invitations making sure everyone was going to be in their cabins at 6 p.m. – and the fact that the killer had to get hold of a gun – means it can't have been spur-of-the-moment.'

'So she planned it all in advance from Los Angeles,' Suzie said.

'But she only got into the UK on the day that Oliver died. It's impossible she could have got all of that in place in time.'

'True,' Suzie agreed, 'but she's still the only person who didn't know about his cancer.'

'Or so we presume,' Judith said. 'There's only one way to find out for sure. We need to speak to her.'

Chapter 15

It wasn't immediately obvious to Judith how they could find out where Lizzie Jenkins was staying. Did she have a room in a local hotel? Or had she rented a house? Or maybe she was staying in London and there'd be no way of contacting her without getting the address from Tanika? All Judith knew for sure was that Tanika had banned Lizzie from leaving the UK while the investigation was ongoing.

Judith was feeling deeply frustrated. There was so much she needed to talk to Tanika about: whether she'd made any progress in working out who'd sent the fake invite; whether or not the scarf they'd pulled from the river really belonged to Verity; and whether or not she'd found the murder weapon yet. Trying to catch the killer without access to the police left Judith feeling as though she was being forced to fight with one hand tied behind her back.

★

With the case stalled, Becks was able to spend more time at home with Chloe and Hugo. Unable to dispel her feelings of unease about her daughter's boyfriend, she decided to broach the subject with Colin when she took him his morning cup of tea in his office.

'I'm not sure what I think about Hugo,' she said. 'There's something . . . I can't put my finger on it.'

'You've never liked him, have you?' Colin said.

'That's not true.'

'It's because he's posh, isn't it?'

'What?' Becks said, appalled. 'No.'

'He went to a posh school, his family are loaded. I agree, it's a bit of a culture shock, but it's none of our business.'

'We're her parents, of course it's our business!' Becks snapped. Many years before, she'd come to terms with the fact that Colin had barely lifted a finger to help raise their children. Now that they were ostensibly adults, he seemed to feel his duties as a parent were over.

'And remember,' Colin added, 'when you and I met, I was the one with the money. If it was OK for you to go out with me, surely it's OK for Chloe?'

It was true. Colin had been a high-flying banker when he and Becks had fallen in love. His subsequent call to the ministry had been a surprise to them both – although it had very much been more of a surprise for Becks.

'I had a job too,' Becks said in a voice of deadly calm.

'So there we are!' Colin said triumphantly. 'It worked out for us, so why don't you think it will work out for Chloe and Hugo?'

'I don't know!' Becks said, barely keeping a lid on her irritation. 'That's why I want to talk to you. I'm trying to work out what it is that's worrying me. It's like he's so polished the whole time – and so attentive – and then, every now and then, and only for a split second, he'll drop the mask and I can see this calculating look in his eyes. And then he goes all charming and polite and well-mannered again. It's blink-and-you'll-miss-it, but I can't shake the feeling that we're not seeing the true Hugo.'

'Is this because he suggested that Chloe drop out of uni?'

'God, no – I've no problem with that. Or at least, I don't think I have,' Becks said as she considered whether Colin could be right. 'Actually, maybe that is part of it. Hugo's already got his position in society, hasn't he? He's got money, contacts galore from school and his family – it doesn't matter if he gets a degree or not. It's different for Chloe.'

'The way she tells it, she couldn't wait to drop out.'

'I know that's what she's saying, but it doesn't make it right that he suggested it to her when she's someone who will need a degree, and a good one at that, if she's going to make her way in the world.'

'Nonsense! Everyone will want to employ Chloe. She's the daughter of a famous crime-fighter.'

Despite herself, Becks smiled. Perhaps Colin was right and she was being too harsh on Hugo. After all, like Chloe, he was just a young person trying to work out what to do with his life, even if his starting point was one of excessive privilege. And it wasn't as though he lacked motivation. He'd thrown himself into organising the 'big trip' to Asia with far more verve than Chloe. He'd spent hours with Colin making sure that the work he and Chloe were going to do would be both useful and ethical. He'd created spreadsheets to cover budgets and travel itineraries, the house was full of various travel books he'd got out of the library, and Becks couldn't deny that it was wonderful to see someone take control of Chloe's somewhat laissez-faire life.

Hugo had also set up what was proving to be a very successful crowdfunder to raise money for the trip. With almost daily updates and video diary entries, he was keeping his and Chloe's supporters informed of the progress of their campaign. Becks knew it was only because of his diligence that they'd been able to raise so much money from their family and friends. But the biggest contribution to the fund was coming in from the congregation at All Saints'. Hugo and Chloe had delivered a talk about the orphanage in Vietnam they were going to be working in, and Becks had been deeply moved by how generous the town had been in supporting her daughter.

Following her conversation with Colin, Becks went downstairs to check in with Chloe. She found her in the kitchen, making toast and a big pot of tea for herself and Hugo. Before she could stop herself, Becks asked if Chloe was sure she was doing the right thing, dropping out of university.

'Why won't you let me be happy?' Chloe snapped, loading the breakfast things on to a tray and storming out of the kitchen. Becks heard her daughter's footsteps stomp upstairs and sighed. Why had she immediately asked the one question she'd told herself she shouldn't ask? In her heart of hearts, she knew she'd been triggered by the sight of her daughter making breakfast for her boyfriend in the same way she'd just taken a cup of tea through to Colin.

★

As for Suzie, she got on with her life as a dog-walker and once-a-week local radio presenter, but she still couldn't shake the feeling that there was something 'bad' about to happen to Judith. Because she was her own worst enemy, Suzie decided to make her weekly radio phone-in entirely about her listeners' supernatural encounters. It turned out that there were many, and by the time she left the little studio, she'd whipped herself up into a frenzy of worry. As soon as she got home, she rang Judith to check whether the prophecy from the tarot cards had come true. Judith, for her part, told her for the hundredth time that she was talking nonsense. But then, the following day, something happened that shook Judith's confidence to its core.

She was in the Little Theatre with a few other actors, waiting for Mrs Eddingham to arrive so they could start a rehearsal. To pass the time, she was looking at the various framed photos of the MADS committee on the wall. In the most recent photo, Oliver was standing in the middle, with Verity, Toby and Duncan gathered around him. Everyone's smile was relaxed, their body language perfectly friendly. It was impossible to imagine that the three people standing with Oliver were currently suspected of shooting him dead.

Judith's gaze shifted to another committee photo, this time featuring Mrs Eddingham. As she continued to look at all of the committee photos, while some faces came and went, Oliver, Duncan and Mrs Eddingham seemed to be a permanent fixture. It was strange seeing their faces get younger, their bodies slimmer, Judith thought. But then she saw that the oldest framed photo wasn't a formal picture of the committee at all. It showed Duncan and Oliver standing in front of what looked like an old prefabricated hut, Oliver's arm around Duncan's shoulders.

Verity, who had noticed Judith's interest in the wall of photos, came over.

'The history of the MADS,' she said with a sad smile. 'The history of all of us.'

'What's this photo of Duncan and Oliver?'

'That's how the MADS started. Before the council gave us this theatre.'

'What was it like in the early days?'

'You'll have to ask Duncan, it's all before my time. But the way Oliver told it, he and Duncan had always been involved in theatre when they were at school. Then, when they left, they wanted to set something up in the town, with Oliver doing the people side of things and Duncan doing the tech stuff. When Oliver qualified as a building surveyor, he discovered that the town council had a spare building – it was due to be condemned or something – but he got them to let him and Duncan use it, and they operated out of it for the first few years. There wasn't any rehearsal space – they had to use Liston Hall for that, and for their performances. But they kept their lights and costumes in the hut. Once they'd established themselves and shown the town council what a good job they were capable of doing, they were able to get the lease on this building, and that's when things took off for the MADS.'

'Actually, Duncan mentioned something to me and I wonder if you can help me clear it up. He said that he'd heard some of your arguments with Oliver. It's how he found out that Oliver had cancer. He overheard you.'

'That's typical Duncan. I know he's supposedly great at sorting out problems for people, but when it came to me and Oliver, all he seemed to do was stir things up.'

'Like what?'

'Like parking his boat opposite our house so he could spy on us.'

'Is that what he was doing?'

'Evidently. He's already told you that Oliver and I argued, which is hardly very loyal of him.'

'To be specific,' Judith said, 'he told me that you told Oliver his cancer was "punishment" for what he'd done.'

'What on earth do you mean?'

'That's what Duncan said he overheard.'

'But that's absolutely poisonous! I would never have used that sort of language with Oliver. Don't get me wrong, he infuriated me, and yes, we argued, but I never crowed about his cancer. It was a horrible thing for him to endure. For both of us to endure.'

Toby came over and joined the women.

'Verity, could I ask for some help with my exits in Act Two?'

'Of course,' Verity said with a bright smile as she headed back to get her copy of the script with Toby in tow.

Judith frowned. Who could be believed? Duncan, who said that Verity thought Oliver's cancer was a suitable punishment? Or Verity, who said that Duncan was trying to cause trouble? And there was something else too. There'd been the faintest whiff of cannabis when Toby had come over and stood next to her. Judith remembered how he'd mentioned that he used to smoke spliffs but had stopped when Oliver had told him that it was bad for him. Had he started smoking drugs again, and if so, why?

There was so much for Judith's mind to turn over, and she decided she wanted to get away from the hubbub of her fellow cast members.

There were little Juliet doors on either side of the stage. She went through the nearest one and climbed the few short steps up to the backstage area. She was finally on her own with the old ropes and dusty drapes. It was all very romantic, Judith thought. As she stepped onto the stage, she saw the briefest flash of metal – and the sense of something very heavy whooshing past her – before there was a crash as a theatre light smashed onto the floor a few inches from where she'd been standing only seconds before.

She was too terrified to speak, but when she looked up, she saw Duncan Wood on the rigging gantry directly above her.

'What are you doing there!' he said, his face white as a sheet.

'What happened?' Judith managed to stammer.

'Didn't you see the sign?' Duncan said. 'At the entrance to the stage. No one's allowed here while I'm rigging lights.'

'I'm sorry,' Judith said.

'I could have killed you,' Duncan yelped.

Judith looked down at the heavy stage light on the floor a yard from where she was standing.

'Yes,' she said. 'You could have done.'

Judith looked back up at Duncan and held his gaze, and then he turned away and started to scurry down the caged ladder that led to the stage.

Suddenly, Judith didn't want to be anywhere near Duncan. Before he reached the bottom of the ladder, she turned and left the stage, heading back down the steps and through the door into the brightness of the auditorium.

The doors to the main entrance banged open as Mrs Eddingham arrived in a profusion of apologies. Judith drifted over to join her. She'd not had a rehearsal with Mrs Eddingham since she'd started trying to find out where Lizzie Jenkins was staying, and she was hoping that she'd be able to have a quiet word with her.

However, Mrs Eddingham's tactic on arriving late to rehearsal was the same as the one she employed when she forgot her lines, or missed her cue: she launched into a monologue and kept on talking so no one had a chance to ask her what she was doing. The subject of today's speech covered the time Mrs Eddingham had mistakenly auditioned for Liverpool's Gay Sweatshop Theatre Company; how she should have been in the very first episode of the Peter Davison *Doctor Who*; how she'd inadvertently caused a union walkout at the BBC by unplugging a camera at Broadcasting House; and how Michael Parkinson was the most courteous man she'd ever met in the entertainment industry.

Despite Verity's best efforts, she wasn't able to get the cast to stagger through the scene even once. Then, with only minutes to go before the end of the rehearsal, Mrs Eddingham suddenly announced they should all go back 'on book' for one proper run-through of the scene. She then whipped out her copy of the play and proceeded to perform it very slowly and loudly – which was at least the correct interpretation of her part – but her moves were from the previous production she'd done as Lady Bracknell, and didn't fit the new set design.

'Why isn't my chair here?' Mrs Eddingham asked imperiously, in no way breaking out of character to do so.

'Your chair's stage left, Mary,' Verity said for the dozenth time.

'It should be centre stage,' Mrs Eddingham huffed.

And throughout it all, Judith wasn't paying attention to anything that was going on around her. All she could keep thinking was, had Duncan just tried to kill her?

Chapter 16

By the time Mrs Eddingham had agreed she'd consider performing her scene from stage left after all, it was time for the rehearsal to end. And Judith still hadn't had a chance to talk to Mrs Eddingham about Lizzie Jenkins. Against her better judgement, she caught up with her as they were leaving and suggested they go for a cup of tea together. Mrs Eddingham was delighted to accept the offer and the two women repaired to Strawberry Grove, where they furnished themselves with cups of tea and large slices of Victoria sponge cake, and settled onto a sofa.

'Now, Judith, you're doing very well in your part.'

'Thank you,' Judith said, touched by Mrs Eddingham's support.

'Although I do have a few notes.'

Before Judith could respond, Mrs Eddingham launched into a speech about how the hardest thing an actor has to do on stage is know what to do with their hands, even though no one in real life ever considers what they're doing with them.

'So I recommend you get yourself a clutch bag to hold,' Mrs Eddingham said, moving on to her peroration. 'Although I don't think Miss Prism would have a bag of any sort, now I think about it, and I suppose it might interfere with the revelation about the handbag later on, so I think you should just hold your hands together in front of you. Yes, that would suit the modesty of your part very well. Hold your hands together thusly.'

Mrs Eddingham cupped her hands together as though she were holding a very delicate bird inside them.

Judith tried to take offence, but she couldn't help but smile at Mrs Eddingham's misguided advice. She could see it came from what Becks would call 'a good place' – even as Suzie would point out how irritating that place was. Thinking of her friends reminded Judith of her task.

'Verity is very impressive, isn't she?' she said, by way of an opening.

'She's a breath of fresh air, I completely agree.' Mrs Eddingham said. 'I loved Oliver, of course I did, but he did like to hold forth, and you could get to the end of a rehearsal without him having drawn breath even once.'

Judith marvelled at how Mrs Eddingham didn't realise she was describing herself as much as Oliver.

'Was he a good director?'

'He had energy, I'll give him that,' Mrs Eddingham conceded. 'But it was always a touch chaotic. He'd change his mind. I remember a production of *A Christmas Carol* we did that he insisted had to be modern-dress, and then, at the last minute, he balked and said we were going nineteenth century after all. Even though there wasn't time for Roger to grow any side-whiskers, and Sue – his wife – had to spend the week before opening night sewing frills and ruffs all over his M&S suits and shirts. And his ideas were always too ambitious. When we did *Little Shop of Horrors*, he insisted that the cast build Audrey II – the big puppet plant – all together. It would be a bonding exercise, he said. But – again – a week before curtain up, we had this puppet that was nothing more than a wheelie bin with dozens of pairs of dark green tights stuffed full of paper as its branches. It was terrible. The Marlow Bar and Grill had to step in and hire us a proper puppet from the Valley Players in Hughenden. And the Valley Players have felt they've had bragging rights over us ever since.'

'Everyone's stories about Oliver are so vivid,' Judith said, trying to staunch the flow of words.

'Of course, his death is so very shocking,' Mrs Eddingham agreed with barely disguised glee. 'I don't know how the MADS will continue. You've seen Verity – you're right, she's impressive in her own way, but she gets stuck on the simplest things, like that silly chair. Whoever heard of Lady Bracknell being at the side of the stage in Act Three? You see,' she continued, taking a delicate bite of Victoria sponge and then wiping the non-existent crumbs from her lips with a paper napkin, 'if Oliver's been the heart of the club these last four decades, I've been its head. For all that Verity is now trying to mount her little coup, I've been on stage in every production, usually in a leading role – which is only to be expected, seeing as I'm the only member of the company with anything close to professional experience. Much as I love everyone else who joins in, of course. But it's not the same – it just isn't.'

'What about Toby? He's off to RADA, isn't he?'

Mrs Eddingham sniffed her disapproval.

'You don't think he's a good actor?' Judith asked.

'He's confident, I'll give him that. But since you're asking, no,

I don't. It's all "show" with Toby and very little "truth". If I were being generous, I'd say he's got some talent, but it's limited. I'm surprised an institution as auspicious as RADA has taken him. There, I've said it, but you can't sugar-coat in our profession. In the long run, it's unkind to let someone get their hopes up needlessly.'

If that was Mrs Eddingham being generous, Judith wondered what a critical appraisal from her would look like.

'I'm afraid to say that Toby's talents are what Trev would call shallow. Sorry, I should say, "Trev" is Sir Trevor Nunn – I got to know him at Stratford in the 1968 season.'

'You performed with the Royal Shakespeare Company?' Judith said, impressed.

'Not exactly – I was there as an usher – but Trev made sure all the front of house staff felt part of the company. The point is, Oliver, wonderful Oliver, was always attracted to shallowness. Seeing as he was so shallow himself. Especially when that person hung on his every word like Toby did. Oliver loved his acolytes.'

'You really didn't like him, did you?'

'What? No, I loved him! His failings were what made him human. And he was so much fun to be around, and got the productions done when anyone else would have faltered. He was a Mephistopheles figure, that's all I'm saying.'

Judith took a sip from her cup of tea and decided it was time to get down to business.

'You say you've been with the Marlow Amateur Dramatic Society since the start?'

'Our inaugural production was *A Midsummer Night's Dream*. I was Titania, of course, and Oliver was playing Bottom. The funniest thing happened to his donkey ears on the first—'

'Does that mean you knew Lizzie Jenkins back then?' Judith asked, cutting in.

'Now why would you be asking about her?' Mrs Eddingham asked, her eyes alight with mischief.

'Is it such an interesting question?'

'It's the only question worth asking. I'm surprised it's taken you so long to ask it.'

'Why?'

'Because I can tell you categorically, if you want to know who killed Oliver, then it's her – Lizzie will have killed him.'

'You know that?'

'It wouldn't have been any of the others, I can assure you.'

'Not even Verity?'

'She thrived on the drama of living with Oliver, don't let anyone tell you different. She loved losing her temper with him, always being in the right – it's why she's enjoying being a director now. For Verity, it's all about controlling her environment – being in charge – which is why she and Oliver were such a bad match. But you're right to ask about when Lizzie first joined us. She was about seventeen when she walked through the door of the theatre and she was already quite beautiful. And when it comes to real talent, she had it from the start. You couldn't take your eyes off her, she was . . . luminous. I wasn't remotely surprised when she became a film star. She was absolutely radiant. But what was so interesting was that she wasn't aware of it at all. You see, she came from a horrible family. I don't remember all the ins and outs of it, but her father was in prison for some reason, and I think her mother was abusive. Which made her all the better an actor, in my opinion. There was a real danger to her when she performed. And fragility. Mesmerising, beautiful and brittle all at once. Her first leading role for us was as Eliza Doolittle in *Pygmalion* and she was wonderful.'

'But why is asking about her the only question worth asking?'

'Because Oliver fell completely under her spell. He was playing Henry Higgins – of course he was. I should say, this is long before Verity came on the scene. And it's about the only time I ever saw him obsess over someone who wasn't himself. Oliver normally has to be top dog, you see. In charge. But he was slavish in his devotion to Lizzie. Even though she must have been at least ten years younger than him. It was totally inappropriate, because he was in his late twenties and she'd just dropped out of school.'

'She didn't make it through school?'

'I think her mum threw her out. Lizzie's got many qualities, but she's not the sharpest knife in the drawer. Or not academically, at least. The point being, Oliver couldn't wait to offer her his spare room. She moved in with him. And before too long, they became lovers.'

'Why has no one mentioned this before?' Judith asked, amazed.

'It's impolite, considering everything Verity's gone through. And it's so far in the past, who'd want to bring it up all these years later? But we all knew about it at the time, and the two of them didn't do anything to hide it. And I know people say it was a more innocent time, but none of us were happy about it. A vulnerable seventeen-year-old girl shacked up with an older man – it was so obviously wrong. But the two of them didn't care. If you asked Lizzie about it at the time, and I did, she'd say she was in love with him.'

'How long did this last?'

'She stayed with us for a year or so. Did only two further productions. A stunning Peter Pan in that year's panto, and the prettiest Gwendolen in *The Importance of Being Earnest* you ever saw. I was Lady Bracknell in that production as well. But then she didn't turn up for auditions for the next play. I remember it was such a surprise. And Oliver refused to talk about what had happened between them. All I ever got out of him was "she's gone", or words to that effect.'

'I can't believe I didn't know any of this,' Judith said.

'There aren't many here whose memory of the MADS goes back that far.'

'And you think there was still unfinished business between Lizzie and Oliver?'

'She turns up out of the blue all these years later and he's shot dead the same day? You mark my words, it's no coincidence. She killed him.'

'When did Verity join the MADS?' Judith asked.

'It was not long after Lizzie left. The production after, or maybe the one after that. She doesn't stick in the memory quite like Lizzie does. Although she was a fine actor in her own way.'

'Verity told us she had no talent.'

'Nonsense! She could completely lose herself in the part she was playing. There was nothing flashy about her like there is with Toby. She'd immerse herself like a proper character actor should. It was such a shame when she stopped treading the boards – she was the real deal, though I say so myself.'

Knowing how much antipathy Mrs Eddingham had towards Verity as a director, Judith knew how much this had cost the older woman to say.

'How did she and Oliver get together?'

'Well, they're closer in age, to begin with. And after Lizzie disappeared from our lives, I think that Verity was his – now what does my granddaughter call it? Oh yes – "rebound" relation-ship. And Oliver's not stupid, he was always attracted to quality. But Verity's a very serious person. Proper. And for her it was important that she and Oliver marry, so they got married. And then, after a few years, she gave up acting altogether. I never understood it myself. It was almost as if she was doing everything in her power to have as little as possible to do with the MADS.'

'I wonder what Lizzie Jenkins would say about what you've told me,' Judith said ruminatively.

'Why don't you ask her?'

'I'd love to, but I've no idea how to get hold of her.'

'That's easy enough, she's staying at the Danesfield Hotel.'

'How do you know that?'

'I've a great-niece who works at the spa there. She couldn't wait to tell me that Lizzie Jenkins was staying at the hotel. And she's in the gym – or spa – or having treatments every day.'

'Now that is *very* interesting,' Judith said as she popped the last piece of Victoria sponge cake into her mouth.

Chapter 17

Lizzie Jenkins was sitting in the circular Jacuzzi at the Danesfield House Hotel, trying to control her feelings of guilt and shame. She'd been in a spin ever since Oliver had died, and she'd even started taking sleeping pills again so she could find some kind of peace at night. When she'd presented herself to the hotel concierge, she'd had a sense of grim inevitability as she'd asked for the details of a private doctor in Marlow who'd see her.

A nice-looking woman got into the Jacuzzi and sat opposite her. Lizzie came out of her reverie and gave a quick but cold smile. She could see the flash of recognition in the other woman's eyes and wondered if she'd have to get out – the constant price of fame. As Lizzie was contemplating whether the woman opposite was about to strike up a conversation, the ceiling lights were blocked by a very tall woman stepping up to the Jacuzzi's edge and a big foot slapping down into the water. The new arrival couldn't take her eyes off Lizzie, and she realised she'd definitely have to get out before one of these two women started talking to her. Lizzie lifted herself out of the water.

'Not so fast,' Judith said as she appeared at the edge of the tub and carefully lowered herself in to join Becks and Suzie.

'We meet again,' she said with a deadly smile.

'You're that woman,' Lizzie said, trying to work out what Judith was doing in her Jacuzzi.

'And these are my friends,' Judith added.

Becks coughed and pointed apologetically at her mouth.

'Sorry,' she said. 'Some bubbles went up my nose.'

'You can't just march in here,' Lizzie said. 'It's a private hotel.'

'We've paid for day access to the spa,' Suzie said like an East End gangster as she sat in her frilly green swimsuit in amongst the froth.

'We wanted to hear your side of the story,' Judith said. 'Because everyone else has been talking about you, and I think you'll benefit from having your say.'

'About the night Oliver died?'

'About so much more than that.'

'And you want to do that in a Jacuzzi?'

'It's as good a place as any,' Suzie said, scooping up some bubbles and then blowing them off her hand in delight. 'Jacuzzis are brilliant.'

'This is crazy, I've told the police everything I need to.'

'That's right,' Judith said. 'Everything you need to, but not everything that's relevant. For example, you've not mentioned your affair with Oliver Beresford.'

'I didn't have an affair with him.'

'When you were seventeen.'

'You know about that?' she asked.

The water bubbled around the four women.

'It was a pretty dark time,' Lizzie conceded.

'Was your dad really in prison?' Becks asked.

'Who's been talking? It's that cow, isn't it? Mary Eddingham. She always was a vicious gossip – you can't believe a word she says, she's a nasty fantasist. If you're looking for someone who'd have wanted to kill Oliver, don't look any further than her. She's been completely sidelined from the MADS. She wasn't even invited onto the boat, that's how out of favour she is.'

'But is it true?' Becks asked. 'Was your dad in prison?'

'That was . . .' Lizzie said as she tried to work out how to explain. 'He beat up a guy in a pub. Some bloke. He'd not even met him before.'

'He was violent,' Becks said.

Lizzie nodded.

'I'm so sorry.'

'It's what it was. And Mum was a junkie. I've written all about it in my autobiography.'

'Yes, I saw online that you'd written an autobiography,' Judith said.

'A lot's happened to me in my life,' Lizzie said.

'Tell you what I don't get,' Suzie said. 'How did you end up getting involved in the local am-dram society?'

'You want to know? OK, there was this woman at the youth club in Marlow. Up by Great Marlow school. We used to go there after lessons had finished. I was basically disruptive and made her life miserable.'

'You were hurting,' Becks offered.

'I belittled her, made jokes about her weight, and made every-one turn against her – I shudder at how nasty I was.'

'What was her name?' Becks asked.

'No idea. I was so wrapped up in myself back then. I've blanked her. It's weird. All I remember is how much I wanted her to hurt, but she's a void in my memory now.'

Judith was already getting the impression that, in Lizzie's world, everyone who wasn't her was possibly something of a void.

'I was a mess. My mum hadn't enrolled me in sixth form and I'd not seen any of the letters from the council. And the woman at the Youth Club was a saint. Even with how I was treating her, she said I should use the club as my postal address while I tried to sort my life out – little good it did me. It was too late for me to go back to school. That's when she tried to get me to join as many local clubs as possible. But I wasn't interested. I signed on with the job centre instead. And whatever she suggested, I did the opposite. Except amateur dramatics.'

'Why did you do that one?'

'To this day, I don't know. I think I kind of went along to laugh at it. But it was full of people who didn't treat me like a problem, and who didn't know about my dad and my mum. It felt – I don't know – safe. Not that I let on. I pretended I hated it, of course I did, but I kind of knew it was where I belonged the moment I arrived.'

'And Oliver Beresford?'

'Listen, I'm not proud of that. It's about the only thing I've not put in my autobiography. My therapist would say that in those days I thought everything in life was transactional. If you had sex with someone it meant they loved you. And I was pretty, you know? But with zero self-esteem. It was a toxic combination.'

'He took advantage of you,' Becks said.

'He was the powerful man in the room. I was always attracted to power. And I was desperate to get away from home. So I moved in with him. It was only for a year or so, and it was hellish, but it was better than home.'

'Why was it so hellish?'

'I know I'm wrapped up in myself, but I'm nothing compared to Oliver. And at that time, his work wasn't going well. He'd just qualified as a surveyor or whatever and he'd been given a crap job. Checking over a load of council buildings for asbestos – it was grim work. And dangerous in its own way. He was stressed and difficult to live with, but I knew I'd at least be safe. Physically. He never hit me. And there were good times as well. He could come up with these grand gestures. Like hiring a sports car for a day, even though he couldn't afford it, and driving us out to the countryside for a picnic. There were real highs in there. And he helped me apply for drama school.'

'He did?' Judith asked, noticing that Oliver seemed to have a habit of helping his acolytes apply to drama school. First there was Lizzie and, latterly, Toby. She wondered who else he might have helped over the years.

'Yeah,' Lizzie said, and for the first time she looked uncomfortable.

'What is it?' Suzie asked.

'What?'

'You look guilty.'

'I'm not guilty, it's just not something I like thinking about. The thing is, I didn't get in to drama school, and it kind of sent me into a spin. Look, it's all in my autobiography. You can read all of the sordid details for yourself.'

'Then we will. Thank you. So how come you came back to Marlow?'

'There's no mystery. I got a begging letter from a guy called

Toby Vincent. From Marlow. I get sent begging letters the whole time, but it was from someone in the MADS. And it made me start thinking about the old days. And I realised I was happy to give him cash to go to RADA. He could go when I couldn't, if you see what I mean. But I wanted more than that. I wanted to come home. The process of writing my book had slain a load of ghosts for me and I reckoned it was time to face my past. To say thank you to the MADS for the start they gave me.'

'And to thank Oliver Beresford,' Becks added.

'Even Oliver Beresford,' Lizzie agreed.

'Even though he was patronising to you,' Suzie said, remembering what Lance had told them.

'He was always patronising.'

'But he was particularly bad that night, wasn't he?'

'Not that I noticed.'

'Where exactly were you standing when Oliver Beresford died?'

'Are you serious?'

'It's an easy question,' Judith said. 'Where were you?'

Judith and her friends all saw the moment when Lizzie's brain froze and her mouth twitched. 'I was in my cabin!' she blurted. 'God – bloody hell, don't put me on the spot like that again.'

'You're lying,' Judith said.

'I'm not! It's those stupid invites everyone received! They make it look like I'm guilty, when I'm not!'

'Then who was the "Lizzie Jenkins" who sent the notes if it wasn't you?' Suzie asked.

'I don't know – someone who was setting me up.'

'Why would anyone want to set you up?' Becks asked.

'I've no idea.'

'And why did you insist that the boat had to have cabins?' Judith asked.

'What's that?'

'Lance Goodman said you told Oliver that when he hired a boat, it had to have proper cabins, and a driving position that was also enclosed.'

'I never said anything of the sort.'

'Are you saying Lance is lying?'

'If he's saying that that's what I told Oliver, then yes.'

'Why would he lie to us?' Becks asked.

'You'll have to ask him yourself.'

'Are we supposed to believe that everyone else is lying and you're the only person who's telling the truth?' Judith asked.

'Why would I lie about any of this?'

'Because you shot him,' Suzie said, summing up the situation as she saw it. 'You got on the boat that night with a plan to kill Oliver Beresford, and that's what you did.'

'That's not what happened!'

Judith leaned closer to Lizzie.

'What *did* happen?' she asked.

'I . . .' Lizzie said, floundering, and then her countenance cleared as she came to a realisation. 'I don't have to do this,' she said, and stood up, water sloshing off her.

'You killed Oliver Beresford,' Suzie said again.

'You weren't there, you don't know what happened that night!' Lizzie said as she scrambled out of the Jacuzzi. Grabbing a white robe from a nearby peg, she didn't even have time to put it on as she strode out of the pool area to the safety of the changing rooms.

Judith sat back in the Jacuzzi like a Mafia don following a particularly satisfying shakedown and looked at her two friends.

They were all thinking the same thing.

Was Lizzie Jenkins their killer?

Chapter 18

Once Judith and her friends left Danesfield House, they agreed they needed to read Lizzie's autobiography as a matter of urgency, so Suzie drove them over to the Marlow library. Fortunately, there were three copies available and they took them out, agreeing to meet up the following day to discuss it.

It was no surprise to any of them, as Judith poured them all cups of tea the next morning, that Judith had read the book twice, Becks had read it only once, but had taken copious notes that she'd organised under headings, and Suzie had been forced to admit that she'd not quite finished it yet.

'I have to say,' Becks said, holding up her notes, 'Lizzie wasn't joking when she said her life was rough. That sort of poverty – and lack of love – would haunt you your whole life.'

'Do you know what I noticed?' Judith asked. 'Lizzie told us that she didn't put her affair with Oliver in her book, but it's so much more than that. She doesn't refer to Oliver Beresford even once. And the MADS is only mentioned in passing. She describes everything about her home life in wincing detail, and then suddenly she's in New York. If it hadn't been for Mrs Eddingham talking to me, her whole interlude with the MADS and Oliver would have been airbrushed out of history.'

'That shows she can't have got over him,' Suzie said.

'That's what Mrs Eddingham believed,' Judith agreed.

'It's what happened after she left Marlow I found the most shocking,' Becks said.

'Yeah – sorry,' Suzie said without any hint of regret, 'I didn't get to that bit.'

'It was about the third chapter, Suzie. How much of the book did you actually get through?'

'I knew you two would read it, so I went to the Marlow Youth Club yesterday.'

'You did?' Judith asked, impressed.

'I used to go to it when I was a teenager. And I remembered there was a book you had to sign in and out of when you came and left. I wanted to see if they still had anything from when Lizzie was there. Or some photos from that time. Or the name of the woman Lizzie said she terrorised. If her old youth leader still lives in Marlow, she could tell us more about Lizzie's life back then.'

'Did you find anything?' Becks asked.

'No – sadly. The guy I spoke to said they had a big clear-out of all their old archives and records about ten years ago. Everything they had went to the man who runs the Marlow Museum. He's called Joshua Smith. I'll speak to him the next time I'm in town.'

'That's an excellent idea,' Judith said. 'I can't help feeling that whatever we can dig up on Lizzie's past in Marlow is going to be useful. And Becks and I can summarise what we learned from her book anyway. Lizzie went to New York when she was eighteen. And Becks is right. It's there that her life fell apart. She started taking heroin and wound up living in a squat with some rather scary people.'

'Even now,' Becks said, 'all of these years later, you can feel her self-loathing on every page. When she ran out of money, she basically ended up sleeping with men to get her next fix.'

'Then how did she get to be the glossy Hollywood star of today?' Suzie asked. 'That makes no sense.'

'A massive slice of good luck. She was spotted on the street by a fashion photographer. The way Lizzie tells it, there was a thing called "heroin chic" at the time, and she, as a heroin addict, embodied it perfectly. Before too long, she was on the front page of every magazine and dating a rock star. She led a rock and roll lifestyle for a bit. And then, one day, she woke up in hospital. She'd taken an overdose and it was the jolt she said she needed. Her modelling career in New York meant she'd already had interest from a talent agency in Los Angeles, so she went "out to the West Coast" as she puts it, cleaned up her life and started getting acting jobs. Within a year, she was getting good parts, and she hasn't looked back since.'

'Until now,' Suzie said. 'Because coming to Marlow is very much "looking back".'

'You're right,' Becks said. 'It's definitely telling that she doesn't mention Oliver Beresford even once in the whole book.'

'And the first time I met her, she had to admit that she owned a gun – even if it was back in Los Angeles,' Judith said.

'So she knows her way around a pistol,' Suzie said. 'And remember, it's her name on all of the letters telling everyone to go to their cabins for 6 p.m. And she was the one who wanted proper cabins on the boat according to Lance. And an enclosed driving position. But are we saying she was able to get all this organised when she only flew in from the US at lunchtime?'

'Then here's an idea,' Judith said. 'What if she had an accomplice?'

'But who?' Becks asked. 'It can't have been Oliver, can it? Seeing as he's the person who ended up shot.'

'No – I suppose that's right,' Judith said. 'I wonder if there's someone else it could have been? Who else did she even know? Apart from Duncan Wood and Mrs Eddingham, there's no one who goes back that far, is there?'

'Can I just check something,' Becks said. 'Are we sure we're happy doing this? Because we can't pretend we haven't started investigating the case again.'

'What's the problem?' Suzie said indignantly. 'All we've done is read a celebrity autobiography.'

'And stalked the prime suspect to her Jacuzzi – not forgetting the other people we've talked to about the case. We haven't even remotely followed Tanika's instructions.'

'No,' Judith said thoughtfully. 'You're right – it's not a good look, is it? And I promise you, the absolute last thing I want is to get Tanika into trouble.'

'So maybe Suzie shouldn't go digging around in the youth club records?' Becks said.

Before anyone could answer, Judith's landline started to ring.

With a little huff of effort, Judith got herself out of her chair, went over to the phone and answered it.

'Hello,' she said. 'Mrs Judith—'

'Judith, you've got to come at once!' a desperate-sounding Verity said before breaking down in sobs.

'What is it?' Judith asked.

'I didn't know who to call – please, you've got to come!'

'We can be with you in ten minutes. Don't worry, whatever it is, we can help sort it out.'

Before she'd even hung up, Becks and Suzie were heading to the front door to get their coats, and, with Suzie driving, they screeched up the driveway of Verity's house in record time. The three friends piled out of Suzie's van and ran for the front door. As they arrived, Verity flung the door open, looking terrified. Her eyes were red-rimmed with tears.

'What's happened?' Becks asked.

'It's better if I show you,' Verity said, disappearing back into the house.

The women followed her into the front room that overlooked the riverfront garden. One of the windows had been smashed, and there were shards of glass sparkling on the carpet under the jagged hole. In the middle of the floor was a dirty old brick. Someone had thrown it through Verity's window.

There was a piece of paper lying on the floor next to it and an old rubber band to the side.

'What happened?' Becks asked.

'Someone threw a bloody great brick through the window,' Suzie said, surprised that Becks felt that it was a question that needed asking.

'No, I see that,' Becks agreed. 'But who threw it?'

'I don't know!' Verity said. 'I was just tidying up – trying to get the house straight – and that's when there was this crash and the brick smashed through the window.'

'When exactly was this?' Judith asked.

'I don't know – twenty minutes ago. But you have to look

at that note,' Verity added, pointing at the brick, too frightened to approach.

Judith went over and picked up the piece of paper. It was a simple sheet of A4 that was folded in four. She opened it and the message arrived in a rush of thick letters.

Judith held up the paper so her friends could see the message for themselves.

Outside, they heard a car crunch to a stop on the gravel. Judith looked out of the window and saw Tanika get out of it.

'It's the police,' she said, surprised.

'I rang them before I rang you,' Verity said. 'Whoever did this is unhinged – but I knew you'd get here before the police did. I need people around me I can trust.'

'We'd better make our excuses,' Becks said, willing Judith to leave with her eyes.

'I want you to stay with me,' Verity said. 'The police already think I'm involved in Oliver's death.'

'They do?' Suzie asked.

'It's something to do with a scarf that someone found in the river the day after Oliver died.'

'Oh?' Judith asked, thrilled that Verity had brought up the

subject without any prompting from her. 'What was so special about it?'

'That's what I don't understand – it belonged to me. The police got me to go in to the station to identify it.'

'I'm sure there's some perfectly innocent explanation for why it ended up in the river,' Becks said.

'That's what I said, although I wasn't wearing it that night, so I don't know quite how it got there.'

'When did you last wear it?' Judith asked.

'I don't know. I haven't worn it in months, maybe even a year.'

'Where did you keep it?'

'In my bedroom.'

'You didn't leave it somewhere else? Suzie asked. 'Like at the theatre? That's what I always do, leave my coats, scarves and gloves on the back of chairs when I go out.'

'I suppose it's possible, but I'm convinced it was in my drawer, upstairs. I saw it a few months ago when I was looking for a pair of gloves.'

'So who could have taken it?'

'I've no idea. Why would they take it, that's what I don't understand. And it gets so much worse than that. The police told me the scarf had something on it that came from the gun that was used to kill Oliver.'

'Do you mean gunshot residue?' Becks asked.

'That's the phrase they used. They said there was gunshot residue on the scarf from the exact same pistol that had been used to shoot him.'

Judith, Suzie and Becks struggled to hide their surprise.

'Your scarf was being held by the killer as they shot your husband?' Suzie asked.

'That's what the police said – and they kept asking me where I was at 6 p.m. when he died. I told them I was in my cabin, but I can't prove it, can I? Of course I can't, I was on my own! I thought the scarf was going to be the worst of it, but now this note says I killed him!' Verity had a sudden revelation. 'I'm being set up, aren't I? Oh God, is that what's going on? The person who did this to Oliver is trying to frame me for his murder!'

There was a loud knock at the door and the women heard Tanika call out, 'Are you there, Mrs Beresford? It's Detective Inspector Tanika Malik.'

'I think discretion is the better part of valour,' Judith said to her friends before turning to Verity. 'Can we use your back door?'

Chapter 19

Judith, Suzie and Becks left Verity's house by the kitchen door, but Judith led them down the garden to the riverside rather than heading to the driveway.

'Are we trying to avoid Tanika?' Becks asked.

'We are,' Judith said. 'But I'd also like to know where Duncan is.'

'You think he's the person who threw the brick?'

'I don't think it's what he would do. If Verity and Toby are to be believed, it's far too direct for him. But he might have seen who did it.'

'Not that the brick's necessarily the biggest thing we found out,' Becks said.

'I know what you mean,' Judith agreed. 'That revelation about the scarf is dynamite, isn't it? Although it's interesting, given that Lizzie's explanation for the "Go to your cabin at 6 p.m." messages is that she's being set up. And now here's Verity saying the same thing about the scarf. Someone's setting her up.'

'She's got a point,' Suzie said. 'If she were the killer, do you think she'd dump her scarf in the river when it's covered with evidence that she shot Oliver?'

'Maybe he wrestled it from her after he was shot?' Becks suggested.

'But the second shot was straight to the heart, wasn't it?' Suzie said. 'And it killed him instantly.'

'Then perhaps the tussle happened after the first shot and before the second. He had those wood scrapings in his palms and bruising to his wrist, didn't he?'

'He did,' Judith agreed. 'If only there'd been a witness who could tell us what happened on the back of the boat.'

'Instead of everyone being in their cabins,' Becks said.

As the women reached the water's edge, they saw Duncan at the back of his houseboat on the opposite riverbank. He was in the process of stowing a pair of oars.

'Good morning!' Judith called across the water.

'Bloody hell,' Duncan said with a start. He'd clearly not seen the women approach. 'Where did you lot pop up from?'

'Sorry to interrupt,' Judith called across the water. 'I just wondered if you've seen anyone suspicious near Verity's house this morning?'

'What's that?' Duncan said, putting his hand to his ear so he could hear better.

'Have you seen anyone near Verity's house this morning?' Suzie bellowed.

'Right,' Duncan said in appreciation. 'I very definitely heard that. And no, I've not seen anyone around. Why are you asking?'

'Did you hear the sound of glass smashing at any time?'

Duncan paused before he answered.

'No, can't say I have. And I'm sorry about that whole stage-light thing, Judith, but you've got to be careful in a theatre, they're dangerous places. Anyway, I've got to get on, see you around,' he said, vanishing down the steps into his boat.

'That's interesting,' Judith said. 'The pane of glass the brick went through was large, it would have made a loud noise when it was smashed. I wonder why Duncan didn't hear it.'

'Or why he didn't want to talk to us,' Becks said. 'There's no question he looked uncomfortable.'

'I suppose it was a surprise, us suddenly appearing like that. What is it?' Judith asked Suzie, who was studying her carefully.

'What did he mean when he said you have to be careful in the theatre?'

'Why are you so interested?' Judith asked, before realising why Suzie was so interested. As breezily as possible, she explained how Duncan had mistakenly dropped a stage light that had nearly landed on her.

'This is it, isn't it?' Suzie said, her eyes wide. 'I told you your life was in danger.'

'You're not saying the cards made Duncan drop it on me, are you?'

'I'm not saying anything – it's the cards that are speaking.'

'But this is good news, isn't it?' Becks asked.

'I nearly get killed and you think it's good news?' Judith asked.

'It could mean the curse is over, since it failed.'

'Hold on, the light wasn't cursed. It either fell by mistake or Duncan dropped it on purpose, those are the only two options.'

'And I don't see how it can be the end of the curse,' Suzie said.

'There is no curse!' Judith said.

'The light missed you,' Suzie said, ignoring her friend. 'The cards make it clear that something bad is actually going to happen to you. It won't be a near miss. It's something big and direct, and it will be a real threat to your life.'

'I don't know how many times I have to say this, but three

cards pulled at random from a pack can't predict the future. I'd much rather you concentrated on the fact that Duncan might have dropped the light on me because he's trying to stop me from revealing that he's the killer.'

Judith's words hit home, and the three women looked over at Duncan's boat. It was sitting blamelessly in the autumn sunshine. Judith shivered.

'Come on,' she said. 'Let's go back to the van.'

The women skirted the garden to get back to the driveway, got into Suzie's van and decided to repair to Judith's house. After Becks whipped up a round of toast with dripping honey and a large pot of tea, they went through to the makeshift incident room Judith had constructed on the wall of her sitting room.

In the past when they'd been trying to find killers, Judith and her friends had always worked in the room she normally kept locked at the far end of the house. However, since she'd got rid of her vast archive of newspapers in pursuit of catching Geoffrey Lushington's killer, Judith found that she no longer wished to go into the room at all. She preferred to bring her investigative work into her far more comfortable sitting room.

'I wonder if there's a way of discovering where everyone was when the brick went through Verity's window,' Judith said. 'We already know Duncan was in the area – we saw him on his boat.'

'It's Lizzie's location we need to know,' Suzie said. 'Seeing as she's the killer.'

'I wonder if there's a way of finding that out?' Judith asked. 'Not that she's definitely the killer, Suzie.'

'We all saw how flustered she got when we asked her where she was when Oliver died. She's the killer.'

'We don't know that for sure.'

'OK, I'll do you a deal. If she *isn't* the killer, I promise I won't mention tarot cards or the curse they placed on you again.'

'Really?' Judith asked. 'You promise you'll drop the subject?'

'I promise.'

'Even though you originally thought the killer had to be Verity?' Becks asked.

'What's that?' Suzie asked.

'At first you thought the killer was Verity, and now you're saying it's Lizzie. Are you sure you won't change your mind again?'

'No way. Lizzie's the killer, you mark my words.'

The doorbell rang and Judith frowned. She wasn't expecting any visitors or deliveries. She put down her cup of tea and went to see who it was. She opened her front door to find a very sour-looking Tanika standing outside.

'Ah,' Judith said.

'You thought I wouldn't discover you were at Verity Beresford's house?'

'I suppose it was always going to be a bit of a stretch.'

'Suzie's van was parked on the driveway with her name written down the side of it in big pink letters. And the first thing Mrs Beresford told me was that the three of you had just left.'

'But she invited us to her house,' Judith said with a rare hint of desperation. 'She rang me and said I had to go and see her. She sounded so upset that we could hardly refuse her.'

'How very convenient for you.'

'And we left by the back door so we wouldn't get you into trouble. We've been as good as gold. I promise you, we've taken what you said to heart. We've not dared do anything that would get you into trouble.'

Tanika's eyes narrowed.

'What have you dared to do then?'

'What's that?' Judith said, pretending that she hadn't quite heard what Tanika had said.

'Don't you try that "little old lady" act on me,' Tanika said as she pushed past Judith and entered her house.

'Oh, you don't want to go in there,' Judith said, as she followed Tanika through the hallway and into her sitting room.

As Tanika entered, Suzie froze, a slice of honeyed toast halfway to her mouth as Becks pinned a card that had *BRICK THROUGH WINDOW* written on it to the wall right next to a photo of Verity Beresford.

All the other photos and index cards from the case were pinned to the wall all around her, red wool creating a spider's web of links between all the evidence.

'Oh God!' Becks said, as she saw Tanika – and then she hid the ball of red wool she was holding behind her back.

Chapter 20

'It's not as bad as it looks,' Judith said.

'You said you wouldn't get involved!' Tanika said.

'I'm so sorry,' Becks said. 'But it was too intriguing, and we've sort of got into the habit of trying to solve crimes.'

'And we're good at it,' Suzie said with a flare of defiance.

'We've done our best not to step on your toes,' Becks added. 'We've not been following up on leads. We didn't even mention to Verity that it was us who found her scarf in the river.'

'Although she mentioned the scarf to us,' Suzie said.

'And I promise, we wouldn't have gone to Verity's house if she hadn't said we had to.'

'It's true,' Judith said. 'We've tried to make sure we didn't cause you any problems.'

Tanika sighed.

'It's just nice to be with people who are supportive,' she said. 'Do you mind if I sit down?'

'Of course not,' Judith said, indicating that Tanika should take her favourite wingback by the fireplace, and Becks went over to the tray of tea things and poured a fresh cup.

'It's hard enough trying to work out what happened on the boat that night without worrying I'm going to get stabbed in the back if I make a mistake.'

'It's that Brendan chap. I bet he's the only person pushing this. I don't trust him one bit. And you shouldn't, either.'

'It doesn't help that we've not been able to find anything in any of the suspects' lives that's even remotely suspicious. Toby Vincent is behind in payments on two credit cards, Duncan Wood has nine points on his driver's licence – and that's about it. And there's nothing that suggests any of them have any kind of problems with Oliver Beresford that would be worth killing over.'

'But none of them liked him!' Suzie said.

'That's not enough to build a case. He was too up himself for most people – so what? Loads of us have to deal with unlikeable people all the time, but we don't kill them. And as I'm sure you've worked out for yourself, this was a pre-meditated murder, not a spur-of-the-moment loss of temper. Whoever did this had been planning it for some time. Getting hold of a gun, sending those fake invitations . . .'

'Then what about Oliver's nefarious activities and dark secrets?' Judith asked, stirring a spoonful of sugar into her tea.

'That's a far better question. Because if we've not found much in the suspects' lives, there's a mystery at the heart of Oliver's life we can't solve.'

'What is it?' Suzie asked eagerly.

'Every week he disappeared for three days.'

'How do you mean?'

'Exactly how it sounds. He vanished.'

'Is this when he travelled?' Judith asked. 'Verity said that Oliver surveyed properties around the UK on Wednesdays, Thursdays and Fridays every week.'

'She told us the same thing. But when we spoke to his boss, he explained that a couple of years ago, Oliver stopped working for them full-time. Since then, he's only worked two days a week. Mondays and Tuesdays.'

'What?' Suzie said. 'He's been lying to Verity all this time? What did Verity say when you spoke to her about it?'

'She was as shocked as we were to learn that Oliver wasn't working on those days. She said he'd always return home on the Saturday morning with stories from his life on the road.'

'Did you believe her?'

'I never believe anyone, but her surprise seemed convincing.'

'And you've not been able to find out where he was going for yourselves?' Becks asked.

'I'm afraid we haven't.'

'Hang on, but you're the police!' Suzie said.

'I know – but wherever Oliver was going, he was going to great lengths to keep it a secret. On those three days of the week, he didn't use his debit or credit cards, so we have no record of where he was spending his money.'

'That's impossible,' Suzie said. 'You can't go three days every week without spending money.'

'I know,' Tanika agreed. 'But he managed it. We've found no digital footprint for where he was.'

'This is massive!' Suzie said. 'He was up to no good, you mark my words.'

'But is that definitely the case?' Becks asked. 'I mean, I know it looks suspicious, but Verity's admitted that she and Oliver didn't get on. What if he was just trying to get away from his marriage? A break from home life for three days every week – I imagine there's a long list of husbands and wives who'd sign up to that.'

Becks' friends all avoided making eye contact with her.

'How about we tell you what we've found?' Judith said as a way of moving the subject on.

'Yeah, go on,' Tanika said. 'What have you got?'

'Well, we've spoken to Lizzie Jenkins and she couldn't have behaved more guiltily if she'd tried. She also said that we "weren't there" when Oliver died, and that we didn't know "what had happened". It was rather a slip of the tongue on her part, as far as we could tell. There's definitely something about where she was that night – or what she did or saw – that she's not telling us.'

'Then you'll be interested to know, Lizzie Jenkins wasn't quite truthful about when she arrived in the country, either,' Tanika said. 'She told us she arrived shortly before midday, but when we checked, we discovered that her plane touched down at 8 a.m.'

'So why did she lie about when she arrived, unless she's guilty?' Suzie said. 'Do you think she could have killed Oliver with the help of an accomplice?'

The question took Tanika by surprise.

'Like who?' she said.

'It could be any of them,' Judith said, 'but we were wondering about Toby Vincent. It was Toby who originally contacted Lizzie Jenkins – they've got a pre-existing connection, and lines of communication.'

'But why would Toby want to kill Oliver?' Tanika asked.

'There you've got me. He's about the only person we've met so far who unreservedly liked him.'

'Although you should know,' Tanika continued, 'we found some circumstantially incriminating evidence against him. When my officers searched the *Marlow Belle*, they found a bullet in the corner of the cabin Toby used. It had rolled under the single bed. And before you ask, it hadn't been fired, but it was the same calibre and make as the bullets that were used to kill Oliver Beresford. Naturally, he strenuously denies any knowledge of how the bullet ended up in his cabin. Says anyone could have left it there. There were people in and out of his cabin the whole trip.'

'Hold on,' Suzie said, trying to get her head around the news. 'You found a bullet in Toby's cabin, and it's the same make of bullet as the two that were used to kill Oliver?'

'That's right.'

'And you're saying that information's *circumstantial*?'

'The thing is, Toby's right. He challenged us by saying there's no way we'd be able to find his fingerprints on the bullet – and we couldn't. In fact, the bullet doesn't have any fingerprints on it, it's been wiped clean.'

'Is he saying that someone is setting him up?' Judith asked.

'It's curious you should say that,' Tanika said. 'That's exactly what he's saying. His line is that whoever put the bullet in his cabin is trying to frame him for the murder.'

'Which makes him the third person to claim that the killer is trying to set them up. First there was Lizzie with her invitations, then Verity with her scarf – and now Toby with his bullet. It all seems to be developing into something of a theme, doesn't it?'

'Have you found the murder weapon yet?' Suzie asked.

'Police divers are still looking, but nothing so far.'

'Or have you got any idea what sort of gun it was?'

'Nope. We know that it fires nine-millimetre bullets – that's all we've got. All in all, you can see why my team aren't behind me.'

'What about witnesses on the riverbank?' Becks asked.

'That's one of the most frustrating aspects of the case. We've had boards up on the Thames path appealing for witnesses to come forward, and we've found a few people who remember seeing the *Marlow Belle* at some point that afternoon, but no one who was nearby in the crucial minutes before or after 6 p.m.'

'He definitely died at 6 p.m.?' Becks asked.

'The pathologist confirmed that that's when Oliver Beresford died. Or thereabouts.'

'And what about the brick that's just been thrown through Verity's window?' Suzie asked. 'Do you know where Lizzie was when it happened?'

'We checked up on all the suspects immediately,' Tanika said. 'And they're all accounted for. Lizzie Jenkins was having some kind of hot-stone massage at Danesfield House; Toby Vincent's workmates have confirmed that he was at the garage; a local farmer saw Duncan Wood working on his boat at about that time; and Lance Goodman was at the pharmacy in Marlow Bottom picking up a prescription. We've checked with the pharmacist and she confirms his story.'

'None of them could have thrown it?' Suzie asked.

'They've all got alibis, yes.'

'Then who could it have been if everyone's accounted for?'

'I'm sorry to say, I've no idea.'

'What about forensic evidence on the brick?' Becks asked.

'Ah,' Tanika said, 'that's where it gets even more baffling. The paper's generic copier paper, the ink is common to any number of laser printers – so there's nothing we can say about the paper or ink – or the rubber band, for that matter. But we've managed to lift a set of fingerprints from the paper.'

'They belong to someone from the case?' Judith asked, leaning forward in anticipation.

'They do.'

'That's fabulous news!' Judith said. 'This makes things *much* simpler. If we're lucky, the person who threw the brick is also the murderer.'

'That's highly unlikely.'

'How can you be so sure?'

'The fingerprints we lifted from the paper wrapped around the brick belong to Oliver Beresford.'

'Sorry – what?'

'The only prints on the "You Killed Him" message belong to the murder victim.'

'But that's not possible,' Becks said.

'Oh God!' Suzie said, her hand going to her chest. 'What if it's another message from beyond the grave? First the tarot cards, then the ghost woman in the red outfit, then the near miss of the light falling on you, Judith – and now this. This is getting scary.'

'Oliver Beresford isn't throwing bricks from beyond the grave,' Judith snapped. 'And my life's not in danger, before you say that it is.'

'You're under threat somehow, the cards don't lie.'

'All this means is that the person who threw the brick must have used a piece of paper that already had Oliver Beresford's fingerprints on it. That's all. So it proves that the brick was thrown by someone who knew him, but it doesn't reveal much else.'

'OK, I get that,' Becks said. 'But what I don't understand is, why would someone want to make it look as though the murder victim was accusing his wife of having killed him?'

The women looked at each other. They had no answer.

Chapter 21

Following the revelations about the fingerprints on the paper, Judith found it increasingly hard to get Suzie to talk logically about the case. As far as she was concerned, the supernatural was now woven through Oliver's murder from start to finish, and she even came up with extra theories that helped prove her point. After all, as she saw it, there was the mystery of the vanishing murder weapon that couldn't be explained, and the small matter of two gunshots fired on the boat that weren't heard by anyone.

To make matters worse for Judith, Suzie was also insisting that their investigation was cursed because the Marlow Museum was closed due to a mystery illness which meant she couldn't gain access to the old archives of the youth club. When Judith went to the museum to check out Suzie's story, she saw a sign in the window that revealed it was closed for a week while the curator had a planned operation. It was hardly a supernatural mystery.

The sign listed a phone number in case of enquiries, so Judith rang it and spoke to the museum curator, a man called Joshua Smith. He told her he'd had surgery on his wrist and was recuperating at home, but said he'd be happy to go to the archives and search the youth club records when he felt better. He then ended the call by saying that if he found anything, he'd let her know or bring it to the opening night of the next MADS production. Judith was shocked to discover that Joshua knew she was one of the cast.

'Everyone knows you joined the MADS to try and catch Oliver Beresford's killer,' Joshua said with a chuckle before hanging up.

Judith took a moment to gather her thoughts. As if it wasn't unsettling enough that people knew who she was, she had to admit that she'd compounded the problem by taking part in the next MADS production.

And there was no getting away from it: Judith's theatrical debut was only a week away. She was being called to rehearsals – or costume fittings, or prop rehearsals – every day. It did at least allow her to keep an eye on Verity, Duncan and Toby. In the pressure cooker of an imminent opening night, it was impossible for the three of them to hide their true personalities.

Verity remained something of a rock to everyone. She was capable, organised and there wasn't a detail of the production she didn't intimately know. Judith couldn't help but conclude that of all the MADS, she seemed the most capable of committing a meticulously planned murder. And there was no doubting that she'd had a second lease of life since her husband's death. She was invigorated, engaged and – this is what Judith had ultimately come to conclude – happy.

When it came to Duncan, Judith found that he now kept himself away from her as much as possible. She even tested her theory a few times by making sure she went near him, but he'd slip away every time – a sure sign of guilt, she believed. But guilt about what? Nearly killing her? Or actually killing Oliver?

As for Toby, he remained his usual, friendly self, but Judith had begun to recognise that there were times when he retreated into himself. It mostly happened when he wasn't in the scene that was being rehearsed. He'd go very still, very quiet, and he'd look – to Judith's eyes, at least – worried. If she were a betting woman, she'd say there was something gnawing at him. Was he the killer? It seemed unlikely, given how much he'd looked up to Oliver. Or maybe he was just nervous about the impending opening night?

And then, one day, a man called Rob Hooker visited the cast. Rob was an impish man in his seventies who taught at RADA. He was an old friend of Oliver's, and an expert in Oscar Wilde. Verity had asked him to come and deliver a talk on the historical context of the play, but had kept his arrival a surprise.

By chance, Judith was looking at Toby as Rob entered the auditorium. What she saw on Toby's face was a sudden rush of panic, and there was no question that Rob was the cause. Toby couldn't take his eyes off him as he crossed the room to embrace Verity.

As Verity called the company together and explained that Rob was from RADA and was going to talk to them about the play, Judith watched Toby slip out of the auditorium. What on earth was that about?

Rob dazzled the company with his wit and knowledge for half an hour, tolerantly answered questions for a further hour, and then announced that he had to leave to catch a train back to London. In the hubbub of his departure, Judith caught up with him and quickly thanked him for his talk.

'Can I talk to you about Toby Vincent?' she asked.

'Sorry, who?' Rob said, not entirely listening, as he put on his coat.

'He's off to RADA in September.'

'He is? I don't have anything to do with admissions.'

'But you must know of him. Oliver Beresford was his mentor.'

'Even so, I don't recognise the name. And I can't talk about any aspects of the admissions process, I'm sure you can understand why. Now I must get on or I'll miss my train.'

Judith smiled, but she knew there was something 'off' about Rob's answers. He'd been shifty. So she begged a lift with Verity back to her house, saying she could walk home afterwards, the exercise would do her good. Verity was happy to agree.

'I don't think I've properly thanked you for stepping into the breach,' Verity said as she drove them down the high street towards Marlow Bridge. 'It was good of you to take on the role of Miss Prism.'

'I've enjoyed it,' Judith said with an honesty that surprised her. 'Everyone's so talented.'

'They are, aren't they?'

'There's such a lovely camaraderie. And it also helps that you're able to snag someone as impressive as Rob to come and talk to us.'

'Yes, well, I can't take any credit for that. Rob was always Oliver's friend more than mine. And he's lovely, but he's very much a man's man. The sort of person who has lunch every day at the Garrick Club and doesn't think it wrong.' Judith knew that the Garrick was one of the last gentlemen's clubs in London that refused to admit women. 'I have no sway with him, so it's fortunate that he'd agreed to come and talk to us before Oliver

. . . passed,' Verity added, aware that she was stretching the euphemism of the word 'passed'.

'They'd known each other a long time?' Judith asked.

'Oh gosh, yes. Decades.'

'I suppose Rob helped with Toby's application to RADA.'

'Very much so. As I remember, it was Rob who chose Toby's Shakespeare speech for his audition – not that he helped him with how to perform it. He said that was for Toby to discover for himself. But he made sure Toby didn't choose a text that the panel had heard a million times before.'

Judith allowed a silence to develop. If Rob had been so instrumental in getting Toby his place at RADA, why was he now denying that he'd helped? And why had Toby panicked at the mere sight of him? Judith knew this was a puzzle she'd have to solve. Thinking of puzzles, Judith remembered the other great mystery of the case.

'Can I ask you something?' she asked as they pulled into Verity's driveway.

'Of course.'

'It's to do with Oliver vanishing three days every week.'

'Do you know if the police have worked out where he went?' Verity asked.

'That's the thing – I don't believe they have, and I'm very much asking as a private individual. We're not working with the police, it's important I say that. But what I don't understand is why the police have been able to find no trace of him, with all the resources they have available to them. Why is it proving so hard for them to find out where your husband went every week?'

'I don't understand, either. I've found it quite upsetting to discover that Oliver was pulling the wool over my eyes. And deceiving all of his colleagues at work.'

'You must have some idea of what he was up to?'

'But that's the thing, I don't. I was so glad to see him gone for those three days, I didn't question it.'

'What did he wear?'

'How do you mean?'

'Was he smartly dressed when he left? Or came back? You didn't by any chance find receipts for shopping or food when you went through his pockets to do the laundry?'

'I've gone over it all in my mind, but I can't think of anything that might help. If I could, I'd have told the police.'

'How was he before he left?'

'How do you mean?'

'What was his mood like? Was he happy? Excited? Worried?'

'It all felt very humdrum to me. He'd pack a little overnight bag and then he'd go off in his sports car before I woke up.'

'So he left early?' Judith asked, before realising that she'd replied to the wrong part of Verity's answer. 'Hang on,' she added, 'he has a sports car?'

'He bought it when he turned fifty. Said it was his mid-life crisis purchase.'

'I don't remember seeing it on your driveway.'

'It lives in the garage under a tarpaulin. It was his pride and joy.'

'So he always used it when he left for his mid-week trips?' Judith asked, the beginning of an idea forming in her mind.

'Always.'

'Did he use it at any other time?'

'Not often.'

'Then did you ever drive it?'

'I wasn't allowed to touch it. It wasn't particularly expensive, but it was his toy and he didn't like sharing.'

'Do you think I could possibly see it?'

'Of course. Although I warn you, it's not very interesting.'

There was a wooden car port off to the side of the house that contained an old lawnmower and a few bits of gardening equipment, with a wheelbarrow hanging on the wall. There was also a vehicle under a grey tarpaulin. Judith and Verity pulled the cover off to reveal a dark green sports car that Judith felt wasn't new enough to be fancy or old enough to be classic. Cheap, that's what it was, she thought to herself.

'Lovely,' Judith said for politeness' sake as she moved around the car. 'Have you told the police about this?'

'They know about the sports car, but not that I don't drive it. Sorry, what are you looking for?'

'I'm not sure. Maybe a clue to where the car went every week.'

'Well, I'll let you get on with it. I need to go and write up my notes from today's rehearsal, I'll be back at the house.'

As Verity left, Judith bent down to look at one of the back wheels. The tyre tread was worn away, but she could see a couple of tiny bits of gravel trapped in the grooves. She reached into her handbag, brought out a pencil and used it to prise the gravel into her hand. There were only three pieces in total; each one was only a few millimetres wide, but she could see that they were all bright white. Painted almost.

The driveway to Verity and Oliver's house was made from much larger pieces of natural gravel – far wider than the treads on the wheels of the sports car – so the little pebbles that had got caught in the wheels must have come from somewhere else.

Judith moved to the other wheels of the car and was able to prise out seven more pieces of white-coloured gravel, but there were also two pieces that were a dark green colour. The car had driven over gravel that was made up of tiny pieces of white and green stones. She slipped the pieces of gravel into the pocket of her skirt. She then stood up and looked at the car. Where had Oliver taken it each week that it had picked up white and green pieces of gravel?

Chapter 22

Judith pulled the door to the car open and got into the driver's seat, trying to see if there was anything inside that would help her. She noted that the car had travelled just over seventy-three thousand miles in its life. Seeing the distance recorded in this way gave her an idea. She leaned over and opened the glove compartment so she could pull out the logbook. It was a flimsy document, and she turned to the last few pages. Yes, she was pleased to see that Oliver had taken the car in to Platt's garage for an annual service, and they'd recorded the total distance the car had travelled during that year. She got out her phone and took photos of the annual inspections that covered the last three years. She then took a photo of the milometer on the dashboard. She'd see if she could make sense of the numbers later on.

As she was getting out of the car, a woman's scream pierced the air. Judith was picking up her skirt and running towards the house before she'd even considered what was going on. The repeated screams were coming from the side of the house, and as she rounded the corner, she saw Verity, her hand over her mouth, staring at something hanging by her back door. It was a foot or so long, and shockingly red. Judith approached and saw that someone had hung a skinned rabbit on the door. And there was something sticking out of it, but there wasn't time to take in the horrific sight properly; Verity needed to be moved to safety.

'Let's get you away from here,' Judith said, taking Verity by the arm and leading her away from the back door.

Once they'd reached the front of the house, Verity started shaking and saying to herself, 'Oh my God, oh my God.'

'Don't worry,' Judith said. 'We'll get Tanika here, she'll sort this out.'

Judith phoned Tanika, told her what had happened and the police officer said she'd be with them as soon as possible.

'Come on, let's get you inside,' Judith said to Verity. 'Make you a nice cup of tea.'

As Judith led Verity into her house, she glanced over at Duncan's canal boat on the opposite river bank. Duncan was standing on the back of it, looking directly at them. In his hands were a pair of binoculars. Judith didn't have time to consider what his presence meant; she had to look after Verity. Once inside, she made a strong cup of tea and added a couple of spoonfuls of sugar before splashing in some milk.

'Thank you for everything you're doing for me,' Verity said as she took the tea in trembling hands. 'Who's doing this to me?'

'Have you no idea who it might have been?' Judith asked.

'No, of course not. No one I know would be so cruel. Not just cruel – wicked. Do you think it's the same person who threw the brick through my window?'

'Well, let's see what Tanika says, but I think we can safely assume it is. I'm so sorry. But do you mind if I go and have a proper look at what it was?'

Verity looked down at her tea and nodded.

'As long as I never have to set eyes on it again,' she said.

Judith left the kitchen and went around the side of the house. She steeled herself. She needn't have worried too much. Robbed of its shock value, it was just a skinned rabbit that had been tied to the knocker of the back door. However, that wasn't the end of the story. There was a piece of paper that had been pinned to the dead rabbit by a knife that was stabbed deep into its body. The note was red with blood, but the message was simple enough. As before, it read:

Judith peered more closely at the note, but couldn't discern any further information. As she'd suspected, the person who'd thrown the brick through Verity's window was almost certainly the same person who'd now tied the rabbit to the door. But why did they think that Verity was the killer?

Judith heard the wail of an approaching siren and returned to the front of the house in time to see Tanika arrive with Detective Sergeant Brendan Perry.

Tanika looked mortified to see Judith waiting for them.

'It's a complete coincidence,' Judith said as the two police offi-cers approached. 'I was here with Verity – after rehearsals – when she found a skinned rabbit pinned to the door. But you should know, there's another note that accuses her of killing her husband.'

Tanika instructed Brendan to make sure the area around the crime scene was properly secured.

Brendan could be heard grumbling to himself as he headed off down the side of the house.

'I'm so sorry,' Judith said.

'You're making this very hard for me,' Tanika said as she went into the house to interview Verity.

Judith tried to ignore the twinge of guilt she felt and instead focused on why someone was leaving these messages for Verity. It had always been possible that Verity was the killer, of course. After all, she'd admitted that she hated her husband, so she had a motive. And there was the small matter of her scarf being found in the river covered in gunshot residue from the weapon used to kill Oliver. But what Judith didn't understand was why someone who believed that Verity was the killer would terrorise her like this rather than go to the police. Whoever had been behind the brick and the rabbit was very clearly trying to sow fear, so why was their priority upsetting Verity rather than getting justice for Oliver? Who had Verity upset so much that they'd do this to her? Judith couldn't think of anyone involved in the case who had a bigger problem with Verity than they did with Oliver.

Brendan came back from the side of the house and approached.

'Hello again!' Judith said, trying to establish a lightness to their encounter.

'Mrs Potts, what were you doing here?'

'I'm sorry?'

'I'm a detective sergeant, I've a right to ask the question.'

'You don't need to parade your rank to me, you only have to ask politely.'

Brendan took half a step forward.

'I don't have to do anything other than my job, and my job is to find Mr Beresford's killer.'

Judith pulled herself up to her full height, which meant she barely reached Brendan's chin. She refused to be intimidated.

'Then you're not doing it very well, are you? Oliver Beresford's killer is still out there. And let me tell you something else. I've done nothing wrong or untoward. Detective Malik's made it crystal clear to me I can't be involved. However, I'm a member of the Marlow Amateur Dramatic Society's upcoming production, and Verity is my director. I was here entirely in that capacity when she discovered that awful rabbit pinned to her door. And if you were intent on catching Oliver Beresford's killer, you'd ask me what I learned from my talk with her. Because she revealed to me – entirely unprompted, I hasten to add – that he only ever used his sports car during the three days each week he vanished.'

'We already know that,' Brendan said smugly.

'Verity told me she hadn't told you.'

'His sports car got a speeding ticket down Burchett's Green way, last year on a Thursday – one of the days he was away from home.'

'So you've finally found something out about where he goes?' Judith asked.

'We *are* the police,' Brendan said with satisfaction. 'It was only a matter of time.'

'Well then, I mustn't take up any more of your time,' Judith said. 'You've got important work to do. Processing the scene and helping Verity. Seeing as you don't want me here, I'll pop off.'

With a smile, Judith turned and headed for the road, leaving a very self-satisfied Brendan behind. But what he didn't realise was that his pride had made him reveal a crucial piece of information. Would it be enough for Judith to identify where Oliver had gone to each week? She wasn't sure, but a plan was beginning to form in her mind.

Chapter 23

'You want us to do what?' Suzie said, a Viennese slice paused in surprise halfway to her mouth.

Judith, Becks and Suzie were having afternoon tea in Judith's house. Judith had got them together to tell them about Oliver's sports car and her plan for working out where he'd been going every week.

'It's a long shot,' Judith conceded, 'but I think we could uncover the truth if we all throw our backs into it.'

'Explain it again, would you?' Suzie said.

'Of course. The first point is, wherever Oliver went each week, he drove there in his sports car.'

'Yes, I got that much.'

'Point two – Verity said that he went away every week without fail. And that he'd been doing this disappearing act for the last three years. Now, that can't have literally been true – there must have been other times he used his car, and some weeks when he didn't go away. But here's the thing, we can see the total distance he travelled each year for the last three years because – point three – the garage records his annual mileage in his car's logbook. So, let's say we average those three distances to come up with a rough idea of how far he travelled in a year – which is one thousand, one hundred and twenty-nine miles. Again, this is only a rule of thumb, but if we take that average annual distance and divide it by the number of weeks in a year – fifty-two – then we get a weekly distance he travels of about twenty-four miles.'

'Oh!' Becks said, delighted. 'I understand it this time.'

'That number can't be more than the roughest of rough guides, but it does suggest that wherever he's going, it's not all that far away. For example, he's not travelling to Edinburgh every week.'

'He's travelling twelve miles to his destination, and then twelve miles back,' Suzie said.

'Something like that. Exactly.'

'But that could be in any direction, couldn't it?' Becks said. 'Twelve miles from Marlow in all directions includes High Wycombe and Maidenhead, there must be tens of thousands of homes and businesses in that radius.'

'Of course,' Judith agreed. 'However, Oliver made one mistake. Thanks to Brendan's desire to brag, he revealed that the police finally uncovered a speeding ticket in Burchett's Green on a Thursday last year – which is about five miles south west of Oliver's house. That suggests that his weekly journey took him south-west of Marlow – in the broadest of terms – and if you look in that general direction, at about twelve miles out from Marlow, you're mostly in the countryside, with a few villages dotted about like Twyford and Wargrave.'

'Oh, I get it,' Becks said, finally understanding Judith's plan. 'You want us to knock on every door in every village that's twelve miles south-west from us.'

'It's not as impossible as it sounds. From the gravel I took from the tyres of the car, I think that the person or business Oliver visited has white painted gravel where he parked. But there are also bright green bits in there as well. There's no need to knock on any doors. We can look at the driveway from the road and rule it out if it doesn't have white and green gravel. And I think it's also possible to say that that sort of gravel is quite suburban, I don't think we'd find it down a farm track.'

'Hold on,' Becks said, an idea coming to her. 'We don't even need to physically visit any of these houses. We can go on Google Street View, can't we? We can walk along the streets virtually and look at all the driveways that way.'

'That's a very good idea,' Judith agreed. 'Good thinking, Becks.'

Becks glowed at the compliment as Judith got out an old county A to Z and pulled out the sections that covered the areas around Wargrave and Twyford. There were eleven pages in total and she shared them out, although Suzie could see that eleven didn't divide into three so she made sure she was the person who only received three pages.

'It's not a top priority, of course,' Judith said. 'But we should walk the streets on our maps and cross them off when we have a spare moment or two.'

The problem was, there were still many hundreds of streets in the area Judith had chosen, and nearly every driveway had to be checked out. There was a bit of excitement the following day when Suzie identified a driveway that had bright white gravel in a house by the crossroads of Hare Hatch, but when she went to check it out, she discovered that there were no green-painted pieces of gravel mixed in with the white.

As the women had known when they'd started the task, it was like finding a needle in a haystack, and Becks decided she could do with some help. She waited until Hugo was in the house but her daughter was out. Hugo even made it easy for her to broach the subject.

'What are you up to, Mrs Starling?' he asked as he entered the kitchen looking at his mobile phone.

'Trying to find a house on Google Street View,' Becks said, indicating her laptop screen. 'And it's Becks – please.'

'I was always told to treat my elders and betters with respect,' he said with a smile as he went to the kettle.

'You make me sound like a maiden aunt,' Becks said with a laugh that she realised had an edge of desperation to it.

'You've been so welcoming to me, not like a maiden aunt at all. Colin's been spreading the word about our crowdfunder like no one's business. Did Chloe tell you, we've just broken the six thousand pound mark? The people around here are so generous. We've both been humbled by it.'

'The community of parishes will always support charitable ventures, especially when they're carried out by young people. Although, perhaps there's something you could do for me in return?'

'Whatever you want,' Hugo said with a smile. 'And would you like a cup of tea?'

'That would be lovely,' Becks said, and she then explained how she was looking for a driveway with a white and green gravel driveway while Hugo made a second cup of tea and brought it over.

'So that's why you've got these maps out?'

'I'm marking off the roads on the paper maps as I walk down them on Google Street View.'

'Oh, I get it, you want Chloe and me to help you look?'

'If you have the time?'

'Of course – it's the least I can do.'

'If you get out your phone, I can show you the roads we're interested in.'

'My phone?'

'You were looking at it when you came in.'

'Of course, it's in my pocket. Hold on.'

Hugo fished out his phone and tapped on the icon for Google Maps.

Becks and Hugo identified an area of Wargrave village that he'd take responsibility for.

'What's the deadline for this?' he asked, once he'd marked the streets on his app.

'There's no deadline as such,' Becks said, 'but the more we do, the sooner we'll maybe find out where Oliver Beresford was going every week.'

'It's amazing how you help catch killers,' Hugo said. 'Seriously, it's about the coolest thing I've seen. And it explains where Chloe gets her smarts.'

Becks felt a thrill at the compliment, and Hugo thanked her again for allowing him to help, before leaving with his cup of tea. Becks' smile dropped as soon as he left the room. She now knew for certain that she'd been right not to trust him.

Hugo remained just as charming, still had perfect manners – he was dripping in what she knew her mother would call 'polish' – but she'd seen his mobile phone when she'd made him get it out of his pocket. It was a black Android device, which wouldn't have been worth noting if it weren't for one thing. Every time Becks had seen Hugo with Chloe, he'd had an iPhone. And Becks had spent enough time around criminals to know that people who had a second phone they only used when their partner was out of the house were never up to any good.

She knew she'd have to speak to her friends about this. When Judith texted her later that afternoon to say they should meet up that evening, Becks was quick to say yes.

★

'So what are we up to?' Suzie asked as she and Becks met Judith at the top end of the Wycombe Road.

'I didn't want to tell you the specifics, or I knew you wouldn't want to come,' Judith admitted. 'The actor playing the part of the butler, Lane, in the production is a very nice man called Geoffrey. He's been very friendly to everyone, and he announced this morning that he's something of an amateur photographer, so he's asked all the cast to visit his house tonight as part of the Marlow Art Trail.'

'What a good idea,' Becks said.

'Hold on,' Suzie said. 'What's the Marlow Art Trail?' she added suspiciously.

Judith explained that it was an annual event where local artists opened their houses and displayed the art they'd made in the last year. The idea was that the general public walked from house to house, looking at and buying art made by local artists. The culmination of the whole perambulation was an exhibition in the Liston Hall, a red-brick Victorian community building in the centre of town.

'Are you serious?' Suzie asked. 'We've got to spend the evening looking at a load of amateur art?'

'I'm sure it will be fascinating,' Becks said, 'and it will give you a chance to help me solve a problem I've got.'

As they walked towards Geoffrey's house, Becks explained that Hugo seemed to be running a burner phone behind Chloe's back.

'You're kidding me?' Suzie said.

'I've had my doubts about him since I met him, but I've tried to put them to one side. For Chloe's sake. But this is the first confirmation he's up to no good.'

'What sort of doubts?' Judith asked.

'I don't know, it's hard to put my finger on what it is, but I'm just not sure I trust him.'

'Then you need to confront him about it,' Suzie said. 'In front of Chloe. Ask him why he's got a secret phone.'

'But what if I'm mistaken and he's got it for some perfectly innocent reason? Accusing someone of being untrustworthy isn't something you can easily retract.'

'Then get hold of it when he's not looking,' Judith said. 'And secretly find out what's on it.'

'I'm not sneaking around my own house,' Becks said, but she couldn't help but smile at her two friends' different approaches to problem-solving. Suzie, by nature, was always wanting to confront matters head on, while Judith was instinctively cunning.

The women were still trying to work out what the best strategy for Becks might be when they met Geoffrey, the actor who was playing Lane. They then had to smile warmly as they looked at the hundreds of framed photos he'd taken over the last year that were all close-ups of various parts of cars.

Once they'd left, Suzie rubbed her mouth to get some blood back into her face.

'Bloody hell, I thought my face would freeze from having to smile so much.'

'Yes, the photos were rather . . . samey, weren't they?' Judith said.

'I'm sure they won't all be that bad,' Becks said. 'Come on, let's go to another house.'

'Yes,' Judith agreed. 'We can continue to work out what to do about Hugo as we go.'

Luckily for the three friends, the next house belonged to a talented artist called Bee Skelton. Even Suzie had to admit that she liked her colourful paintings of Marlow and the River Thames. They then carried on to the other houses on the Art Trail, although Suzie's patience soon started to wear thin. By the time they arrived at Liston Hall, Suzie was grumbling that all she wanted was a break from 'all of the bloody art'.

'Don't worry,' Becks said, 'I'm sure we'll be done soon.'

'I mean, I'm sure it's all great and everything,' Suzie said as she looked in dismay at the hundred or so paintings that were hung all around the hall, 'but does there have to be so much of it?'

'There has to be a space for all the artists who don't live near enough to Marlow to take part,' Becks said. 'Or who don't live in houses they can open up to the public.'

'Does there?' Suzie said with a weary sigh. 'Can we at least decide what you're going to do about Hugo?'

'I think I've got no choice but to tell Chloe what I think about him.'

'Even though we all agree that that's a bad idea?'

'It's a terrible idea. I know. But she's about to go to Vietnam with someone who I think is dodgy. I'm her mother, I've got no choice, I've got to talk to her.'

'She won't like it.'

'But if anything happened to her, I'd never forgive myself.'

Before Suzie could reply, Judith bustled over.

'Quick!' she said. 'You've got to see something.'

'What is it?' Suzie asked.

'It's better I show you,' Judith said as she led her friends across the room to a wall that had a big sign at the top that proclaimed 'What the River Means To Me'. The wall was covered in pictures – big and small, colourful and monochrome; oils, pencils and prints – but Judith drew her friends' attention to a small oil painting at the side.

It depicted the River Thames, the trees on the far bank a riot of autumn colours, the water silvered by the early evening light. Chugging through the painting was a wooden pleasure cruiser.

It was the *Marlow Belle*.

'OK,' Suzie said, nonplussed. 'So it's a painting of Lance's boat . . . ?'

'But Lance told us that the night that Oliver was killed was the *Marlow Belle*'s maiden voyage. So if there's a painting of it on the Thames, then it's very possibly from that night. And I know that spot of the river from my swims – that's in between Bourne End and Marlow. Which is where Oliver was shot dead. I think this painting means there was a witness on the riverbank after all.'

'But that's wonderful!' Becks said. 'All of this time Tanika's been trying to find a witness – someone who took a photo that afternoon, or a video for their social media. Everyone films everything the whole time these days, it seemed so unfair that we'd not been able to find anyone who'd recorded the boat that day. But this painting is what we've been looking for all this time. It just took a bit longer for the artist to put the image down on canvas.'

'We need to speak to the person who painted this,' Judith said, peering at the note on the wall to the painting's side. 'Find out what they saw that night. It says here her name is Rebecca Lewis.'

'Then that's lucky,' Becks said. 'We were in her house half an hour ago.'

'You're not saying we have to go back, are you?' Suzie said.

'Don't worry,' Judith said. 'This time when we talk to her about her art, it's because we're trying to catch a killer. We need to find out exactly what she saw.'

Chapter 24

Rebecca Lewis lived in a modest bungalow in a small close off one of the main roads that led out of Marlow. Inside, the house was clean and uncluttered, and not at all how Judith and her friends thought an artist's house should look. But then, Rebecca was also nothing like the stereotypical artist. She was a slender woman in her seventies, had straight grey hair cut in a bob, ice blue eyes, and she gave the impression of being someone who never wasted an emotion or even a word. Ascetic – that was the word Judith thought of as Rebecca led her and her friends into the kitchen area.

'Would any of you like a cup of tea?' Rebecca asked. 'Herbal probably at this time of night, you don't want caffeine.'

'No, of course,' Becks said. 'And it's very kind of you to let us in again, even though the evening's ended.'

'It's a little unorthodox, but if you have any questions about my art, I'm happy to answer them.'

The women worked out what herbal teas they'd like, and Rebecca poured boiling water into cups for them all.

'Your paintings were particularly beautiful,' Becks said, indicating three oil paintings that were on easels by a glass back door that led onto a little garden. The first picture was of Marlow Bridge, the second of the war memorial and the third of Bisham church. Like the painting of the *Marlow Belle* they'd seen in Liston Hall, the lines were clean and the colours were bold.

'Thank you. I only took up painting once I'd retired. I was a science teacher at Borlase for many years.'

Judith took her tea over to look at the paintings and saw a book on a little table by an armchair. She recognised the cover at once. It was a well-thumbed copy of Lizzie Jenkins' autobiography. There was also a pile of what looked like old copies of celebrity magazines that all seemed to have Lizzie Jenkins on the cover.

'Oh, you're interested in Lizzie Jenkins?' she asked.

'Yes I am,' Rebecca said, and Judith could see that she was embarrassed as she went over to the table, picked up the books and magazines, and tidied them away onto a shelf.

'You didn't teach her, did you?' Suzie asked.

'No, I was at Borlase and her autobiography says she went to Great Marlow.'

'Then maybe you know someone who taught her?'

'I don't think I do, it was a long time ago.'

'So why are you so interested in her?'

'Do you mind me asking why you're asking?' Rebecca said, avoiding the question.

'Very well,' Judith said, deciding that two people could play that game. 'Can you tell us about the painting you submitted to the Art Trail exhibition in the Liston Hall?'

Rebecca's face fell.

'Oh,' she said. 'I did wonder if anyone would put two and two together.'

'Did you paint the picture the night that Oliver Beresford was shot?' Suzie asked.

'I did. Shocking though it is to say. Let me explain. Everyone who participated in the Art Trail this year was asked to do a piece on "what the river means to me". So a few weeks ago, I went to my favourite spot on the river – halfway between Bourne End and Marlow – and set up to paint a picture. And before you ask, I didn't see anything on the *Marlow Belle* that was in any way suspicious – or hear anything, for that matter. If I had done I would have gone to the police at once. I didn't know anything untoward had happened. The first I knew about the murder was when I read about it in the papers the next day. That's why I've been reading all about Lizzie Jenkins since then,' she added, nodding to the cleared-away books and magazines. 'I couldn't help myself. Against my better judgement, the whole melodrama has rather drawn me in.'

'What did you see that afternoon?' Becks asked.

'That's the point, I didn't see anything.'

'Hold on,' Suzie said. 'What I want to know is how you managed to paint a boat as it drove past you? Surely it was going too fast?'

'I have a very good visual memory. It's almost eidetic.'

'Sorry – what's that?'

'I have an almost perfect recall for what I see. It's been a great blessing in my life. And a curse in some circumstances.'

'You can remember everything you see?' Suzie asked, amazed. 'What colour are our eyes?'

Rebecca closed her eyes to think and said, 'Your eyes are brown, and your friends' are blue in one case, and hazel-flecked, I'd almost say with gold, in the other.'

Rebecca opened her eyes to see astonished looks.

'If I've seen it, I can recall it,' she said.

'No way!' Suzie said. 'That's brilliant! How can it be a curse?'

'When I taught science, it took every ounce of will to remember that while I found it easy to remember formulas and so on, lots of youngsters struggle. It always felt to me like insolence when they couldn't remember the simplest of facts. Not that it was, of course, but that's how it felt.'

'Wow,' Suzie said, remembering with a shudder all the teachers who'd been like Rebecca during her childhood. 'What made you go into teaching?' she asked.

'My father was a vicar, I've always felt I had to give my life to service. And I've always helped youngsters – it's been something of a vocation for me – even before I became a teacher. But since I retired, I've tried to do things I've never done before.'

'Like painting,' Becks said.

'The principles of colour theory are fascinating when applied to physical paint.'

'You're very talented.'

'That's kind of you, but I can see that what I do is accomplished rather than talented. My work is a bit "painting by numbers", but I like that aspect of it as well.'

'So if you can remember everything, what exactly did you see?' Judith asked.

'Very well. Firstly, I didn't see the boat head out from Marlow, I must have arrived after it passed.'

'But you were on the bend of the river by the fallen oak tree, weren't you?' Judith said.

'That's right. I got there at about 4 p.m. I paint straight onto the canvas, I don't do any sketches first, but I wanted a boat in the picture, so I started on the background. A few boats came past while I was getting going, but they weren't very interesting. I was looking for something that was a bit more quintessentially "River Thames". I was thrilled when I saw the *Marlow Belle* heading towards Marlow. She was just right for me, with the polished hull contrasting with the gnarled wood of the trees behind. I watched it carefully as it passed, locking in every detail. And then I started painting.'

'Did you see anyone on the back of the boat?'

'No – although I saw someone in the driving cabin at the front. A rather stocky-looking man.'

'That would have been Lance Goodman,' Becks said.

'If you say so. I didn't recognise him. But I knew the other person who was with him. Oliver Beresford.'

'Hold on,' Suzie said, 'You saw Oliver?'

'I wasn't paying much attention to the humans on board. I was trying to take in the boat. But yes, I always go to the first night of every production of the Marlow Amateur Dramatic Society, so I recognised Oliver's face. As the boat went past, he was in the driver's cabin talking to the stocky-looking gentleman.'

'Do you know what time this was?' Judith asked.

'Not exactly. I started to pack up my things after All Saints' church struck 6 p.m., but the boat was gone by then.'

'How long before then did it pass you?'

'I don't know. Ten minutes, something like that?'

'Did you get a sense of how the two men were with each other?'

'You mean, was one of them angry? Or threatening? No, nothing like that – although I suppose I was at a distance of thirty yards or so. And the boat was going quite fast. It's why

I didn't feel I needed to go to the police. I don't actually have anything to say.'

'You didn't see anything suspicious at all?'

'Nothing that registered, I'm afraid.'

'What happened on the boat after it passed?'

'How do you mean?'

'We think Oliver was shot on the deck at the back,' Judith said. 'Maybe you saw Oliver come out on the rear deck once it was further upstream? Or maybe you saw someone else?'

'No, I'm sorry, I didn't see anyone on the back of the boat before I lost sight of it around the bend in the river.'

'Then perhaps you heard a couple of gunshots once it was out of sight?'

'No – I didn't hear anything like that. Although the boat made a few loud bangs as it passed. It sounded like its engine was misfiring, not that I know the first thing about engines. But it spoiled the peace and quiet.' Rebecca paused to consider what she'd revealed. 'Do you think I should have told all of this to the police?'

'You were one of the last people to see the victim alive,' Judith said.

'But I didn't really see anything.'

'You're still a witness.'

Rebecca sighed.

'Very well. I'll go and see the police tomorrow. Tell them what I've told you. But it doesn't add up to much, does it? All I can report is that two people were in the driver's cabin talking.'

'Oh no, it adds up to quite a lot,' Judith said. 'You see, Lance told us that he was on his own in his driving position before the murder. He didn't mention any last-minute chats with Oliver.'

Judith turned to her two friends and said, 'I think we need to find out why that is.'

★

It was too late to visit Lance by the time they left Rebecca's house, so the three friends drove to his boatyard the following morning. They found him clearing a pile of wooden pallets by the main building.

'What now?' he said as they approached.

'Good morning to you, too,' Judith said. 'We just want to check a detail with you.'

'If you have a problem, take it up with the police.'

'There was an eyewitness after all.'

Lance pretended nonchalance as he shrugged, 'What eyewitness?'

'A woman called Rebecca Lewis.'

'Where was she?'

'On the riverbank, about halfway between Bourne End and Marlow.'

'She painted your boat,' Suzie said. 'And she said she saw you driving it as you went past. And that you were in your cabin talking to Oliver Beresford.'

'What is this?' Lance asked dismissively,

'I'll tell you what this is,' Judith said. 'This is a witness who says you were with the victim only minutes before he died. Which you told us wasn't the case. You said you'd been on your own in your driving position.'

'I don't have to do this,' Lance said, as he turned from the women and started to head towards the *Marlow Belle*.

'Hey!' Suzie bellowed and Lance stopped in his tracks. 'You don't walk away from me. Ever.'

'Jesus, Suzie, when are you going to get over me?'

'Don't worry, Lance, I'm over you.'

Lance shook his head, stepped up onto the boat and went down into its interior.

Barely missing a beat, Suzie followed him onto the boat, Judith and Becks right behind her. As they were about to go down the steps, Lance reappeared looking flustered.

'You can't come on my boat,' he said, and Judith picked up on his panic.

'Why ever not?' she asked.

'It's private property,' Lance said angrily.

'No – it's more than that, you're worried about us being here, aren't you?'

'Jesus, woman, the police have been all over the boat from top to bottom and they didn't find anything. And you think I'm being unhelpful? OK, I'll admit it – Oliver came and talked to me on the boat about ten to six. He said Lizzie Jenkins had some kind of surprise set for 6 p.m. and would I stay in the driver's cabin for the next ten minutes or so.'

'He said that, did he?' Suzie said.

'Did he say what sort of surprise it was?' Becks asked.

'No. And I didn't think much of it. They're a load of actors, they're always going to be melodramatic. Oliver told me I had to stay out of the way, so I wasn't lying when I said I was on my own at six o'clock. I was. He'd left by then.'

'Hold on,' Judith said. 'You're now saying that Oliver told you that Lizzie had a surprise organised for 6 p.m. and you were to stay out of the way?'

'No,' Suzie said, 'I'm not having this. First you argued with Oliver at the pub – remember, Mrs Eddingham witnessed Oliver saying to you . . . what was it?'

'That if you wanted your secret to remain secret, you'd hire the boat to Oliver, whether or not it was ready,' Becks said.

'And now you're having clandestine meetings with Oliver a matter of minutes before he was shot dead? Why won't you tell us the truth about what happened that night?'

Guilt flashed in Lance's eyes.

'What is the secret you're not telling us?' Judith asked.

Lance licked his lips, his mind racing, and then the women saw the moment he came to his decision.

'I don't have any secrets,' he said. 'And if you think differently, then I only have two words for you. Prove it. Now I've answered your questions, get off my boat.'

And with that, Lance went back down the steps and slammed the door behind him.

Chapter 25

'I can't believe I went out with him!' Suzie said once the women had repaired to Judith's house. 'I dated a killer!'

'We don't know he killed Oliver,' Becks said. 'And if he did, you're not to blame.'

'I'm such a bad judge of character.'

'Nonsense!' Judith said. 'You're friends with Becks and me, and that tells me you've got nothing to worry about on that front.'

'And just because he's lying to us,' Becks said, 'it doesn't mean he's the killer.'

Suzie was so out of sorts that she turned down the offer of a Bourbon biscuit with the cup of tea that Judith brought her.

'It's the fact that he only tells us the truth when we put pressure on him,' Suzie said. 'That's what's so upsetting.'

'I wonder if we could use that against him?' Becks asked.

'How do you mean?'

'Well, if he only tells us things when we put pressure on him, do you know anything we can use as leverage against him?'

'That's a *very* devious idea, Becks Starling,' Suzie said with approval. 'Let me have a think about that. See if I can find something we can blackmail him with.'

'And he's not the only one who's keeping a secret from us,' Judith said.

'Who are you thinking of?' Becks asked.

Judith explained how she'd seen Toby make a sharp exit as soon as he'd seen Rob Hooker turn up at the Little Theatre. And how, when she later spoke to Rob, he'd said he didn't know anyone called Toby Vincent.

'But that sounds plausible,' Suzie said. 'There must be hundreds of people who apply to RADA every year.'

'That's what I thought at first. But later on, Verity told me that Rob helped Toby choose one of his audition speeches. I can't believe that he would help Toby gain a place at RADA and then fail to remember his name. And it also doesn't explain why Toby scarpered as soon as Rob appeared.'

'When you put it like that, it does sound a bit odd,' Becks said. 'I wonder if there's a way of getting to the bottom of why that was?'

'You know what?' Judith said, an idea coming to her. 'I think there might be. Suzie, you keep thinking about how we can get Lance to reveal what he's hiding from us, but leave Rob Hooker to me.'

★

The following day, Judith got the train to London. She'd remembered how Verity had said that Rob was very much a 'man's man' who had his lunch at the Garrick Club every day. It was her plan to catch him at lunch and ask him to tell her why he denied knowing Toby Vincent. The only problem was, the Garrick was one of London's most prestigious gentlemen's clubs. Women weren't admitted.

As Judith stood outside the imposing facade of the club, she rubbed her hands together in anticipation. The building looked like a prison to her – all heavy, soot-smoked stone – although the enormous picture windows that overlooked the street gave a hint of the splendour inside. Judith usually found it a chore fighting against the world that men had constructed entirely for their own benefit, but sometimes it was a sheer pleasure, and today, she decided, was going to be one of those days.

She climbed the steps to the oak and glass front door and pushed it open. Inside, there were further red-carpeted steps that led up to a grand lobby with a sweeping staircase, but her eyes were drawn to a green felt board on her left that held various items of post for the members. There was also a suited man standing to her right.

'Good morning, madam,' the man said. 'My name's Joseph. How can I help you today?'

'Is Rob Hooker in?' Judith asked crisply.

'He didn't mention anything about anyone joining him for lunch.'

Judith felt a jolt of excitement as she realised that Joseph had confirmed Rob's presence in the building.

'He must have forgotten,' she said. 'The dining room's up the stairs on the right?' she added airily.

'No, madam, it's on the left. But if Mr Hooker's not expecting you—'

'Then he's about to get what will be a delightful surprise,' Judith said as she swept past Joseph.

'Madam!' Joseph yelped as he scuttled up the steps to keep up with her, but Judith discounted him; she could already tell that he didn't know how to deal with a woman of advanced years who wouldn't do as she was told.

Judith saw a large door to her left that led into a dining room that was all polished wood, deep red walls and glittering chandeliers. The longest table she'd ever seen ran down the middle of the room, and she could see that it was about a third full, the diners all bunched up at one end. As Joseph finally caught up with her, Judith strode towards the table and was pleased to see Rob Hooker sitting at a place that didn't yet have anyone in the chair opposite him.

'Thank you, I can take it from here,' Judith said to Joseph as she pulled the chair out and plonked herself down. 'I won't be long. Not if Rob answers my questions.'

Judith took in the faces of the men at the table, which ranged from well-bred shock to well-bred horror, although she was amused to see that an ancient man in his nineties was sitting at the end of the table and was too busy trying to get to grips with his soup to have noticed her arrival.

'Now, Rob,' she said, before anyone could interrupt. 'Can I ask you about Toby Vincent? And this time I'd like you to tell me the truth.'

Rob picked up the tail of the napkin that was attached to one of the buttons on his shirt front and dabbed at the corners of his mouth.

'This is a little unorthodox,' he said.

'Then how about you answer my question, and I can end the shame of there being a woman in the same room as all you men.'

'Mr Hooker?' Joseph said, hovering.

'Don't worry,' Rob said with a sigh. 'This lady's my guest.'

'Very well, sir,' Joseph said with relief and left.

Judith noticed that all the men at the table were still looking at her, apart from the nonagenarian, who was now carefully tilting his spoon so he could watch the soup dribble down into his bowl.

'I want to know what the story is with Toby Vincent,' Judith said to Rob.

'What story?'

'I've never seen someone leave a building faster than he did when you arrived to do your talk to the Marlow Amateur Dramatic Society.'

'I didn't notice,' Rob said.

'It's not just these gentleman who'd like me to leave,' Judith said, her irritation flashing. 'I'm also not entirely enjoying myself. And if you don't start telling me the truth, I'll start smashing things.'

'You wouldn't dare,' Rob said.

'Oh, I would, you'd better believe it.'

There was a cough from nearby.

'Rob, old boy,' an old gent with dandruff on the shoulders of his suit jacket said. 'I was prisons minister for three years, and I can tell you, I think she could well go rogue. I recognise the type.'

'Thank you,' Judith said to the man.

'My pleasure,' he replied with a friendly smile.

'I can't talk to you about applicants to RADA,' Rob said. 'It's unethical.'

'Toby's a suspect in a murder enquiry. Not helping catch the killer is far more unethical.'

'Hold on,' a gentleman with ill-fitting dentures two places down clacked. 'Is this the Oliver Beresford case in Marlow?'

'It is,' Judith said.

'Then you'd better answer this lady's questions.'

'You think that's a good idea, Dominic?' Rob asked the man.

'You don't need his permission,' Judith said.

'It would help,' Rob said. 'He's the Lord Chief Justice. And if he's saying I should talk to you, then I'll talk to you. And sorry about the "all-male" thing; it's not how I'd like things to be.'

'I'm sure that's what you tell yourself, and yet here we are in your all-male club. But let's not get bogged down. Why did Toby run away from you?'

'It's no one's fault. It's one of the occupational hazards of doing my job. He was embarrassed.'

'Why on earth would he be? He's off to RADA in September, he should have met you in triumph.'

'Is that what he told you?'

'Of course.'

'Sadly, that's not quite the case. You see, it's a highly competitive process. And we were predisposed to let him in. After all, he's an older man with all that lived experience, we wanted him to join us. Unfortunately . . .'

'He didn't get a place?' Judith asked, stunned.

'He didn't, I'm afraid.'

Judith remembered Mrs Eddingham's description of Toby's acting style.

'He's flashy, but there's no substance there,' she offered.

'That's it exactly. And even his flashiness isn't all that flash. I nearly had words with Oliver afterwards. It was slightly embarrassing, him sending us someone so lacking, but that was Oliver all over. He'd always been desperate for fame, and now that his chance to achieve it for himself had passed, he was hell-bent on trying to bestow fame on others.'

'You know, I don't think Toby's come clean with anyone about not getting a place.'

'It can be a bitter blow when you don't get in. It's not uncommon.'

'But he's a grown-up. I wonder why he hasn't been able to admit it yet. Well, thank you, I'm glad you were finally able to help me. And thank you, Lord Chief Justice,' Judith added to the man with ill-fitting dentures, who smiled happily in acknowledgement. 'I shan't tempt any of you gentlemen with my feminine allure for a second longer. I'll show myself out.'

Judith scraped her chair back and walked out of the dining room without a backward glance.

'And will madam be returning any time soon?' Joseph asked as she passed.

'Only if someone else commits a murder,' she said with a killer smile.

★

Judith went to Paddington station, boarded the next train to Marlow and phoned Suzie and Becks on the way, arranging to meet them as soon as she arrived. As she stepped off the train, Becks and Suzie met her in Suzie's van and told her that they'd already rung Platt's garage, who'd informed them that Toby wasn't working that day. However, Becks had managed to charm his home address from the man in the reception.

'Was that the right thing to do?' Becks asked.

'Oh, I think so, well done,' Judith said as she climbed into Suzie's van. 'Because I think it's time Toby told us why he's been lying to everyone about his RADA place.'

Chapter 26

Toby lived in a small close near to Marlow High Street. The terraced town houses had been built in the 1970s and had white clapboard fronts and sitting rooms on the first floor.

A strong smell of cannabis wafted out from the hallway behind Toby as he opened the door for Judith and her friends.

'Wow, that takes me back!' Suzie said.

'Oh, hi,' Toby said, glassy-eyed.

'That's a very strong smell,' Judith said.

'Just a little smoke at the end of the shift. You want any, ladies?'

'No thank you, but thanks for the offer. We'd like a chat. May we come in?'

Toby seemed to zone out for a few seconds, and then he slowly refocused on the women.

'Sure. Come in. It's a bit of a mess.'

Toby led them up the stairs to what Judith felt was a rather grim room. The sofa was grey and tired, there was a massive TV screwed high on the wall that spewed cables, and the only lighting came from a floor lamp that arched over the sofa and illuminated a coffee table that was covered in old car magazines, cigarette papers, a mess of rolling tobacco and a little cellophane bag that contained dried cannabis.

'I've just got back from London,' Judith said. 'I had lunch with Rob Hooker.'

'Rob?' Toby said with a frown.

'He told me the truth of the situation. That you didn't get a place at RADA.'

Toby's eyes widened as he sat down on the sofa and leaned back onto the soft cushions.

'Whoa,' he said.

'You've been lying to everyone all this time.'

'And I can imagine why,' Becks said, seeing how worried Toby was by Judith's line of questioning. 'It must have been so awful, throwing yourself into the audition process, only to miss out on a place.'

'Huh,' Toby said.

'All those hours of work.'

Toby looked off into the distance as he lost himself in his memories.

'He made me go over the speeches over and over,' he eventually said. 'Oliver. He was a taskmaster. Always saying, "No, do it this way". "No, do it that way".'

'That sounds tough,' Becks said.

'I didn't even want to do it,' Toby said, turning to look at Becks. 'That's the thing. I was happy doing plays and you-know-what with the MADS. It's like I said that first time I talked to you all. I loved that feeling of being on stage. But Oliver told me I should give everything up and turn pro. I didn't believe him. I didn't think I was any good. But he said I was basically the best thing since . . . well, whoever – name someone famous. It was all about him. I see that now. He made me work my arse off. Then I met that Rob guy in London and he took me around RADA. It was . . .' Toby sighed. 'I don't know. Kind of amazing. I had no idea a place like that could exist. Not the buildings, although they were pretty special. It was the people. All they did was act, and write, and think about texts and performance. You know, instead of where the wheel change nut is. Or how to get the oil out of your overalls at the end of a shift. I let my head get turned. I threw myself into those auditions like nothing I've done before. Oliver convinced me I'd definitely get in, so I handed in my notice. I was so sure of myself. Cocksure.'

Toby drifted off.

'What happened in the audition?'

'It was . . . humiliating. I dried. Couldn't do it. I was a mess. Felt like an imposter. And you know what made it worse? They were so nice. But it was patronising, too. You know? They knew I didn't come from any kind of theatre background, so they encouraged me to go again. And again. And every time I tried to do my speeches, I froze. And there was this look on their faces, I'll never forget it. Pity. They *pitied* me,' Toby added with an edge to his voice.

'I don't even remember leaving the building. By that stage it was like a dream. A nightmare. When I got home, I knew I'd stuffed it. But I'd felt pumped up for months – so arrogant – bragging at work about how I was getting out of Marlow. Getting away from my nothing job. And the nothing people who worked there. Everyone at work just bloody lapped it up. Said it was great me going off and following my dream. I couldn't tell them I'd screwed up. And this was the worst bit . . . I was so wrapped up in what Oliver had told me, there was still a bit of me that wondered if RADA were going to offer me a place anyway. Despite my audition. Maybe they saw how great I was. So I didn't tell everyone how badly it had gone. And then, when I got the email telling me I hadn't got in, I didn't know what to do. It was like the worst day of my life.'

'When was this?' Judith asked.

'Last month.'

'That recently? So you'd already contacted Lizzie Jenkins?'

'Oliver told me I couldn't hang around. Said I was guaranteed a place and I needed to sort out funding from famous actors as fast as I could. Everyone else who was going in September would have already started writing their begging letters. I had to get in there.'

'You must have been very angry with him,' Becks said carefully.

'Huh,' Toby said, not disagreeing.

'He'd led you astray.'

Toby's countenance darkened as he considered his answer.

'He made me look a fool,' he said, picking up his rolled spliff from the ashtray, taking a long drag on it and then coughing violently. 'It's good stuff, this,' he said, indicating the little cellophane bag of cannabis on the table.

Suzie looked at the bag and her friends saw her frown. She picked it up to look at it more closely. There was a handwritten label on it.

'You want a smoke?' Toby asked, impressed.

'No,' Suzie said, not taking her eyes off the little bag.

'Well, this explains why you've started smoking cannabis again, doesn't it?' Judith asked.

'I've felt so stupid. So embarrassed,' Toby said, not denying it.

'Or did you take it up again after you killed Oliver?'

Toby seemed more puzzled than shocked.

'No,' he said.

'But it's like you said – Oliver led you astray. Humiliated you in front of all your friends at work. In front of Rob Hooker and everyone else at RADA. He needed punishing.'

'No way,' Toby said, holding up his palms as though he was very slowly trying to stop a bucking horse. 'None of this stuff is life or death. It's pretty bad, but why would I want to kill him over a stupid audition? When things get bad, I can just roll myself another spliff. What does it matter?'

'How did a spare bullet end up in your cabin on the boat?'

'What?'

'The police found a bullet in your cabin – a bullet that matched the bullets that were used to shoot Oliver Beresford.'

'Jesus. I've been over this with the police. I don't know.'

'Where were you at 6 p.m. that night?'

'I was in my cabin.'

'Doing what?'

'Waiting for Lizzie Jenkins. You know all this. She'd sent me that note. I thought she was going to give me my money there and then, you know? But she didn't come, did she?'

'How long were you there?'

'I'm innocent, OK?'

'You have a motive – Oliver humiliated you – and incriminating evidence was found in your cabin on the boat.'

'Listen, I'll tell you how that bullet got there. The killer must have left it in my cabin.'

'Did anyone else go in your cabin?'

'I don't know. What if they put it there on purpose?'

'And why would they do that?'

'To make it look like I was the killer when I'm not.'

'I'm really rather fed up with the lot of you saying that the killer is trying to set you up. Who do you think would want to punish you in this way?'

'I've no idea. About the only person who hates me is Mrs Eddingham, and that's because I took her place on the MADS committee. But she wasn't on the boat, so it wasn't her.'

'Then who do you think shot Oliver?' Suzie asked.

'That's the thing – no idea. Only Verity had a problem with him – everyone knew that. But why would she kill him and frame me for it? You've seen how she is with me, Mrs Potts. We get on.'

Judith had to concede that Toby's point was at least partially true. Unless Verity was putting on an act, she and Toby appeared to have a good working relationship.

Suzie held the bag of drugs up in front of Toby.

'Where did you get this?' she asked.

'You want my dealer's number?' Toby asked. 'Knew you wanted a smoke. You've got the look.'

'Who sold you this?'

'No problem. Share and share alike.'

Toby reached for the phone on the armrest of his armchair and started fiddling with it.

'Some kid,' he said. 'It's his way of making a bit of pin money on the side. That's it,' he said, getting up a contact card on his screen. 'His name's Dylan. Nice guy. Good weed, good prices.'

Suzie thanked Toby for the tip-off and made a note of Dylan's number, saying she'd call him. As she did so, Toby started rolling another spliff, so the women made their excuses and left. As soon as they were outside, Becks turned in panic to Suzie and asked, 'You're not planning on buying drugs, are you?'

'Don't worry, I've never been into drugs,' Suzie said.

'So why do you need his dealer's number?'

'Just something I need to check,' Suzie said in a way that made it clear she was shutting the conversation down. 'Don't worry. I've got this.'

Judith and Becks exchanged a glance. What was Suzie up to?

Chapter 27

The three friends walked down Marlow High Street – the bustle of people shopping, chatting and having a lovely time all around them – and tried to make sense of what they'd learned from Toby. On the one hand it seemed like a major breakthrough. His admission that he blamed Oliver for his failed audition gave him a motive. But on the other hand, there were still elements of his story that didn't quite add up.

'After all,' Judith said, 'we shouldn't forget that Toby was one of the people on the boat who knew Oliver had terminal cancer. And I still can't believe that someone would risk killing someone who'd be dead soon anyway.'

'So we're still looking for someone who didn't know he had cancer,' Suzie said.

'Which isn't much use, is it?' Becks said. 'Everyone on the boat knew.'

'Everyone apart from Lizzie. That's why my money's on her.'

'I thought your money was on Lance,' Becks said with a smile.

'That was just because I found him irritating. Lizzie's the killer.'

'And before then you thought it was Verity.'

'Okay, so I've changed my mind a few times. Come on, Lizzie arrived that morning and then her ex-lover is dead by nightfall? It's why I was happy promising that I'd drop all mention of tarot cards if it turns out I'm wrong. I'm not wrong. Lizzie's our killer.'

'It's so frustrating!' Judith said. 'What are we missing? I can feel that we have all the elements of the case, but we're not putting them together in the right order. Or maybe they're all in the right order, but we're still missing the one thing that would tie them all together. Something we're yet to uncover, or something we don't quite understand the importance of yet. I know, how about we all go for a nice long walk? We so often have our best ideas on a walk.'

'That's true,' Becks said. 'But I think I want to get home. Talking to a stoner who's smoking away his life has made me realise I need to talk to Chloe. And I can't bottle it this time. I need to have the courage to speak my mind to her.'

'And you're sure it's a good idea to question her choice of boyfriend?' Suzie asked.

'Oh no, she's going to hate me. But I'm her mother. If I don't talk to her about the risks of throwing in her lot with Hugo, who will?'

★

Becks left her friends and walked home to the vicarage. When she arrived, she was pleased to see that Chloe was already in the kitchen, her laptop open.

'Hi, darling,' Becks said.

'Mum, I've news,' Chloe said excitedly.

'You're pregnant, aren't you?' Becks said in a panic.

'I wish you'd stop saying that every time I try to tell you something.'

'Sorry, it's just your father and I worry.'

'This is because of Hugo, isn't it?'

'What?'

'You've never liked him.'

'How can you say that? Of course I like him.'

'But I see the way you look at him when you think I'm not looking. It's because he's posh, isn't it?'

'What? No – of course not.'

'He can't help where he comes from any more than anyone can, and if you have a problem with his upbringing, then you need to take it up with his parents, not with him.'

'I don't have a problem with him, it's none of my business.'

'Finally you admit it!'

'But the thing is, darling, I'm older than you. I've seen a lot of relationships over the years – those that work and others that don't, and everything in between. And you're about to drop out of uni and go to Vietnam with him. What if he wants to stay out there and – I don't know . . .' Becks realised she didn't quite have the language to describe her fears. 'You both end up in an opium den?'

'Are you seriously suggesting that's likely to happen? What even is an opium den?'

'I don't know, now you mention it, but we know so little about Hugo.'

'I know *everything* about him.'

'Are you sure you can trust him? In the depths of some jungle somewhere, if you fall and break your ankle, will he stay with you until you're rescued? Or will he try and save himself?'

'Of course he'll stay!'

'He's got a secret phone,' Becks said before she once again lost her nerve.

The words hung in the air between mother and daughter like poison gas.

'What's that?' Chloe said.

'I couldn't help noticing that he's got a second phone. One you don't know about. And that can't be good.'

'Are you serious?'

'I just think you should know he's hiding a phone from you.'

'Do you know where Hugo is right now? He's in the church next door, and I'd really like you to ask me why.'

Becks knew her daughter well. She was lining up her mother's neck for the chopping block.

'OK,' she said, only now remembering that Chloe had started their conversation by saying she had news. 'Why's he in the church?'

'He's looking for you. Because he's spent the last two days – on his own – walking up and down Street View on Google Maps trying to help you. He's clicked through every single street in Twyford, Wargrave, Shiplake and Hurst because you asked him to. And guess what he found?'

Chloe spun her laptop around and Becks saw that the screen was filled with an image of a house with a little hedge in front of it. The edges of the picture were blurred from where they'd been digitally stitched to the adjacent photos, but the central portion of the image was crystal clear. The house had a driveway of bright white pebbles. But there was a thin strip of gravel that marked where the private driveway stopped and the public pavement started.

The little strip of gravel was bright green.

Becks felt elated and terrible both at the same time. She noted the address of the house in Wargrave village as she rang Judith and Suzie and arranged to meet them there. Half an hour later, Becks' car pulled up outside the house to find Suzie's van already waiting. On the way over, she'd kept replaying her conversation with her daughter, and every time she'd felt so mortified by her behaviour that it was like a silent scream of shame inside her. As both Suzie and Judith had been telling her, what was one of the cardinal rules of parenting? You don't get involved in your children's love life. Becks knew she'd betrayed a trust that it would be difficult to get back. What had made her think that telling the truth to her daughter was ever going to be a good idea?

'I can't believe you found it,' Suzie said in excitement as Becks approached.

'It wasn't me who found it,' Becks said, knowing she had to tell the truth. 'It was Hugo.'

'Well, bully for him,' Judith said, and Becks was pleased that her friends hadn't picked up on her feelings of existential humiliation.

'We've had a quick look,' Suzie said, indicating the house behind them, 'and we both reckon it could be the one.'

Judith put her hand in her pocket and pulled out a few green pebbles. 'I snuck onto the driveway and took a few pieces of gravel, and look,' she added, her other hand reaching into another pocket and pulling out a cellophane bag. Inside it were three pieces of green pebble. They appeared to be identical in shape, size and colour to the pebbles Judith was holding in her other hand.

'I think there's a very good chance that this is where Oliver was coming for three days every week,' she said.

'Here?' Becks said, looking about herself. The house looked so very ordinary. Just as all the other houses on the street did.

'I know,' Suzie said in agreement. 'It's a head-scratcher, isn't it?'

'There's an easy way to find out,' Judith said. 'Shall we?'

As Judith led her friends to the house, the white and green gravel crunched satisfyingly under her feet. She saw her reflection in the glass of the front door and straightened her coat. She pressed the doorbell, and a bell rang inside the house.

There was the sound of feet approaching and then the door was opened by a woman who looked blankly at them.

'What do you want?' she asked.

The woman was wearing faded jeans, an old grey T-shirt, and she had dark, shoulder-length hair that looked as though it could do with a wash.

Judith was about to ask the woman if she knew Oliver Beresford when she realised she'd seen the woman somewhere before.

A girl appeared from a door further inside the house. She looked about seven years old.

'Mum, the Wi-Fi's not working,' the girl said.

Judith saw that the girl was standing next to a row of coats on pegs, and one of them was bright red.

In fact, it was a bright red puffa jacket.

'It's you!' Judith said, stunned. 'You're the ghost. The woman we saw in the lane when we left Verity Beresford's house that first time.'

The woman's eyes narrowed.

'I don't know what you're talking about,' she said.

'And you then disappeared from view. Why was that? Why did you hide when you saw us looking at you?'

The woman didn't say anything for a few seconds, and then she snarled, 'Go to your room, Jade.'

The girl began to complain until the woman barked, 'Now!'

Jade trudged upstairs and the woman stepped out to join Judith and her friends, pulling the door closed behind her so they could have some privacy.

'Who are you?' she hissed.

'Tell you what,' Suzie said. 'We can do you a deal. You tell us who you are and we'll tell you who we are.'

'And don't worry,' Becks added, guessing what was underneath the woman's fear. 'We're not the authorities in any way. I'm a vicar's wife.'

'That's right,' Judith said. 'We're just three women from Marlow, we've got no connections to the police at all. But we know all about Oliver Beresford coming to your house. He was here Wednesday to Friday every week, wasn't he? Even though the pair of you tried to keep the whole thing a secret.'

Judith could plot the battle of emotions that was raging inside the woman – between her desire to keep her secret and her desperation to share it.

'Honestly,' Becks said kindly, 'we're only here to help.'

'Ha!' the woman snorted. 'I know your kind – bloody do-gooders, the lot of you. All right, then,' she said, coming to her decision. 'You're right, I did know Oliver, not that that's the name I knew him by. He was always Jack to me. Jack Dawkins.'

'Seriously?' Suzie asked.

'That's what he called himself when we met.'

'But that's the real name of the Artful Dodger,' Judith said. 'From *Oliver Twist.*'

'All I know is it's what he called himself – Jack.'

'Why did he use a fake name?'

'I didn't know it was fake, did I? I only found out what was going on after he bloody died and I saw his face all over the papers. But you want to know who Oliver Beresford was?' the woman said, taking a menacing step towards the women. 'He was my husband, that's who he was. We were married.'

Chapter 28

Judith, Becks and Suzie were too stunned to respond.

'Yeah,' the woman said with a smirk. 'That got you.'

'Sorry,' Becks said, 'you and he were married?'

'These last two years.'

'Can I ask what your name is?'

'Jo,' the woman said. 'Joanne Dawkins.'

'How did you meet?' Judith asked, trying to control her spinning thoughts.

'In a pub. The Horse and Groom at Hare Hatch. He was propping up the bar one day. I'd gone in for a quick sharpener before the school pick-up and we got talking. Him in his fancy clothes and me in a tracksuit, we were a right pair, I can tell you. But he was funny, and he saw me, you know? Even without any make-up or anything, looking like I'd been dragged through a hedge backwards, he was OK – and OK goes a long way in my book. Anyway, I went off and got Jade and didn't think any more of it, but the next week, the same time, the same day, I went into the pub, and he was there again. He said his name was Jack.

I was late picking Jade up that day, and we organised lunch the next week. You can guess the rest.'

'What did he say he did?' Judith asked.

'He said he worked for the government.'

'Doing what?'

Jo's brow creased at the memory.

'He said he couldn't say.'

'Why not?' Becks asked.

'He said it was "hush hush" and that it was to do with "Six" – not that that made any sense to me.'

'Of course!' Judith said as she realised the importance of Oliver's pseudonym. 'In *Oliver Twist*, the character of Oliver is somewhat worthy, whereas the Artful Dodger is far more charismatic. I can understand why he wanted you to think he was Jack Dawkins. Did he really say he worked for MI6?'

'Listen,' Jo said defensively, 'someone's got to be dealing with all those terrorists and bombs, why not Jack?'

'But he didn't look much like a spy,' Becks said.

'He said how he dressed was all part of his "cover". That you wouldn't expect someone who was trying to hide to wear such fancy clothes. It was a double-bluff.'

'This is why he could only spend three days a week with you, isn't it?' Judith said. 'He was off doing "secret" things the rest of the time.'

'When he wasn't with me because he was serving his country, he told me I'd also be serving my country.'

'And you believed him?' Suzie asked.

'Hey, don't take that tone with me. He was good to me. He loved Jade. We were the "Three Js" – Jack, Jo and Jade. When he was around, the house was full of laughs – and why wouldn't

I believe him? He'd turn up with these gifts from around the world. You know, a couple of shot glasses from Turkey. A piece of jade for Jade all the way from Thailand.'

'And when you went out, he always paid in cash,' Judith said, beginning to appreciate the method in Oliver's madness.

'He said he couldn't let his enemies know about us. He couldn't leave any kind of digital footprint. They could use the information against him. That's what he said. I know this all makes me look stupid, but I've raised Jade on my own, you don't know how hard things have been for me. And he was flat out lying to me,' she added bitterly. 'I never expected that.'

'But you must have had doubts?' Suzie said.

'He was so clever. Whenever I asked him about anything that didn't make sense, he always had an answer. Why didn't he have a mobile phone? They could be tracked, that's what he said. Why couldn't I meet his mum and dad? He said he was an orphan. It's so obvious now – looking back at it all – but at the time, I wanted to believe, and I believed. And he married me, didn't he?'

'Yes, I don't see how that works at all,' Becks said. 'You can't get married without official documents, and the reading of the banns. How did you manage to take Oliver's surname of Dawkins if it wasn't his real surname?'

'But you didn't get married in the UK, did you?' Judith guessed.

'That's right, we got married in Greece.'

'Where the requirements to prove your identity would have been so much less.'

'The holiday was booked in my name. He said he didn't dare leave any kind of record. And you're right, the hotel basically didn't look at our documents at all. Why would they? It's not like he was likely to be an imposter, was it?'

'I'm so sorry,' Becks said. 'I can't imagine how hard this must have been on you.'

'It's Jade who it's hit hardest. I haven't dared tell her the truth – that her stepdad was a bloody conman. I just said he's had to go away for a while. I'll tell her we've split up when I've got the strength to, she can never know the truth. It would kill her.'

'Can I ask, did you know about Oliver's diagnosis?' Judith asked, before correcting herself. 'Sorry, I mean Jack, of course.'

'What diagnosis?'

'He had cancer.'

Judith noted that the revelation hit Jo hard.

'He didn't tell you?' Suzie asked.

'He always boasted about how healthy he was. He said he was going to live forever.'

'I'm sorry to say he had late stage liver cancer.'

'No,' Jo said again, trying to make sense of what she was hearing. 'No, he never . . .' she said before trailing off, lost in a confusion of thoughts.

'Tell you what I want to know,' Suzie said. 'Why did you hide from us that time we saw you?'

'I told you,' Jo said. 'I don't remember seeing you.'

'But we remember seeing you,' Judith said. 'Why would you lie to us now?'

Jo didn't say anything, but she looked so shifty that an idea hit Judith like a thunderclap.

'Was it you?' she said.

'Was it me what?'

'Who threw the brick through Verity's window? That's why you won't tell us you were there. You were checking her house out and didn't want to be seen. And – of course! – it also explains why the paper wrapped around the brick was covered in Oliver's fingerprints. It wasn't a paranormal message from beyond the grave, Suzie. Jo used paper that Oliver had handled. While also making sure she didn't get any of her fingerprints on it.'

Suzie scrunched up her nose, unhappy with Judith's debunking of her supernatural theory.

'And of course you'd check Oliver's house out,' Judith continued, now in full flow. 'Once you'd discovered his real identity in the papers after his death, it would have taken a will of steel not to try and find out the truth about the man you knew as Jack Dawkins. And to want to punish the woman he was also married to.'

'OK,' Jo said, tilting her chin up. 'I threw that brick. And I strung up the rabbit, and I don't care who knows it.'

'We'll have to tell the police,' Becks said. 'Although it's possible Verity won't press charges.'

'Oh, she'll press charges all right,' Jo said with a dark chuckle.

'What makes you say that?' Judith asked.

'She's a vindictive cow.'

'And how do you know that?'

'Because we had it out, didn't we? That first time I went there. When I saw you leave her house in your van. You're right, I hid from you. I didn't want anyone to know what I was about to do.'

'Which was?'

'I confronted her. Jack's woman. I went up to her house and gave her what for.'

'You *spoke* to her?'

'And guess what? She knew who I was before I even got to her. She was screaming at me how I had to get off her land – it's like she'd gone mad, like a bloody fishwife. Accusing me of stealing her husband and turning him against her.'

'Hang on, she already knew about you?' Suzie asked.

'She didn't know my name, but she knew all about me. Jack had told her about us.'

'He'd told her?' Becks asked, amazed.

'Some time before he died – that's right. The point is, she found out about Jack and me and then, a few weeks later, he's shot dead on a boat that she's on. She killed him.'

'But if you thought she was the killer,' Judith asked, 'why didn't you go to the police?'

'And have my name dragged through the press? And Jade's too? No way. But I wasn't powerless, was I? That's why I threw that brick through her window. I knew she'd know who was behind it. I wanted her scared. And I got this feeling of power when the glass smashed. The rabbit was just the next stage. She had to know I wasn't going to leave her alone.'

'And you think she killed him?' Becks asked.

'Don't let her nice clothes and big house fool you. That woman's vicious when she gets going, and I saw her get going plenty when she went for me. So I say, bring it on. You tell the police what I did – I don't care – but I want her in prison for what she's done. She killed my husband!'

Judith, Suzie and Becks all looked at each other. Could it be true?

Chapter 29

Judith rang Verity and said that with the opening night of *The Importance of Being Earnest* being only one day away, she was having a wobble of confidence, and could she perhaps come over and have a chat? Verity said that she was at the Little Theatre and she'd be delighted to talk to Judith to settle her fears. When Judith, Becks and Suzie arrived twenty minutes later, they found Verity backstage, building trestle tables in the wings.

'Good morning, Judith,' Verity said as the women came up the steps at the side of the stage. 'It's funny. You spend hundreds of hours rehearsing, learning lines, designing the set, building it – doing the marketing and advertising – all this endeavour, and yet the whole thing can fall apart if Lady Bracknell's handbag isn't in the right place on the prop table. For want of a nail and all that,' she added, but then stopped herself as she saw the looks on the women's faces. 'What is it?' she asked.

'Were you ever going to tell us the truth?' Suzie asked.

Judith looked at her friend and shrugged. It seemed as good a place as any to start their conversation.

'I'm sorry?' Verity said.

'You know who threw the brick through your window.'

'And who pinned the rabbit to your door,' Becks added.

'Judith, I thought you were having a wobble, what is this?'

'I lied to you,' Judith said. 'But then, you've been lying to us all along. It's time to come clean.'

'I've nothing to come clean about.'

'That's not true,' Suzie said. 'You found out your husband had a second wife just before he died. Didn't you?'

A nervous smile darted onto Verity's lips.

'What on earth are you talking about?' she asked.

'It finally explains what Duncan told us,' Judith said. 'The reason why, when you and Oliver were fighting, you told him that he must have got his cancer "as punishment" for what he'd done. You'd found out he was a bigamist.'

'Judith, I'm disappointed in you,' Verity said. 'This is a lie – whipped up by Duncan or whoever – and don't forget I was the one who came to you when Oliver first went missing. I was worried about him and wanted him found.'

'Which was clever of you,' Suzie said. 'After all, why would you be wanting him found if you were the killer? You were trying to make it look like you were innocent.'

'How dare you say that to me!' Verity snapped and strode down the steps that led back to the auditorium, Judith, Suzie and Becks exchanging quick glances and following her.

'Why are you running away?' Suzie called.

'I'm not running away,' Verity said without breaking step.

'We've spoken to Jo Dawkins and, unless you speak to us, the next people you're going to see are the police, and they're going to arrest you for your husband's murder.'

Verity stopped in her tracks and Suzie looked at her friends in satisfaction. That seemed to have done it.

'I didn't kill him,' Verity said without turning around.

'Then tell us the truth,' Becks said.

'I can't . . .' Verity turned and finished her sentence. 'I'm too ashamed.'

'I don't buy it,' Suzie said. 'You must have known all this would come out.'

'I didn't. You have to believe me. But you're right, I knew about his other woman. I'll admit to that. And after Oliver died, I kept waiting for the police to find out about her. But that first day passed. And another day passed. And I found myself hoping that maybe no one would ever know the truth. Are you happy now?'

'No,' Judith said. 'Why on earth didn't you say anything to me after she came to your house and accused you of murder?'

'Her attacking me like that only made me want to keep the secret even more. When I saw what she was like. The sort of person Oliver had betrayed me for.'

'What happened?' Becks asked.

'I was already feeling pretty raw that day. And you'd been asking all those questions about Oliver and me. It was awful. I knew I couldn't tell you about his other woman. I would never tell anyone. And then, after you left, there she was – bold as brass – striding up to my front door. She told me straight out that she was Oliver's wife. I'll never forget it. The adrenaline started pumping – it was like I was taken over by this desire to smash, to destroy. The dam finally broke. All the pain I'd felt, and the horror of Oliver's death – and how it had happened – it all came out right there.

'But she gave as good as she got. She didn't spare me any of the details of her and Oliver's sordid life together. And then she accused me of killing him. It was like being in a nightmare where you can't wake up. She was shouting obscenities at me – these lies, all about me. About how if I'd been enough of a wife, he wouldn't have looked elsewhere. That a man like him deserved more than me. That it was all my fault that he'd found her. And all I wanted was to get her off my property.'

'But you can't have been that surprised to see her,' Suzie said. 'When did Oliver tell you about her?'

Verity swallowed, but didn't answer.

'It's far better you tell us everything,' Becks said.

'A few weeks before he died,' Verity said. 'Sometime after his cancer diagnosis, anyway. He got really down – not that I could blame him – and whenever he talked about what life would be like without him in it, he kept making these cryptic comments about how I didn't know the half of what he was leaving behind. But there was a challenge in how he said it. Like I was too stupid to understand how important he was. I tried to forgive and forget – it was him who'd been given a terminal diagnosis, not me. But the more I ignored him, the more he needled me. In the end I flat out asked him to tell me what it was about him that was so special.

'I'll never forget the look in his eyes as he told me. His mouth was saying all these impossible words, about having a second wife and a step-daughter. But his eyes were looking at me the whole time like he was trying to work out how much pain he was causing me. And I could see the delight it was giving him. The nasty, vicious, narcissist.'

Verity choked back a sob as she finished speaking.

'Nice story,' Suzie said, 'but why should we believe a word you say?'

Verity's eyes widened at Suzie's accusation.

'You found out that your husband had a secret second life,' Suzie continued. 'And a second wife. So you decided to kill him, using your scarf to make sure you didn't get any gunshot residue on your hands. And you came up with those invites so that everyone else would be out of the way at 6 p.m. when you shot him dead on the back of the boat. Your only mistake was that you threw the gun and scarf into the river not knowing the water levels were going down. So your scarf ended up being revealed the next day.'

'No, that's not what happened!' Verity said.

'Then how did your scarf end up covered in gunshot residue in the river?'

'It was his other woman who killed him, it has to have been!'

'You mean Jo Dawkins?' Judith said.

'Think about it. When he got his terminal diagnosis, Oliver confessed everything to me. What if he did the same to her? Told her that he already had a wife in Marlow. Did his other woman know he had cancer?'

Judith and her friends didn't immediately reply.

'You see?' Verity said, warming to her theme. 'Whoever killed Oliver can't have known about his cancer. Who'd bother killing him when he was going to die soon anyway? And maybe she got hold of my scarf when she came to my house. Or she got Oliver to take it to her.'

'But Jo wasn't on the boat,' Becks said. 'She couldn't have killed him.'

'Then he wasn't killed on the boat.'

'He was,' Suzie said. 'There was a fight at the back, his blood was found on the deck, as were the bullet casings from the bullets that were fired into him. That's where he was killed.'

'OK, then if that's where he was killed, she must have been on the boat with us.'

'That's just as implausible,' Becks said. 'Everyone saw everyone else who was on the boat and no one saw her.'

'And what do you think happened after she killed him?' Judith asked.

'I don't know. Maybe she slipped into the river and swam to shore – leaving the scarf in the water to incriminate me, don't forget. And then she started throwing bricks through my window – and hanging up skinned rabbits – so the police would think it was me who was the killer.'

'Do you really think that's what happened?'

'I don't know! But someone killed Oliver and it wasn't me, I know that much. I'm innocent, you have to believe me!'

Judith looked at Verity and realised that for all the poise and self-control she'd shown since her husband had died, Jo Dawkins was right. Verity had a fighting spirit – a bottled fury to her – that made it easy to imagine her pulling a gun on her husband and shooting him dead.

But then, was it possible that Jo was on the boat that night as Verity was now suggesting? If so, someone who was there that night must have covered for her – probably by hiding her in their cabin and keeping quiet about it. But none of the MADS – or Lizzie Jenkins or Lance Goodman, for that matter – even knew of the existence of Jo Dawkins. Why would any of them have wanted to help her shoot Oliver? Although, Judith realised, that wasn't quite true, was it? No one on the boat *apart from Verity Beresford* knew of the existence of Jo Dawkins.

But it was impossible to imagine that Verity could have colluded with her husband's secret wife to have him killed. It was simply impossible.

Chapter 30

Detective Inspector Tanika Malik was in her home, emptying the washing machine. Her husband Shamil was supposed to have done it the night before – in fact, had promised that he'd do it – and yet here she was, doing a chore she didn't have time to do because he'd gone out early to DJ a gig, got home late, and was currently fast asleep in their bed upstairs.

As Tanika loaded the washing into the plastic basket, she looked at the rest of the kitchen. She still had to finish the washing-up from the night before, and the pile of broken-down cardboard from the last few weeks' home deliveries was almost up to the height of the kitchen table. She'd get Shamil to take it to the tip when he woke up, she told herself, as she went to the bottom of the stairs, pausing to look into the sitting room. Shanti was sitting on the sofa reading a book to her velveteen rabbit. Tanika felt as though her heart could burst. The hard work, the sacrifices, the stress and compromises – muddling through, living in a state of perpetual chaos where, no matter how much Shamil let her down, she knew she'd always love him – she knew it was all worth it.

There was a knock at the front door. Tanika shifted the basket onto her hip and went and opened it.

Judith, Suzie and Becks were standing outside.

'Oh,' Tanika said. The arrival of the women couldn't possibly be good news.

'We've got a confession to make,' Becks said.

Tanika sighed.

'It's probably better if we come in.'

Tanika led the women into the kitchen where she put the laundry down on the table. It would have to wait a few minutes longer.

'We didn't want to go to the police station,' Becks said, 'in case we got you into trouble.'

'That's very considerate of you,' Tanika said as she waited for the confession.

When it came, it didn't disappoint. The women explained how they'd found out that Toby had failed to get into RADA and blamed Oliver for leading him on; and how they were sure that Lance was up to something shifty, even though they hadn't been able to work out what it was. But they saved the best until last.

'Oliver Beresford was a bigamist,' Judith said.

Tanika didn't believe it at first. Not just the fact that he was living a double life – a double life that Verity knew about before he died – but she was amazed at the legwork the women had put in to find the driveway with white and green pebbles.

'You did all that on your own?' she asked.

'We did,' Suzie said proudly.

'Although it was Hugo who made the key breakthrough,' Becks added, wanting to be fair. 'He's Chloe's boyfriend.'

'And you're sure that none of you want to retrain as police officers?' Tanika asked.

'No thank you,' Judith said. 'But now you know where to look, I'm sure you can find a way of "discovering" all this information in a way that doesn't make it look like we were involved.'

'It's crazy I'm not allowed to hire you as civilian advisers,' Tanika said. 'The way you keep going, you're worth your weight in gold.'

Tanika offered the women a cup of tea, but they could see that they'd interrupted her morning chores, so they said they'd leave her to get on with her day.

'Are you ready for tomorrow?' she asked Judith.

'What's that?' Judith said, before she realised that Tanika was referring to the play. 'Actually, I'm dreading it. When we did the technical rehearsal, everyone seemed to have forgotten their lines and entrances and exits.'

'I'm sure it will come together for opening night. I can't wait to see it.'

'You're coming?'

'There's no way I'd miss your debut on the Marlow stage.'

There was a knock at the door and Tanika could see a man's shape through the opaque glass.

'Oh God!' she whispered to the women. 'It's Brendan!'

Tanika shoved the washing into Suzie's hands and ushered the women into the sitting room before going back to the front door.

Shanti looked up from the sofa and beamed at the sight of the three women.

'Hello, Shanti,' Becks said. 'What are you reading there?'

As Becks and Suzie went and sat with Shanti, Judith drifted to the window and loitered by the curtains. Peeling them back the tiniest fraction, she spied on Brendan.

'—for calling on you without ringing first,' Judith heard him say.

'Don't worry about it,' Tanika said from the hallway.

'Only I knew you'd want to know as soon as possible. The dive team has recovered a handgun from the riverbed of the Thames. About half a kilometre upstream from where his body was found. And it's the same calibre – 9mm – as the gun that was used to kill him. It could be the gun we're looking for.'

'Have they been able to do a test firing?'

'Not yet, although it will happen as soon as you authorise it. The dive team say it's an army-issue semi-automatic and is waterproof. So it should be working OK if we use fresh bullets. Even after all of this time in the water.'

'It's army issue?' Tanika asked.

'And not just any army. Apparently, this type of handgun was only ever used by the Argentinian armed forces. Don't worry, they'll be able to tell us all about it when they process it.'

'OK, then how about you wait in the car. I'll be straight out.'

Judith watched Brendan return to his police car and then slipped away from the window and plonked herself down on the sofa next to the others as Tanika entered.

'Did you hear that?' she asked.

'What's that?' Judith asked innocently.

Tanika indicated with a nod of her head that she didn't want to say in front of Shanti, so the women got up and joined her in the hallway.

'They've found the pistol in the river,' she whispered.

'Don't tell us any more!' Judith said, holding up her hand.

'And don't worry if you have to go with Brendan,' Becks said. 'We can hang out your washing for you.'

A man appeared at the top of the stairs with tousled hair. He was still in his pyjamas.

'Why's there a police car outside?' Shamil asked with a yawn. 'Oh, hello, ladies,' he said, seeing Judith and her friends.

'Can you hang up this wash?' Tanika said, taking the basket up the stairs.

'Sure,' Shamil said with no apparent awareness that he should have done it already.

'And Shanti's in the sitting room. Can you look after her? I've got to go to work.'

'You've got a lead?'

'Looks like it.'

'Then go, I'll hold the fort here.'

'And we'll let ourselves out once the coast is clear,' Judith said.

'Thanks,' Tanika said as she looked at the people who were gathered in her hallway: one eccentric seventy-nine-year-old widow; a middle-aged dog walker; the wife of the local vicar; and a man who still believed he could make it as a club DJ. This was her support team and she couldn't help but smile to herself at how ramshackle it was.

'What is it?' Becks asked as Tanika headed for the front door.

Tanika looked at everyone, her hand on the door.

'Wouldn't change a thing,' she said. 'Although you'd better hide when I open the door.'

Judith and her friends scooted into the sitting room again as Tanika went outside and joined Brendan in his police car. As it drove off, Judith went back into the hallway and announced to Shamil that they couldn't stay; they had somewhere they had to be.

'We can't interfere with the police getting the gun,' Becks said as they headed down the road to where Suzie had parked her van.

'Of course not,' Judith agreed. 'But we can speak to the owner of it.'

'She didn't say who owned it.'

'As it happens, she didn't, but Brendan did – not that she realised that that's what he was doing. I suggest we go and talk to him.'

Chapter 31

As Judith and her friends strode across the field opposite Verity's house, they were pleased to see smoke rising from the chimney on the back of Duncan's boat. Judith rapped her knuckles on one of the windows as soon as they arrived.

'Duncan, I know you're in there,' Judith called out.

There was no sound from inside.

'I can get him out,' Judith whispered to her friends. 'I've realised I've got a diary clash,' she called out, 'and won't be able to perform on the last night of the run.'

Judith turned to her friends and gave them a big wink as they heard movement inside the boat, and a few seconds later, Duncan's head appeared at the back hatch.

'Verity won't be happy,' he said and then coughed into an old hankie.

'Can we come on board so I can explain?'

Duncan frowned, but disappeared back down the steps.

'All right, you'd better come in,' he said from inside the boat.

Judith beamed a smile of triumph to her friends, and they walked up the gangplank to the back of the boat before heading down the steps into the main cabin.

'Actually, I haven't entirely been truthful,' Judith said once her eyes had acclimatised to the gloom, 'I'm looking forward to doing every performance.'

'Then why did you say you wouldn't be able to do it?'

'Because you tried to kill my friend here,' Suzie said with a nod at Judith.

'What?' Duncan said, his eyes widening.

'When you dropped that light on her.'

'That was an accident! And it wasn't my fault anyway, I had signs up everywhere warning that I was rigging the lights that day.'

'We're not saying you'd started that day actively planning to kill Judith,' Becks said. 'But she was getting in the way, wasn't she? Asking difficult questions. So when she walked underneath you and you had a heavy object in your hand . . . ?'

'I don't need this,' Duncan said angrily. 'You don't know the pressure I'm under!'

Duncan looked wildly at Judith, and then he started to cough again, pulling out a hankie that he wheezed into.

'OK,' Judith said once he'd got his breathing under control. 'What pressure?'

'The play! Don't tell me you're like all the other actors? Because I'll tell you the point of that accident we had on the stage. I'm up in that gantry rigging and focusing all those lights on my own. Does Verity lift a finger? Or Oliver before her? It doesn't matter who's in charge, they're only interested in what goes on on stage. But no one would be able to see anything without my lights. And sound. And me making sure the set gets built and can fit in the theatre. And fire safety buckets, and you wouldn't understand anyway,' he said, finishing his rant with a scowl.

Judith tilted her head as she looked at Duncan. He was right about one thing. She hadn't considered that he was also working to a tight deadline.

'This is private property,' Duncan said, 'and I want you off it, all three of you.'

'You don't want us to go,' Suzie said.

'I just said I did.'

'Because otherwise we won't be able to give you the warning you need to hear.'

'Don't try to intimidate me.'

'Seriously, you'd know if I was intimidating you, this isn't intimidation. Although you should know, we told the police on the way over here that the gun belonged to you.'

Duncan froze.

'Oh!' Suzie added, pretending surprise at what she'd just said. 'That's me being intimidating, isn't it? So yeah, this is a chance for you to get your story straight before they arrest you.'

'Why are they going to arrest me?' Duncan asked, but the women could see that he was panicking.

'I think you know why,' Suzie said.

'I don't, I promise you.'

'OK, then let's play a game,' Judith said. 'I'll tell you that the police have recovered the murder weapon, and it's a pistol from the Argentinian armed forces. And then you tell me how your uncle's gun ended up being used to kill Oliver.' As she spoke, Judith moved over to the photograph of Duncan's uncle wearing army fatigues. 'After all, who owns a trophy from the Argentinian armed forces, if not someone who fought in the Falklands War?'

'It's not as bad as it sounds,' Duncan said.

'I should hope so,' Suzie said, 'because it sounds pretty bad.'

'Look – you're right. Uncle Ray had this old drawer in his cupboard at home that had all his old soldier's clothes in it. And his medals . . .'

'And an Argentinian gun,' Becks said.

'The Bersa Thunder 9. All he'd say was that he'd taken it from an Argentinian soldier, but he got this look when he talked about it that sent shivers down my spine. When he died, my aunt said at the wake that Uncle Ray had left all his military stuff to me. I could go upstairs and take it. I left that day with two bin bags stuffed full of his possessions, and the pistol was wrapped up in the heart of it.'

'So who used it to kill Oliver if not you?' Becks asked.

'I don't know – I've been racking my brains since the murder.'

'Oh – you knew it was your gun that was used?'

Duncan moved over to a drawer in a desk and pulled it open. Inside was an old cardboard box full of bullets.

'I've always kept it in here.'

'In an open drawer?' Judith asked.

'I live on my own on a canal boat. It makes sense to have it to hand. As soon as I heard Oliver had been shot, I checked the drawer and saw it was no longer there. I've been in a blind panic ever since.'

'Which explains why you've been keeping your distance from me these last few weeks. As you told us the first time we came here, you've always known we've been trying to work out who killed Oliver, and you were worried I'd find out that it was you who owned the murder weapon.'

'But the point is, it was never under lock and key. Don't you see? Anyone could have taken it.'

'Of the people who were on the *Marlow Belle* that night, who has been on your boat?'

'All of them. At one time or another.'

'Have you ever mentioned the gun to them?'

'No, it's always been my secret. But I can tell you that everyone on the committee – going back decades – have been in here. And the gun's been in that drawer the whole time. Any of them could have found it and then taken it before the murder.'

'What about Jo Dawkins?' Judith asked.

'Jo who?'

'She's a woman who lives in Wargrave,' Becks said. 'Has a young daughter called Jade. Has she ever been on this boat?'

Duncan shook his head.

'The name doesn't ring a bell.'

'Then how about Lance Goodman?' Suzie asked.

'The boat captain? No way – he's never been here – I don't know him.'

'You don't?' Judith said, surprised. 'He told us that all the people on the river know each other.'

'That's normally true, but I've never got to know Lance.'

'That's odd, because he very definitely told us that he knew you. What about Lizzie Jenkins? Could she have taken your gun?'

'No way. The first time I met her was that evening at the drinks reception. And there's no way she'd have known where I lived before then. She only arrived in the UK that day.'

'How can that have been the first time you met her? Surely you must have known her when she was a teenager?'

'Oh, you know about that, do you?' Duncan said, and the women could see that he was embarrassed at being caught out in a lie. 'I only meant that it was the first time I'd met her in decades.'

'What was she like when you first knew her?'

'Irritating. Young. She's one of those pretty girls who's basically messed up. Knows she can catch any man – because it's true – and it makes them arrogant.'

'She came from a difficult background,' Becks said.

'So what? My childhood was no bed of roses. And we all have things happen to us in our life that must be overcome. Doesn't mean you need to manipulate people.'

'She manipulated people?' Suzie asked.

'Girls like that are always manipulative. Was it really my gun that was used?'

'The police will be here soon enough,' Suzie said. 'They can tell you.'

'Well I'll tell them what I've told you. Someone must have taken it. All I can do is hope that they believe me. It's not like I have a motive anyway.'

'You found him irritating,' Becks said.

'I'm not a big fan of you three, but it doesn't mean I want to kill you.'

'But you were in the middle of a feud with him.'

'Are you serious? You're going to tell the police I killed Oliver because he didn't return a book of theatre reviews to me?'

'Then it's something else,' Judith said.

'What else? You've spoken to everyone in the MADS, and

you've seen how everyone is with me and how I am with them. You can't pin anything on me – and you know it. Now, seriously, the three of you have to leave. If the police are coming here, I need to get on with learning my prompt copy of the script and practise my sound and lighting cues for tomorrow night.'

Judith looked at Duncan and realised that he was right. It might have been his gun that had been used to kill Oliver, but she didn't have a definite motive she could pin on him. It seemed so unlikely that he'd kill an old friend over a petty argument. She sighed in frustration.

'Very well,' she said. 'We'll leave you to get on with what you need to do. But make sure you tell the police about your uncle's pistol when they get here. Because if you don't, we will.'

As Judith and her friends went up the steps that led back to the deck, Duncan coughed.

'You should get that cough seen to,' Suzie said.

Judith paused mid-step, her friends bumping into her as something Lance had said to them the first time they'd met popped into her head. It was his story of seeing Oliver at the doctor's surgery. Why had that just occurred to her? She remembered that Lance had said that you can always tell when someone's ill – properly ill – and then she realised the significance of the memory in a sudden rush.

'Is that your motive?' she said, turning on the step to look back down at Duncan.

'We just agreed,' he said. 'I don't have one.'

'You've got cancer, haven't you?'

Duncan's mouth fell open in shock, but he didn't say anything.

'Which is why you cough and splutter so much. But you've kept your diagnosis secret, haven't you? Even when we asked you about Oliver's cancer, you didn't tell us about yours. Why was that? It must have been because your diagnosis was in some way incriminating. But how can that be?' Before Duncan could reply, Judith answered her own question. 'Is it because your cancer is connected to Oliver's somehow? What was it Verity told us? That Oliver had got his from spending so much time around old council buildings making sure their asbestos was removed.'

As soon as Judith mentioned the council buildings, she realised what the connection was.

'That's why you couldn't tell anyone, isn't it?'

'Nothing you're saying makes any sense,' Duncan said.

'It was all there, I just had to put the pieces together.'

'He's got a point,' Suzie said to her friend. 'Becks and I don't know what you're talking about, either.'

'We don't,' Becks agreed.

'Very well, let me explain. When Duncan and Oliver founded the MADS all those years ago, they worked out of an old council building. There's a photo of them both standing in front of it in the Little Theatre. I think it was one of the buildings that Oliver was supposed to condemn, wasn't it? Because it contained asbestos. But he didn't tell Duncan about it because he was so desperate to get his amateur dramatic society up and running.'

'You're right,' Duncan croaked, and then he went over to his sink and turned on the tap. He picked up a glass and filled it with water. The women could see that his hand was shaking, and he held the glass in two hands as he drank from it.

He put the glass down and looked at the women.

'After Oliver's diagnosis,' he said, 'he was angry. And bitter. I could understand it. And then one day, I irritated him for some reason and he told me he'd have the last laugh. I may have moved my boat to ruin his view, but it was nothing compared to what he'd done to me. His doctor had told him his cancer was probably brought on by the asbestos insulation he'd been exposed to during the three years he and I spent in that building. He was supposed to condemn it, but he didn't worry about his health back then. Or mine. All he cared about was having a theatre company so he could be famous, and he didn't care what price he paid for that fame. Or who he destroyed in the process.'

'And because he now had cancer, he crowed to you that you might have it as well?' Suzie asked, appalled.

'He said I'd not been well for months and he wasn't wrong. I went to the doctor's and discovered I have thyroid cancer. Because of Oliver's warning, I caught it early – I suppose I should be grateful to him at least for that. I'm booked in for surgery in a few weeks' time. Hopefully it will be enough.'

'I'm so sorry,' Becks said.

'Your words don't really help.'

'That's not what I mean. It's true I'm sorry that you were exposed to asbestos in the past – that's a terrible thing. Especially since it was Oliver's fault. But that's not why I was saying sorry. When the police get here, they're going to point out that you were on the boat when Oliver died. And that he was killed with your gun. And that you have one of the most compelling motives of anyone that night. They're going to say that you killed Oliver Beresford because you believe he'd already killed you.'

'That's what they're going to think, but it's not what happened,' Duncan said, his eyes shining with tears. 'It's why I couldn't tell anyone about my gun going missing. Or that I had cancer, and that Oliver was to blame for it. It's why I've been staying out of your way, Judith. And I'll even admit there was a bit of me that dropped that light . . .' Duncan trailed off, before regathering his thoughts. 'I'm not saying I tried to hit you with it, but I've never dropped a light before, I think it was my subconscious that knew I had to get you out of the way. And when I saw you it slipped out of my hands. I'm so sorry,' he said, and then buried his head in his hands and started crying.

Becks went to Duncan and put her arm around his shoulders.

There was a knock on the window and the women looked over to see Brendan standing on the riverbank with two uniformed officers.

Chapter 32

Judith and her friends were in a subdued mood as they left Duncan with the police. After spending the last few weeks hearing how selfish Oliver Beresford had been, it was still shocking to learn just how far he'd been prepared to go in his quest for personal glory. But while Suzie and Becks wanted to discuss what this latest revelation meant for the case, Judith knew that she was expected at the Little Theatre for a final costume and props check that afternoon. Then she had to run the lines of the play at speed with the rest of the cast in an exercise she'd been told was called a 'line bomb'. And she knew she'd be too tired to work on the case later that evening, once she'd been released from her commitments to the play. She also had an instinct that she needed time to let the facts of the case settle. There'd been so much that they'd recently learned, and she was sure that letting her subconscious sort and sift everything could only be of benefit. So she left her friends and they agreed they should meet up the following morning.

The next day, as Becks and Suzie arrived bright and early at Judith's house, Suzie was in an excited mood.

'I've got news,' she said as she sat down with a cup of tea. 'Or think I may have news. But first I've got to ask, how are you doing, Judith?'

'Me?' Judith asked surprised.

'How were your rehearsals yesterday? Are you ready for the show tonight?'

'Not remotely,' Judith said. 'And I didn't get a wink of sleep last night. All of the facts of the case kept whizzing around my head, and just before dawn I realised why. I think the killer's toying with us.'

'How do you mean?' Becks asked.

'Every time we look for a motive for someone who was on that boat, we find one. And every time we then look for evidence against that person, we find that as well. Duncan, we now know, blames Oliver for his cancer – understandably so. And then, as if that wasn't enough, it was his gun that was used to kill him. I mean, in any other case, that would make him the killer, wouldn't it? But then we've got Verity, who'd found out that her husband was a bigamist of all things, and we also found her scarf covered in gunshot residue from the murder weapon. And then there's Toby, who Oliver humiliated with his RADA audition, and it turns out one of the bullets from the murder weapon was found in his cabin on the *Marlow Belle*.'

'You're right,' Becks said. 'It's all very neat and tidy. Even Lizzie has a key clue that suggests she's the killer, doesn't she? It was her who gave everyone the invitations that got them out of the way.'

'Even though we don't know what her motive is,' Suzie said. 'Although we can guess it's connected to her and Oliver in the past.'

'That's it exactly!' Judith said. 'It's almost as if the killer is putting on a play for us. A play where everyone is guilty.'

'It would explain why all of the suspects keep saying they think they're being set up. They *are* being set up.'

'But one of them's the actual killer, so why would they set themselves up, that's what I don't understand. And it's not quite true that everyone on the boat has a motive, is it? We still haven't found a connection between Lance and Oliver – even though he's clearly got a secret of some sort he's not telling us.

'I think that's where I jump in,' Suzie said. 'Because I reckon I know what Lance's secret is. And if I'm right, we'll be able to use it as leverage against him. Just like you said we should, Becks.'

There was a knock at the front door and Suzie looked at the clock on the mantelpiece.

'Perfect timing!' she announced.

'You've not invited someone to my house, have you?' Judith asked, appalled.

'I think you'll like this person. You like hardened criminals.'

The knocking got louder and Suzie rubbed her hands together in anticipation.

'Come on,' she said, as she got up and led her friends to the front door.

Becks and Suzie were surprised when Suzie opened the door to a teenage boy with choppy hair and dimples in his cheeks. But not as surprised as Suzie.

'Oh,' she said.

'What?' the teenage boy said as he looked at Suzie, Judith and Becks.

'This is your hardened criminal?' Judith asked.

'No way, this is all wrong,' the teenager said, and he turned and started to walk away towards an orange bike he'd left propped up against the wall.

'I know you!' Suzie said as she strode after the young man.

Becks and Judith knew they no longer had control of the situation, so they followed Suzie.

'Dylan Hatfield, you stop right there,' Suzie barked as she caught up with the teenager and grabbed him by his shoulder. He twisted out of her grip, and started to push his bike to get away.

'You stand still or I'll tell your mum and dad on you.'

Dylan stumbled and stopped before Suzie had finished talking.

'That's right, I know your parents. They hired me to walk Misty a few times back in the day.' Suzie turned to Becks to explain. 'She's a lovely Bernese mountain dog – they have the sweetest natures. And I rang you to do a deal, so let's do a deal.'

'Not if you know me,' the boy said.

'Marlow's a small town, I bet this happens all the time.'

'Yeah, but not with . . .' Dylan said, before indicating the three older women standing in front of him.

'Suzie, can you please tell me what's going on?' Judith said.

'That's easy,' Suzie said. 'You remember I took the number of Toby's dealer from him? Well, I've been trying to set up a purchase of some weed from him and we finally managed to agree on a time and a place. Here. And now.'

'You're a drug dealer?' Becks asked Dylan incredulously.

'It's a sideline,' he mumbled.

'But you deal to Toby Vincent?'

'We don't do names. And it's not dealing. It's only a side hustle.'

'It's dealing,' Suzie said. 'I want to know where you get your supply from or you'll be in big trouble.'

'You can't threaten me,' he said with a scowl.

'Yes I can,' Suzie said as she reached into her back pocket and pulled out her phone. 'I've still got your mum's number in my phone, I think I'll ring her right now and tell her all about what you're getting up to.'

'His name's Andy Ford,' Dylan blurted. 'That's who I get the weed from. Andy Ford.'

'Hang on, we know that name,' Judith said as she racked her brain for why the name was chiming with her. 'He's the lock-keeper at Cookham, isn't he?'

'The lock-keeper at Cookham deals drugs?' Becks said incredulously.

'That's not the answer I was expecting,' Suzie said to Dylan.

'He's the guy who supplies me, OK?' Dylan said, trying to project a sense of swagger.

'Then if he's your supplier, where does he get his drugs from?' Suzie asked.

'I don't know, OK?' Dylan said. 'And it's only weed – that's all. It's natural, and it should be legal anyway.'

'You expect us to believe that you just deal weed?'

'Can I go now? I've got to get home, I've got to take Misty for a walk.'

In asking the question, Dylan managed to look about thirteen years old and Suzie didn't have the heart to hold him any longer.

'Go on, then,' she said. 'Scram.'

'And stop dealing drugs!' Becks called after Dylan as he got on his bike and cycled off.

'Drug dealers, they're like policemen, aren't they?' Judith said as they watched Dylan go. 'They're getting younger every year.'

'But what does this mean?' Becks asked Suzie. 'How is this linked to Lance?'

'I think there's an easy way to find out,' Suzie said.

★

Lance Goodman was sanding down a boat in his main workshop as Judith, Becks and Suzie walked in like gunslingers arriving in a Wild West bar.

'What are you lot doing here?' Lance asked, already irritated.

'We know why you've been acting so guiltily,' Suzie said. 'I recognised your handwriting on a bag of cannabis that Toby Vincent had. And there was a vertical line through the zero of 30%, which I remembered is how you wrote your zeros. So I knew it was you, I just had to prove it.'

'I don't know what you're talking about,' Lance said, but the women could already see that he was worried.

'You're working with Andy Ford at Cookham Lock, aren't you? And then you use local people to distribute it. Like school-kids. And that's not cool, Lance. Not cool at all.'

'None of this is true.'

'It was your handwriting on the baggie. Why are you denying it?'

'And we were able to lift your fingerprints from the label as well,' Judith said, not entirely truthfully. Her words had the desired effect, though. Lance staggered back half a step.

'So go on, then,' Suzie said. 'Where do you get the weed from? Is Andy the grower or are you?'

'You've got to stop asking these questions,' Lance said.

'It's you, isn't it?' Judith said, a memory coming to her. 'The first time we came to talk to you, we saw you coming out of the half-submerged barge you've got in the little tributary behind this building. You were carrying a silver insulation panel – which seemed odd at the time, but makes perfect sense now. You need heat and light to grow cannabis, don't you? The panels are there to keep the heat in and stop the barge from appearing on any thermal cameras if a police helicopter comes looking. Come on, ladies,' Judith said as she turned on her heels and started to head out of the building. 'We can go to the barge and see for ourselves.'

As the three women strode out of the building, Lance caught up with them.

'OK, I admit it, you're right,' he said.

Suzie stopped and turned with a deadly smile.

'A full and frank confession. Now.'

Lance looked from Suzie to her friends and then back to Suzie again. He saw no mercy.

'But it's not big-time or anything,' he said, wanting to get his excuses in first. 'It's just something I cooked up with a few mates.'

'Like the lock-keeper at Cookham, Andy Ford.'

'That's right. And the guy who runs Hurley Lock. It's the three of us, that's how small it is. I grow the weed in an old barge – you're right – and prepare and bag it. And then, every few months, I drop off supplies with them both. And then they sell it on. But it's low key – it makes a few tens of thousands a year, no more than that. And between the cut I give the two lock-keepers, it doesn't amount to all that much.'

'I wouldn't call making tens of thousands of pounds a year "not that much",' Suzie said.

'And Oliver knew about it, didn't he?' Judith said. 'Which is why he was threatening you in the pub with revealing your secret. Isn't that right?'

'Jesus, how did you work it all out?'

'If it hadn't been for the tip-off from Mary Eddingham, we wouldn't have been able to work it out at all.'

'So you admit it?' Suzie asked, wanting to keep the pressure on.

'You want me to say the words?' Lance asked. 'OK, I admit it. When I told Oliver the *Marlow Belle* wasn't ready to be hired, he said that he had a friend who was throwing his life away on weed. And he'd done some digging – to get his friend off it – and found out that I was the source of it all. So if I didn't hire him the boat, he'd go to the police.'

'And here we are once again!' Judith said, exasperated. 'You finally admit the truth when you're forced to.'

'Listen, I'll do a deal with you,' Lance said, desperation in his voice.

'It's a bit too late for that.'

'Just promise me you won't tell the police about my sideline.'

'And why would we help you?' Suzie asked.

'In return, I'll tell you who killed Oliver Beresford.'

'You don't know who did it.'

'But that's the thing, I do. I've always known.'

'Seriously? Then who was it?'

Lance took a deep breath before he answered.

'It was Lizzie Jenkins. I saw her kill Oliver Beresford.'

Chapter 33

No one spoke for a few seconds.

'Lizzie Jenkins?' Suzie said to double-check she'd heard correctly.

'That's right.'

'I knew it!' she said in satisfaction.

'Why didn't you tell us this before now?' Judith asked. 'Or the police?'

'I didn't want them digging around in my life. But since you now know everything, there's no point keeping it a secret any longer. Maybe I can get the police to take it into consideration? If I make a full confession? Or they'll let me do a plea bargain like you see on the telly.'

'So what happened?' Judith asked, wanting to keep Lance focused.

'Look, it was about 6 p.m. – or a few minutes before. Oliver came to my cabin. Like I said the last time we spoke. But what I didn't tell you was that he was in a panic because he'd seen a woman on the riverbank. He said there was someone painting and I had to speed the boat up. We had to make sure no one could see the *Marlow Belle* from the riverbank at 6 p.m. It made no sense to me, especially seeing as we'd be around the corner of the bend in a few minutes anyway. We'd be out of sight soon enough. But he said we only had a few minutes to play with – I had to get the boat up to maximum speed. It meant I'd be breaking the speed limits of the river, but I looked back and I could see the person he was talking about. There was a woman with an easel doing some painting. So I opened up the throttle. The woman was soon behind us, and once we'd got around the bend in the river and we couldn't see her any more, Oliver said I could go back to the normal speed. But he also said I had to stay in the driving position, and if I breathed a word of any of our conversation later, he'd tell the police about my drug-dealing.'

'He blackmailed you?' Becks asked.

'Basically – yes. He said I had to stay put in my cabin. And I agreed – I was planning to stay there anyway. The only problem was, he'd got me interested. I mean, why had he been so edgy about there being a witness on the riverbank? Why was 6 p.m. such an important time?

'After he left, I stayed in the cabin, like he asked, but I didn't check in on the engine – even though that's what I told you and the police. There's a little window at the back. If you look through it, you can see across the top of the cabins to the stern. If anyone's on the deck back there, you can see them from about the shoulders up. When I looked, Lizzie was standing there on her own. I didn't think much of it until Oliver joined her. I couldn't hear what they were saying over the noise of the engine – and the driving position's enclosed anyway – but I could see that they were talking, and pretty intensely. And Lizzie was getting angry,

I could tell that as well. And then, she attacked him – just like that. It came out of nowhere as far as I could see, but she was suddenly attacking Oliver and he was struggling to fight her off. It's all a bit hazy in my memory, but there are things I know I saw. They were grappling up close when she took a step back and lifted her arm. That's when I saw she was holding a gun. I froze, it was like everything went into slow motion. But it also all happened before I even knew it had happened, if you know what I mean. Oliver backed away from her, his hands held up – and then she pulled the trigger. I heard a bang and saw the flash from the muzzle and Oliver dropped to the deck.'

'The first shot,' Suzie said. 'The bullet that went in his side.'

'I thought she'd killed him there and then, but then he staggered back to his feet and started grappling with Lizzie again – trying to get the gun from her, I reckon, and that's when I saw her pull the gun again, get up close to him and shoot him a second time.'

'The second shot. The killing shot.'

'Got it in one. This time, when Oliver dropped out of view, he didn't get up again. That must have been when he went into the water. I couldn't see. But Lizzie stood there for a few seconds, and then she disappeared back below deck. I realised I was in danger – there was a killer on the boat – what should I do? So I locked the door to the driving position and . . .'

'Yes?' Judith asked.

'I waited.'

'You didn't ring the police?'

'My mind was racing. I had some weed on the boat. Quite a lot of weed. I was planning on taking it to Hurley Lock after I'd dropped everyone off in Marlow. I couldn't let the police onto the boat – although it seems crazy that that's what I was thinking. I get it now. But I was also in shock. And then, Oliver's wife – Verity – appeared on the back of the boat. And Lizzie Jenkins joined her. They were chatting like nothing had happened, and Verity was opening a bottle of champagne. And then Duncan joined them, and they were all laughing and having a nice time. And then, Toby as well. I couldn't believe it. How could Lizzie be so calm, she'd just shot a man dead – like, only two minutes earlier. I even began to wonder if it was something they'd staged. You know, as part of their amateur dramatic society. I unlocked the door, went through the boat and joined them on the deck at the back. Everyone was chatting and drinking like nothing had happened. So I looked to see if there was any blood on the deck. But it was hard to see for sure, as I'd painted the wood dark red. Even so, I thought I could maybe see some spots of blood.

'I went back to my driving position as fast as I could and locked myself in again. Then, as soon as we got back to Marlow and I'd dropped everyone off, I turned the boat around and drove home as fast as I could. There was no way I was going to go on to Hurley after that. I got the drugs off the boat and then I waited. And the thing is, the more I thought about it, the more I realised no one could say I'd done anything wrong. I'd not been involved in the murder in any way. And as long as I didn't try and clean the boat or cover up what had happened, I'd be in the clear, wouldn't I? The only person who knew I'd seen the murder was me, and when the police arrived, I knew I could keep my lips sealed.'

'But instead of the police, you got us,' Judith said.

'You can say that again,' Suzie said.

'Suzie,' Lance said with a whine in his voice. 'You know me. I'll admit it, I'm not always honest, but I'm not a bad man.'

'You are a bad man.'

'But not a criminal.'

'You're literally a criminal.'

'You know what I mean, stop splitting hairs! I wouldn't do anything that harmed anyone. You know that about me. And the only person I've harmed with my lies is me, isn't it? Because I could have gone straight to the police, but I didn't. I reckon there's nothing I'll regret more in my life. Because I'm telling you, I know who killed Oliver Beresford. I've always known. It was Lizzie Jenkins. I saw her pull the trigger.'

'You're prepared to say that in court?' Judith asked.

'I'll swear it on the bible. She's the killer.'

Chapter 34

'We have to phone Tanika and let her know,' Becks said as they raced to Suzie's van.

'Of course,' Judith agreed. 'We have to ring her at once.'

None of the women reached for their phones as they bundled in, and it was only as Suzie pulled off, wheels spinning on the gravel, that Becks finally made the call. She explained to Tanika how they'd used the news that Lance was a drug dealer to finesse the truth out of him – that he'd seen Lizzie Jenkins murder Oliver – and then Judith took the phone from Becks and told her that they were heading straight for the Danesfield House Hotel to make sure that Lizzie didn't abscond. Before Tanika could tell Judith that it was a matter for the police, Judith hung up and handed the phone back to Becks.

'Hold on!' Suzie called as the sharp turning for the hotel appeared up ahead on the Henley Road. Without slowing down, Suzie swung out onto the other side of the road – wheels squealing – and jammed her foot on the accelerator to go up the steep drive that led to the hotel.

The suspension was still bouncing as Suzie slammed on the brakes at the entrance to the hotel. The women got out as a red-coated doorman appeared. Suzie scrabbled in her bum bag as they approached him, and then she pulled out her expired police warrant card.

'Police,' she barked as the three women strode past him.

Once inside the wood-panelled reception area, the women approached the check-in desk, Suzie holding up her warrant card, her finger blocking the date in the bottom right-hand corner.

'Police – we're looking for Lizzie Jenkins.'

'You're the police?' the smooth check-in attendant asked, raising an eyebrow.

'If you can tell us where she is,' Judith said, 'I'm sure we can handle this discreetly.'

The attendant took a few seconds to come to his decision, but he could see how unhinged the women in front of him were looking and he decided to take the line of least resistance.

'She was in the grounds about half an hour ago,' he said. 'There's a seated area that overlooks the Thames. She asked for tea to be taken to her.'

'Thank you,' Judith said, the women already striding off through the hotel – past the guests having afternoon tea in the orangery – and out onto the hotel's grand terrace.

'Come on,' Becks said, leading off towards a clump of trees at the bottom of the lawn. 'Colin married a pop star here last year – I had a good poke around. I think I know where she'll be.'

As they entered the copse, the women saw a wooden pergola with outside seating. Lizzie was sitting there on her own, looking down at the turmoil of the water passing over the weir at Hurley Lock.

The women arrived, but Lizzie didn't look up – which suited the three friends, as they all needed a few seconds to regain their breath.

'There was a witness,' Becks said, deciding that when it came to extracting confessions from killers, the vicar's wife should take the lead.

Lizzie looked up and only seemed to recognise the women dimly.

'Lance Goodman, the boat captain,' Becks said. 'There was a window at the back of his driving cabin. He'll testify in court that he saw you shoot Oliver Beresford.'

'Your best chance at this point is to come clean,' Suzie said. 'To tell the truth.'

'I'm sure you want to,' Becks added.

Lizzie pulled a bent cigarette from a packet in her hand and lit it with a gold lighter. As she inhaled on it and then blew out the smoke, she looked down at the swirling water as it rushed over the weir.

'I didn't mean to,' she said.

And there it was. The confession. In those four words.

'Is that what you meant when you told us we didn't know what had happened that night?' Becks asked. 'If there are any mitigating circumstances, it's possible they will help you.'

'You were right all along,' Lizzie said, her eyes not lifting from the water. 'Oliver was the reason I came back. I wrote two whole chapters about him in my book. About how he saved my life and took me in when no one else would. How he helped me fall in love with the theatre. I thought – when I was writing it – that it was all true.

'When I handed the first draft in to my publishers, they got a team of lawyers to fact check it line by line to make sure

I wasn't going to libel anyone. It's standard when you write an autobiography. And in the process they got in touch with RADA to confirm the dates of my application. They replied with the dates, but said that I was incorrect when I said in the book that they'd turned me down. They'd offered me a place.'

'What?' Suzie asked.

'I can't tell you what that was like. My whole life flashed in front of my eyes, and all I could think was that I'd been supposed to go to London and train, and what would have happened if I'd been allowed to. That whole spiral I got into when I didn't get in – or thought I hadn't. The drugs, the abuse – everything bad that happened to me – wouldn't have happened.'

'But if they offered you a place, why did you think they hadn't?' Judith asked.

'I couldn't work it out. So I got in touch with them and they said that all offers of places were sent out by post. This was before the internet and mobile phones. And I never got the letter.'

'It was lost in the post?'

'No, they said they sent out their letters of acceptance by recorded delivery. Someone signed for that letter, so they knew it had arrived. When I never replied to them, they offered my place to someone else.'

'And you were living with Oliver at the time,' Judith said, understanding finally coming to her.

'You're right. It was Oliver who'd intercepted the letter and then didn't tell me I'd got a place. He was so jealous that he kept it a secret from me. But then, I remember that time so well. Our lives had got seriously rocky. He had all of these delusions of grandeur, you know? Telling me how he was going to be famous. How he was going to set the world alight. How people would still be talking about him in a hundred years' time. And I didn't help. When things were bad, I'd tell him he'd never be famous because he wasn't a good enough actor or director. But then, I was falling apart, and there wasn't much holding me together in the first place.'

'That doesn't excuse what he did,' Suzie said.

'I know. Which is why I went back to my book and ripped out every single mention of him. And I thought I could leave it at that. But I couldn't stop thinking about how that one act of his went on to destroy my life for so long. I lost my twenties. The prime of my life. All gone because of him.'

'I'm so sorry,' Becks said.

'How did you end up coming back to Marlow?' Suzie asked.

'A coincidence,' Lizzie said. 'Or a sign. You tell me? I got that letter out of the blue. The begging letter.'

'From Toby Vincent,' Judith said.

'It was full of news from the MADS, and how Oliver had been a big inspiration for him. And how he'd helped him apply to RADA. It seemed like fate that he'd write to me like that. I realised it was the perfect excuse. A reason to come back to Marlow and tell Oliver I knew what he'd done to me all of those years ago. I needed closure.

'Then, when I saw him again – on the boat – I struggled. I felt my legs go, just seeing him. He looked the same. I mean, he was older and fatter, but his spirit was the same. His bluster. And worst of all, I could see there was no remorse in him. He didn't regret what he'd done to me. He said as much to me when the boat set off that afternoon. He sidled up to me and said he still thought "fondly" of our time together. And that he had a surprise for me. I was to go to my cabin on the boat at 6 p.m. sharp.'

'He said that, did he?' Judith said, surprised.

'Don't worry, all will become clear.'

'You can explain the invitations? And why you didn't have one?'

'I've always been able to. But at the time, I didn't know what was about to happen. All I knew was I had to go to my cabin at 6 p.m. Which suited me fine, because I wanted to talk to him in private as well. You can imagine why.

'But first we had the party to get through. I tried to enjoy it, but it was hard. I had the coming confrontation with Oliver on my mind. But I've been in situations like that with the public for years. I can fake an interest in people as easily as breathe. As we got to 6 p.m., everyone seemed to slip off. I now know they had received those fake messages from me saying they should go to their cabins.

'I went to mine – like Oliver had asked me to – and he came in at six o'clock, sharp. He was hyper – wired – and then he pulled a gun on me, pushing it into my ribs. Before I even knew what he was doing, he clamped his hand over my mouth and said if I made a noise, he'd shoot me.'

'It was Oliver who brought the gun on the boat?' Suzie asked, amazed.

'Of course!' Judith said, finally understanding. 'I've been racking my brains trying to work out who'd come up with such a theatrical plan to commit murder, and we never considered the most theatrical person who was on the boat that night. The victim, Oliver Beresford. He was the author of this whole thing, wasn't he?'

'You're right,' Lizzie said, reliving the horror of what had happened to her. 'Oliver told me that ever since I'd said I was coming back, he'd been planning his final exit from the stage. He had terminal cancer, he said. It all came at me in a rush. It was only much later I was able to work out what happened in those next few minutes. But he said he'd had to watch me head off to the States and get all the fame that could have been his. That should have been his. After all he'd done for me. And then, when my book came out, I'd failed to mention him – not even once. And now I was going to pay the price. Because if I was too selfish to tell the world that it was him who'd made me the actor I was, he was going to make sure he went out in a blaze of glory.

'I was so confused – so scared – but he bundled me out of my room and took me to the back of the boat. I managed to blurt out that he was the one who'd wronged me – he'd destroyed my acceptance letter from RADA – but he laughed in my face, saying he'd not destroyed anything, and anyway this wasn't about me, this was about him.'

'He said it wasn't him who destroyed your letter?' Judith asked.

'He was manic, he wasn't listening to me. And it's like I said, my fear meant that everything was coming at me through a fog. I struggled to understand what was going on. But he said that his first real success as an actor for the MADS had been as the star of a murder mystery, and he'd make sure that his last performance was in a murder mystery as well. But it would be one that would echo down the years – the decades, he added. An impossible murder.'

'Of him?' Suzie asked.

'No – he said he was going to kill me. And that he'd spent weeks setting up everyone else on the boat so they'd be suspects. First, with a mystery note that I'd apparently sent to them all, including himself. So everyone would say they'd been in their cabins at six o'clock when I'd been shot. How could any of them have done it? And why would they kill me?'

'He then said he'd planted key evidence that would make it look as though each one of them could have been the killer. The pistol belonged to Duncan's uncle, he said. And he'd previously fired it holding a scarf that belonged to his wife, which he'd dropped in the river a few minutes before. And he'd also planted an unused bullet in Toby's cabin. As for the boat captain, he said that his drug-dealing would come out, if only because he'd made sure Mrs Eddingham overheard him threatening him in a pub. And he knew she'd spill the beans at the first opportunity – she hated him, he said. My death would be front-page news around the world, he told me. The biggest mystery death of a Hollywood celebrity since Natalie Wood, and that had been on a boat as well.

'He was babbling by this point, but he said that with me being shot when everyone had alibis – seeing as they were in their cabins – and with all the incriminating evidence that would then be found by the police, it would be impossible for a jury to come to a unanimous decision as to who the killer was. And the genius of his plan was that it didn't actually matter what the outcome was anyway. Even if – by some chance – it all went wrong and he was convicted of my murder, he'd still be dead from his cancer long before he ever went to prison. His last words to me were that, if he had to die, he was going to die famous.'

'His last words?' Judith asked.

Lizzie took one last drag on her cigarette and flicked the butt into the river before finally looking at the women.

'He only made one mistake. He didn't know this wasn't the first time I'd had someone pull a gun on me. You can't be into the sort of drugs that I was into without hanging out with dangerous people. So, even as he was telling me his story, I was waiting for his concentration to waver – even for a split second. And when it did, I jumped and managed to wrestle the gun from him.

'And then, time kind of messed up, I was throbbing with adrenaline – and looking at the guy who'd screwed up my life. And who thought he could now shoot me so he could live out some crazy death-wish fantasy. It wasn't a red mist that descended, it was like I was jolted with electricity. He backed away from me, I pulled the trigger and he dropped to the deck. But then he sprang to his feet and attacked me – it was terrifying. He was so much stronger than me – I knew I only had seconds before he got the gun from me and shot me dead – so I pulled the trigger a second time and this time he went down and stayed down.

'I felt this surge of power – against him, against all the men who had wronged me. I could see that if he wasn't dead, he soon would be – there was blood all over him – and I dropped the gun and just stood there. I couldn't believe what I'd done. But, thanks to Oliver, I knew everyone was in their cabins, so I made my decision. I heaved his body into the water. The boat was powering on, and I raced down to my cabin and closed the door behind myself as fast and as quietly as I could.

'And then, it all played out like a dream. I heard movement outside. Someone was heading to the deck at the back. I braced myself for a scream or something. I didn't know what I was expecting, but it wasn't the sound of a champagne cork popping.

I stuck my head out of my door and saw Verity pouring herself a glass of champagne. I went out and joined her, expecting her to see the blood on the deck, or to say she heard the gunshots – but it was like nothing had happened. She gave me a glass of champagne – although she did say something about me not going to see her in her cabin, which I didn't understand then, but do now. Before I could find out what she meant, Toby came up on deck and Verity gave him some champagne too. And they chatted to me about my work. Then the boat captain, Lance, came out, wanting to know if we were having a good time. It was . . . terrifying. Surreal.'

'What about the gun?' Judith asked. 'You said you dropped it on the deck.'

'It must have gone in the water when I pushed his body into the river. Half an hour later, we reached Marlow and the boat captain dropped us off. And that's it. I went back to my hotel and tried to work out what had happened. That night was almost worse than actually shooting Oliver. I was going mad with worry. I'd killed a man and no one had even noticed. And the more I thought about it, the more I realised that, since no one had seen me pull the trigger, maybe I'd got away with it.

'And I deserved to! It was kill or be killed – and for what? I hadn't done anything to deserve his anger. It was the other way round. He'd destroyed my life. It was self-defence, what I did, don't you see? He attacked me and I had to defend myself!'

The strength of Lizzie's words forced her up out of her seat, but as she stood, the women saw Tanika heading over to them through the trees with Brendan and two uniformed police officers.

'Elizabeth Jenkins?' Tanika said as she arrived. 'I'm arresting you for the murder of Oliver Beresford. You have the right to remain silent—'

'I know how this goes,' Lizzie said, all the fight going out of her. 'I've been in enough movies. And don't worry, I admit it. It's a relief. I killed Oliver Beresford. I'll make a full confession.'

Chapter 35

The news that Lizzie Jenkins had confessed to the murder of Oliver Beresford spread through Marlow like wildfire. When Judith went shopping in the supermarket, she could see that everyone was talking about it, and she kept herself to herself as she stocked up on a few bits and bobs for the performance that evening. She'd been told to go to the theatre for five thirty, and she knew there was no way she'd be able to get through the evening without a few snacks to keep her energy levels up. As she considered what to buy from the biscuits and crisps aisle, she found herself noting that there were still a few loose ends to the case that were niggling her. Even so, a confession was a confession. And when it matched what Lance had told them, there wasn't much left to say on the subject.

As for Becks, when she got home, she discovered that the arrest of Oliver's killer wasn't the only drama she was going to face that day. She found Chloe weeping in the kitchen, Colin at her side, comforting her.

'What's wrong?' Becks asked as she dropped her handbag and coat to the floor.

Chloe looked up at her mother, and as Becks went to her and wrapped her in her arms, she threw a puzzled look at her husband. He smiled wanly like he was totally out of his depth, which he was.

'It's Hugo,' Chloe sobbed.

Becks froze.

'What's he done to you?'

'Nothing – it's not like that. He's gone.'

'How do you mean?'

'He's buggered off,' Colin said.

'He's done a runner?' Becks asked, her confusion crystallising into fury.

Chloe nodded, her tears wet on her mother's shoulder.

'You were right,' Chloe said. 'I should have listened to you, this is all my fault.'

'No it isn't,' Colin said. 'There's only one person to blame in this, and it's not you.'

'I asked him about his second phone,' Chloe sniffed. 'I couldn't stop myself. Not after what you'd told me. And he got angry. Said I should trust him, or didn't I love him? I felt so bad. I thought it was all your fault.'

'When was this?' Becks asked.

'Yesterday. And then, today, I had to go out, and when I came back, he was gone. He'd packed up. There was a note saying that if I didn't trust him, it was all over.'

'It's not only that, is it?' Colin said. 'Tell your mum about the crowdfunder.'

'He's cleaned it out. Taken all the money.'

'*What?*' Becks said.

'It was nearly eight thousand pounds.'

'Half that money belonged to you.'

'More than half,' Colin said. 'Most of that money came from the parish – the thief.'

'I should have listened to you,' Chloe sobbed into her mother's shoulder.

'I didn't know for sure he was untrustworthy,' Becks said, knowing that that's precisely what she'd believed. 'I just wasn't sure he had your best interests at heart.'

'But you could see it and I couldn't.'

'I've been around the block a few times,' she said with a world-weary smile at her husband. 'Experience gives you a bit of perspective.'

Colin got up and went over to the hob.

'Don't worry, you're not the only one he conned,' he said as he fished out a milk pan. 'I was as taken in by him as you. Now, how about a hot chocolate? The sugar will do you good.'

'I dropped out of uni for him,' Chloe said.

'I know it feels a bit overwhelming right now,' Colin said, 'but today's not the day for recriminations. Or thinking about the future – or what this all means. You need to look after yourself. Make sure you remember how great you are, and how you're better off without him. Besides, you've only missed a few weeks, I bet the university will take you back next term. And if they don't, then I'm sure they'll let you defer. You can spend the rest of the year travelling – if that's what you want to do – and then go back to uni next year. Whatever you want, I bet you'll be able to do it. Your mum and I will be here to support you. And maybe it's a bullet dodged. Better to find out he's capable of betraying you now than when you're halfway around the world.'

'I thought he was the one.'

'How brilliant that you go into relationships with such generosity. In time you'll meet the person who matches your love, and that person will deserve to be "the one" for you.'

Becks didn't quite know where this version of Colin had been hiding for the last however many years, but then her eyes were drawn to the gas ring that the milk pan was sitting on.

'You'll scald the milk,' she said, heading to the hob.

'I've put it on low,' Colin said.

'But it's on the wrong ring, the lowest setting of this one is still too hot. Here, let me do it,' she added, putting the pan onto a smaller gas ring and firing it up. Colin moved over to sit with his daughter.

'I want a relationship like yours,' Chloe said, wiping tears from her cheek.

'You do?' Becks said, not entirely sure she'd heard correctly.

'And you will,' Colin said. 'I promise you, you will.'

As Becks stirred the hot milk in the pan, Colin comforting their daughter, she was overcome with a feeling of warmth – towards her daughter, her home – and yes, even to Colin. And then she felt a sharp stab of guilt, knowing she'd inadvertently caused her daughter's pain. Even so, she told herself, Chloe was better off without Hugo in her life. She'd get over this, even if it was a bitter lesson to learn.

Once she'd had her hot chocolate, Chloe went into the front room to watch TV under a duvet, which allowed Becks and Colin just enough time to get ready for Judith's theatrical debut with the MADS. And while they both felt bad about leaving their daughter in her hour of need, Chloe insisted that all she wanted to do was sit about and eat crisps. They both knew that feeling.

They held hands as they walked to the Little Theatre. And when they arrived, they were thrilled to see dozens of people already chatting and milling about outside the entrance. There was a real buzz of excitement. But they were surprised to see Judith standing outside the theatre as well.

'What are you doing out here?' Becks asked.

'Oh – sorry,' Judith said. 'Thought I'd get some fresh air.'

'Aren't you supposed to be backstage?' Colin asked.

'I'm not on until Act Two,' Judith said.

'Judith Potts,' Becks asked with a smile, 'are you nervous?'

'Me? Never! Of course not.'

'This is wonderful! You've stood up to murderers, but you can't stand up in front of an audience.'

'You're right – when you put it like that. I just have to pull myself together, don't I? Thank you.'

'The show will be brilliant, Judith,' Colin said. 'And you'll be its star.'

'I don't think that will be the case, but thank you for saying so. Where's Chloe? I was hoping to meet the famous Hugo.'

'Ah, there's been a hitch on that front,' Colin said, and then explained how Hugo had done a runner and cleared out all the money in his and Chloe's crowdfunder account.

'Isn't that theft?' Judith asked.

'I'd say so,' Colin said. 'And I blame myself. He seemed so nice and well brought up, I didn't bother looking at him properly. I shouldn't have taken him at face value and instead probed his character. And his background. And history. But then, not all of us can have the sleuthing instincts of my wife.'

'I'm not sure I'm proud of being so suspicious of him,' Becks said ruefully. 'Anyway, we can't stay out here, Judith, we've got tickets to the hottest theatrical debut the town has seen in decades.'

'Don't put it like that!' Judith said and stamped her feet to gee herself up. 'But you're right. I catch killers, I can stand on a stage.'

Judith headed towards the open fire doors at the back of the building. Becks and Colin went in through the front and were met by a woman in a light blue sash who checked their tickets and let them into the auditorium. In among the thrum of people getting drinks from the trestle table at the back, Becks and Colin could see Suzie holding two glasses of red wine. They approached.

'You don't have any drinks,' Suzie said. 'Here have mine, I'll get some more,' she added, handing over her two glasses to her friends and heading back to the table.

Becks could see Verity hovering at the back of the hall with a notebook in her hand. And on a raised dais behind her, Duncan was checking all the cables going into and out of the lighting and sound desks.

Suzie returned with another two glasses of wine.

'I've still got mine,' Becks said.

'These are for me,' Suzie said, before taking a slurp from one of the glasses. 'Come on, we need to sit down, it's going to start soon.'

★

As Suzie, Becks, Colin and the audience started to take their seats, backstage the cast were wound up with excitement and Judith was struggling to control her nerves. To take her mind off what was about to happen, she thought about Hugo's betrayal of Chloe. Judith knew well that under even the glossiest of exteriors, skulduggery could lurk. She found herself twisting the wedding ring on her left hand as her thoughts began to slip into the past, and the truism that if you married in haste you repented at leisure. Not that that had quite been the story of Judith and her husband.

Despite the heat backstage, a chill ran down Judith's spine. The story of Chloe and Hugo had got to her, she could feel it. So she made the conscious decision to let go of her wedding ring and instead watch the action on the stage. And, as she did so, she realised that the play had started and her fellow actors were already full of confidence and getting lots of laughs from the audience.

Most revelatory of all was Mrs Eddingham as Lady Bracknell. It was true that she didn't entirely seem to know what she was doing, or where she was going, but she picked up on her cues, dominated the stage, and was able to bring the house down with a raised eyebrow. Judith was delighted to discover that all Mrs Eddingham's grandstanding had indeed been based on her being a very good actor.

At the end of Act One, Judith went to have a quick word with the star of the show.

'You're amazing,' she said.

'None of us are amazing until we get to the end of Act Three,' Mrs Eddingham said. 'But I can't wait for our scene, Judith,' she added with a smile. 'I think you'll be wonderful tonight.'

Judith didn't quite share Mrs Eddingham's faith, but she knew that she had no choice but to try her best. In Act Two, she stepped out into the lights and briefly froze before heading downstage to where she needed to stand for the scene. It helped that her character was supposed to be prim and proper, so Judith knew that she didn't have to do much more than move when she was supposed to move and say her lines when it was her turn. It was up to the others on the stage to drive the scene forward. After a while, she even managed to relax enough to watch Toby's performance dispassionately. To her eyes, his acting still seemed as charismatic as ever, but she had to accept that she didn't know anything about stage acting, and perhaps Mrs Eddingham and Rob Hooker were right when they said he wasn't – after all – very good.

By the time of the second interval, Judith realised that she was having more fun than she'd had for years. She also knew that she'd never perform again. It was already obvious to her that she'd find the week of performances exhausting. It just wasn't in her nature to parade herself in front of an audience like this. Amateur dramatics, she decided, was a bit like cycling a tandem bike. It was a lot of fun, but there was no need to do it twice.

Feeling more and more confident in everyone's performances, Judith was able to enjoy her scenes in the third act even more. It was so strange that she was catching killers in the morning and performing in the evening. She even found her thoughts turning to the caddish Hugo again. And thinking of him led her to the briefest flicker of hesitancy regarding Lizzie's story of how she killed Oliver, but Judith let her thoughts flutter and die. After all, she told herself for the hundredth time, Lizzie had confessed to shooting Oliver dead and Lance had witnessed her do it, that was the beginning and end of the matter.

But there was something that kept drawing her thoughts back to Hugo. As Judith tried to work out why, she became vaguely aware that Mrs Eddingham was looking at her, and she had a sudden realisation that she'd just been asked a question. She snapped out of her reverie, but luckily the audience thought it was all part of the act and laughed warmly at Miss Prism's inattentiveness.

Judith spoke the next line of the play and tried to relax as the scene progressed, but the jolt of adrenaline she'd received when she realised she'd dropped her cue was now coursing through her and she couldn't stop herself from feeling agitated. And the knowledge that Chloe hadn't considered that Hugo was a wrong 'un was driving the sense of panic she was feeling. In fact, she was almost disassociating from herself as she stood on the stage. She seemed to be both performing her scene and flying off on darting runs in her mind at the same time. She could see that Mrs Eddingham was looking at her with increasing concern as she lost herself in her thoughts – but, like a swallow coming back again and again to dip at a pond for a drink, she kept flitting back to Lizzie's confession. What was it about it that was troubling her?

'Prism!' Mrs Eddingham-as-Lady-Bracknell barked from across the stage, and Judith snapped her attention back to the people in front of her. 'Where is that baby?'

'Lady Bracknell,' Judith-as-Miss-Prism said, 'I admit with shame that I do not know. I only wish I did. The plain facts of the case are these. On the morning of the day you mention, a day that is forever branded on my memory, I prepared as usual to take the baby out in its perambulator. I had also with me a somewhat old, but capacious handbag in which I had intended to place the manuscript of a work of fiction that I had written during my few unoccupied hours. In a moment of mental abstraction, for which I never can forgive myself,

I deposited the manuscript in the bassinet, and placed the baby in the . . .'

Judith trailed off rather than say the last word of her speech – 'handbag' – and Mrs Eddingham-as-Lady-Bracknell looked at her in confusion.

'What's that, Miss Prism?' she said in her most authoritarian voice.

But it was too late. Judith was no longer Miss Prism – she was barely Judith, in truth – she was the single thought that Miss Prism had done things in the wrong order. The baby should have been put in the bassinet and then the manuscript put in the handbag – but *Miss Prism had done those two things the wrong way round*, and that's when the flickering thought she'd been chasing caught fire.

'Bugger me!' Judith said.

'Miss Prism!' Mrs Eddingham exclaimed.

'I put them in in the wrong order,' Judith said, either as Miss Prism or as Judith, no one knew, least of all herself. 'It should have gone baby then manuscript, but it went manuscript then baby.'

'Miss Prism, what on earth are you talking about?' Mrs Eddingham said, desperately communicating to Judith with her eyes that she needed to get back to the script. 'Where did you put the baby?'

'Sorry, sorry,' Judith said distractedly as she considered the logic of what she'd just realised.

'Did you, in fact, put the baby in a handba—'

'Lance?' Judith called out, interrupting Mrs Eddingham.

'Miss Prism!' Mrs Eddingham all but shrieked.

'Sorry, Lady Bracknell,' Judith said as she turned to look at the audience, 'is Lance Goodman here?'

There were murmurings in the audience as everyone realised that Judith had derailed the performance. From her position at the back of the auditorium, Verity rose from her seat, but Judith didn't much care what Verity thought. Before she could speak, a woman called out, 'He's at the back.'

The woman was Suzie.

Judith smiled to herself as she realised that Suzie had noticed Lance's position in the house.

'Lance,' Judith said, 'please stand up and make yourself known.'

There was a scrape of a chair and a figure rose to his feet.

'You want to do this now?' Lance said, irritated.

'Are you sure you saw Lizzie shoot Oliver twice?'

'What is this?'

'Not three times? Not one time, but two times?'

'If it gets the play back on track, then yes I am. I saw Lizzie shoot him twice.'

The audience were now spellbound as they watched the conversation between Judith and Lance like spectators at a tennis match.

'Then I need to speak to Verity, Duncan and Toby.'

Judith looked about herself and saw Toby hovering in the wings. 'Ah, perfect!' she exclaimed. 'Toby, were you very definitely in your cabin at 6 p.m. when Oliver was killed?'

'I've told you,' Toby said, deeply embarrassed.

'And you, Verity? Duncan?'

'We both got the same message,' Duncan called out from the back of the auditorium. 'You know that's where we were.'

'Verity?'

'Yes,' she snapped, furious that Judith was ruining the performance.

'Someone should call the police,' Mrs Eddingham said.

'No need,' a female voice said from the middle of the audi-torium, and Tanika stood up. 'I'm already here. Detective Inspector Malik,' she added, by way of explanation. 'What is it, Judith?'

'I've got one last question,' Judith said. 'Did anyone who was on the *Marlow Belle* see Duncan's pistol on the deck at the back of the boat when you returned from your cabins after six o'clock?'

None of the witnesses said anything.

'This is crucially important,' Judith said. 'Lizzie Jenkins said she dropped the gun after shooting Oliver. Verity, you were first one out after 6 p.m., weren't you?'

'Very well,' Verity said, 'since you're asking, I didn't see a gun. But I can't say I was looking.'

'Duncan? Toby?'

'No,' Duncan called out from the back of the auditorium, and Judith could see Toby shaking his head in the wings.

'What did Toby say?' a woman's voice from the audience called out. 'We can't see him.'

'He shook his head no,' Judith offered.

'Thanks,' the voice replied.

'But was that true of you, Lance? Are you telling me you didn't see a gun when you went to the back deck after Oliver had been shot?'

'I didn't see any gun,' Lance said. 'And I was looking for one.'

Judith looked about herself, at the actors on the stage – trying to ignore the furious Mrs Eddingham – and then she looked down at the great and good of Marlow who had come to the opening night. As much as she was sorry that she'd interrupted everyone's evening, she now knew that she'd had no choice.

Despite her confession, Lizzie Jenkins hadn't killed Oliver Beresford. It had been someone else. And they were in the room with Judith right now.

It was time to reveal who the killer was.

Chapter 36

There was one problem. While Judith believed she'd identified Oliver's killer, as she stood on the stage under the lights with what felt like the whole town of Marlow looking at her, she couldn't work out what their motive had been. Which was a bit awkward. It was one thing to stop a performance to reveal a killer, but she couldn't very well do this if she couldn't explain why that person had pulled the trigger. After all, it made so much apparent sense that Lizzie had done it. The moment Oliver tore up Lizzie's letter of acceptance from RADA, he'd destroyed her life so thoroughly that it was understandable she'd want him dead all these years later. Although, Judith found herself remembering, it was odd that when Lizzie had confronted him about it on the *Marlow Belle*, he'd said that it hadn't been him who'd destroyed her acceptance letter.

'Are you all right there, Judith?' Becks called out from the audience, and Judith realised she'd been standing in silence for quite a long time.

'Hold on, nearly there,' Judith said to buy herself a few more seconds, but she realised that the answer wasn't going to come to her. And in the act of letting go, the truth slotted into place for her as satisfyingly as popping the lid onto a tin of travel sweets.

'Ha!' Judith said to herself, almost in wonder. It was so obvious, she realised, when you thought through the logic of it. She'd been right to think about how Chloe hadn't looked properly at the character of Hugo. And she'd been right to think about the letter of acceptance from RADA.

'I must insist you carry on with the play or vacate the stage,' Mrs Eddingham said with all the authority of her part.

Judith looked at Mrs Eddingham and realised that the older woman had no idea that she was about to reveal the true identity of the killer. Judith walked towards her.

'Don't you want to know who shot Oliver Beresford?' she asked.

'Of course not! I want to finish the play,' Mrs Eddingham said in rising panic.

'Then all I can say is I'm sorry, because it's time for the game to stop.'

'What game?'

'Indeed. What game?'

Judith turned from Mrs Eddingham and strode down to the front of the stage, pinning a woman who was sitting in the front row with her stare.

'Isn't that right, Rebecca Lewis?'

Rebecca Lewis, the ex-teacher and amateur painter, stared up at Judith from her position in the front row like a rabbit caught in the headlights.

'It was you who killed Oliver Beresford.'

There was a gasp from the audience as they realised that the drama they were witnessing was significantly more compelling than the comedy of manners they thought they'd be watching.

Rebecca pointed to herself, unable to believe what she'd just heard.

'W-what?' she stammered.

'You murdered Oliver Beresford,' Judith said, grateful that Rebecca had told them when they'd spoken that she always attended the opening night of every MADS production.

'No she didn't,' a voice called out from the darkness, and Lance stood up. 'I saw Lizzie shoot him. Twice.'

'I don't dispute that she shot him,' Judith called back, 'but consider this. Just because she fired two bullets, how do we know they found their target? Any more than Miss Prism's baby found its target of the bassinet? You see, Detective Inspector Malik told me that Oliver had been shot twice, and that the first bullet had been fired from close range into the stomach. It was the second shot, fired into his heart, that killed him. And that was fired from a little way away.'

'How can you know that?' a male voice called from the audience.

'It's to do with the distribution of gunshot residue on the victim's clothes,' Tanika said from her position in the auditorium, and there was a little 'ooh' of appreciation from the audience. 'And the absence of any scorching to the entrance wound. Judith's right, the first shot into Mr Beresford was into his side from point-blank range. The second bullet – the one that killed him – was fired from a distance of a few feet away. Possibly further.'

'And there you have it!' Judith said, having no problem with taking centre stage now she had a murder to solve. 'The first shot was fired from near and the second shot was from far. But when Lance told us about what he'd thought was the murder, he said that the first shot was fired by Lizzie from a little distance away and Oliver dropped to the deck before springing back up and grappling with her. At which point she shot him a second time, *from close range.*

'At the time, I didn't think much of it. After all, in all the shock of what he'd seen, it hardly seemed surprising that Lance had misremembered the exact order of events that night. But the thing is, when Lizzie confessed to the murder and told us what had happened, she corroborated what Lance said. She said she first shot Oliver from a few feet away. He dropped to the floor, as Lance also told us. He then leapt up and attacked Lizzie, and it was only then that she delivered the *coup de grâce* of a bullet from up close, at which point he dropped to the deck for the last time.

'I'm not sure I'd have quite worked it out until I was delivering the speech as Miss Prism, where a mix-up of a manuscript being put in a pram while a baby was put in a handbag led me to think, what if that first bullet had gone to a different place. In other words, it didn't go into the stomach? What, in fact, would have happened if it had missed altogether? Because if that first shot missed, then suddenly all of the stories that night – from the witnesses to the pathologist's report – finally concur. After all, it always struck me as slightly odd that Oliver, after being shot in the stomach, attacked Lizzie. I can't help feeling that if I were shot in the stomach, I'd drop to the floor and then stay there. So, let me tell you what happened that night. It was always Oliver's plan to murder Lizzie Jenkins.'

'No!' Verity said from the back of the auditorium.

'I'm sorry, Verity, but it's true. He knew his cancer was going to take him anyway, and he'd decided to go out in a blaze of glory. To finally get the fame he'd felt he'd deserved his whole life and never achieved. He was going to be part of a murder case that would baffle and amaze for decades to come. Or, that was the idea, because his greatest character flaw – wanting to be the centre of attention – was also why his plan didn't work. Rather than shoot Lizzie straight away, he had to tell her what he was doing. Which gave Lizzie the few seconds she needed to gather herself and then choose her moment to wrestle the gun from him.

'Then, what happened next? Well, of course, we don't quite know for sure, but we do have both Lizzie's and Lance's testimony that the next few seconds ended with Lizzie firing the gun for the first time at Oliver from a bit of a distance. But, as the detective inspector has confirmed, the pathologist's report said that the first bullet that went into Oliver was fired from point-blank range. Therefore, *the first bullet that Lizzie fired must have missed him altogether.* Where it ended up, we'll never know. Perhaps it went straight into the river. Or off into a field. But Oliver dropped to the deck in fear – which was an entirely understandable response considering someone had just shot at him, even if the bullet had missed. Then, as soon as he realised he hadn't been wounded, he jumped up and attacked Lizzie to try and get hold of the pistol, which was when she shot him from close range – the second bullet that was fired that night, *but the first bullet that hit him.* And, as the pathologist later reported, this bullet went into Oliver's side. Which explains the evidence on the *Marlow Belle* when the police worked the scene the following day. Oliver's blood was spattered on the deck, and two bullet casings were found.

'But let's go back to the seconds after Lizzie had fired her second bullet. Exactly what happened next will be hard to prove with Oliver no longer here to tell us, but I think we can guess the gist of it. While Oliver bled out, Lizzie had to make a decision. Confess to what she'd done – that she'd shot Oliver in self-defence

– or try to get away with it. And Oliver was lying on the deck, inches above the water. I can see why she made a snap decision to tip him in. I don't approve, of course, but I understand why she might have done it. He'd tried to murder her. It was, to her mind, the least he deserved. The only thing she didn't know was that she'd shot Oliver in the side of his torso, rather than killed him outright.

'But, unbeknownst to her, he grabbed the pistol as he went over the side. It was the logical thing to do. Despite the excruciating pain he must have been in, he knew that the gun was the evidence that Lizzie had just shot him. It was covered in her fingerprints. She would go to prison for his attempted murder, so he grabbed it and made sure he kept hold of it as he was pushed into the Thames.

'But let's also remember that the boat was returning to Marlow against the current. Once he was in the water, Oliver would have been swept away. Did he pretend he was already dead? Or thrash about trying to save himself? Lizzie will be able to tell us in due course, but either way, she knew he wouldn't be alive for long. Not in the middle of a river with two bullets in him – as she thought.

'Don't get me wrong – he'd have been bleeding badly, but he was alive as the current bore him back towards Cookham. DS Malik told us that no water was found in his lungs and it was therefore her belief that he was dead before he went into the water. However, we can now presume that no water was found in his lungs *because he was alive as he hit the water* and he simply kept his mouth closed.

'Which is where you come in, Rebecca. You see, you were the only person who was nearby. And you were painting on that little beach at the bend in the river. So let's play this through, shall we? Because Oliver was still alive when he went into the water, and he was still alive when he arrived at the beach where you were painting. Which is when you took the gun from him and shot him dead from the distance of a few feet. This was the third bullet that was fired that night, but only the second that entered his body. The killing shot that pierced his heart and meant he was dead even before he hit the ground.'

A man cleared his throat in the audience to get everyone's attention and said in a nasal voice, 'I think you'll find it's not possible to fire a pistol after it's been submerged in water.'

'The pistol in question was a Bersa Thunder 9 issued to the Argentinian army – they're waterproof. Do try not to interrupt,' Judith said.

There was a smattering of applause and a gentle murmur of approval at Judith's put-down, which allowed her to return her attention to Rebecca.

'Then, having killed him, it couldn't have been simpler. Oliver was already at the water's edge. You pushed him back into the Thames and let the current bear him off again, knowing his body would wind up somewhere further downstream. As for the pistol, that was just as easy to dispose of. You packed up your painting things and took the gun with you as you walked back to Marlow. When you'd got enough distance between you and where you'd killed Oliver, you threw the gun into the middle of the river. You thought the gun would never be found and, if it ever was, any fingerprints and DNA on it would have long since been washed away.'

'Why are you telling these lies about me?' Rebecca said, as much to the people next to her in the audience as to Judith.

'Because they're not lies. And it's deeply ironic for poor old Oliver, because he'd gone to so much effort to create a grand tableau. The sensational murder of the Hollywood star, Lizzie Jenkins! Which finally explains why the police found one of the invitations from Lizzie Jenkins in Oliver's pocket after he died. He was going to murder Lizzie and then quickly slip into his cabin so that he – like Verity, Duncan and Toby – would have the same alibi that seemed to put them all in the clear. They were told to go to their cabins by Lizzie Jenkins for 6 p.m., so they all had to be innocent, didn't they?

'But he had also ensured there was evidence that separately implicated everyone on the boat – thus raising the additional possibility that they had all been in on it together. It was going to be the crowning production of his life. But the whole thing fell apart when Lizzie wrestled the gun from him. Instead of him shooting her, she shot him. And then he didn't even die at her hand – which would at least have been a sensational ending for him. Instead, he drifted downriver, wounded but not fatally so, where he was finally killed by a retired science teacher. And not as part of any grand plan, either. It was totally unplanned, a spur-of-the-moment decision.

'Because you didn't set out to commit murder that day, did you?' Judith said directly to Rebecca. 'How could you? You couldn't possibly have known that Oliver was going to try and shoot Lizzie on the back of a pleasure boat that afternoon.

'And here I must apologise to the people who were on the *Marlow Belle* that night. I was so sure that the murder must have happened on the boat that I overlooked the woman who'd been nearby that night. Rebecca was so obviously an upstanding member of the community, why should I have been suspicious of her? Just as my good friend Becks had no reason to be suspicious of her daughter's upstanding boyfriend. But the sad truth is, you can't trust anyone.'

'So why did she kill him?' a voice called out from the audience.

'Shh!' a few other voices hissed.

'No, it's a good question,' Judith conceded. 'And one that made no sense to me until just now. You see, it was one thing to work out that Rebecca had to have been the killer. But you're right – *why?* That was the question. So I tried to remember everything Rebecca told us on the one occasion we met her, on the night of the Art Trail. And I have to confess there was nothing she said that remotely suggested she could have had a reason to want to kill anyone, let alone Oliver Beresford. Or so I thought. You see, Lizzie's not been in Marlow since she was a teenager, and she was only here for one day before Oliver died, so it always felt that the answer must lie in her past. Which was when I remembered that Rebecca had a well-thumbed copy of Lizzie's autobiography – along with lots of other magazines where Lizzie featured as a main story – which I only now realise was a bit odd. After all, Rebecca told us she'd only become interested in Lizzie since the murder of Oliver. But if that was the case, why was her copy of the autobiography so well read? Why did all her magazines go back so far? And why did she immediately tidy them away when we started asking questions? So I began to wonder if Rebecca might have known Lizzie before she left for the States.

'But I didn't see how that could be the case. Rebecca taught at the wrong school. However, she made one slip of the tongue. She said that she was the daughter of a vicar and that she'd always "helped the young" before she became a teacher. Which reminded me that Lizzie had told us there was a youth leader at the Marlow Youth Club whose life she'd made a living hell when she'd gone there as a teenager. Which is a good opportunity to ask – Joshua Smith, are you here?' Judith said, putting her hand to her forehead so she could shield some of the light from her eyes.

There was the sound of a chair scraping back and an older man in a cardigan towards the back of the auditorium stood up.

'I am,' he said.

'Lovely. How's your injury?'

'Much better, thank you, but I don't imagine that's why you want to speak to me.'

'No, I wanted to know if you'd found any of the youth club's historical records and brought them to the performance tonight?'

'As it happens, I have, and I did.'

'Then lead me to them,' Suzie said, getting up and pushing along her row to get out. 'You can give them to me.'

'Good idea,' Judith said as Suzie and Joshua left the auditorium together. 'We could do with some corroboration. Now, where was I?' Judith asked.

'You were telling us why that woman killed Oliver,' a man called out.

'She was being rhetorical, Roger,' a woman said.

'Sorry, Sue.'

'And now we come to the key event in the past,' Judith said, ignoring both Roger and Sue. 'That was so wicked that the ripples of it could still lead to murder all these decades later. The fact is, after Lizzie was thrown out of her home by her mum, a youth leader welcomed her to the Marlow Youth Club. But Lizzie told us this person *also suggested she use it as her postal address* so she could sort out her schooling options. Which is where we – in the present day – made a terrible mistake, Lizzie included. We knew that RADA sent her the letter telling her that she'd got a place to study with them. And we know it arrived, because it was sent recorded delivery. But we presumed that it was sent to Oliver's address, as that's where Lizzie was living at the time. But back then, Lizzie's life was chaotic, and it would have been perfectly in character for her not to have changed her postal address to Oliver's house. Which meant that when her letter arrived, it didn't go to Oliver's house, it went to the youth club. Didn't it, Rebecca?'

Rebecca was looking straight up at Judith as though she was looking at a ghost.

'When it arrived, you saw that it was addressed to Lizzie and had the RADA logo on it. With that letter, you knew you held Lizzie's future in your hands. Quite literally. This young teenager who had made your life a living hell and who'd bulled you mercilessly. You made a snap decision. You binned the letter. To your mind, it was what she deserved, even if it was petty.

'When did you start regretting what you'd done? Not immediately, of course – you didn't know how that one change in Lizzie's life would affect her. Before long she'd left Marlow, so I don't imagine you thought of her again for a long time. But when she started making it as an actress in Hollywood, you must have realised that this was the same Lizzie Jenkins whose letter of acceptance you'd torn up. Perhaps you felt relieved to see that she'd succeeded as an actor after all. Or maybe you'd already started to feel guilty for what you'd done to her.

'If I were to guess, it was only when Lizzie published her autobiography that you finally understood the pain you'd caused her. The years of abuse that followed. The drug addiction. You realised that you were to blame for all of it. Which is why your copy of her autobiography had been read over and over. When did you first know that Lizzie was back in Marlow?'

'I don't have to answer that question,' Rebecca said.

'Very well. You told us you'd not seen the *Marlow Belle* go out that afternoon as you started to get your painting things together on the riverbank. But I think that's a lie. I think you saw the boat go out, and you saw Lizzie Jenkins drinking champagne with the others on the deck at the back.'

Rebecca didn't say anything, but Judith noticed the tiniest shift in her chin that felt like the beginnings of a nod.

'It must have been such a shock, seeing her back in Marlow. And as you started painting the scene, I think your mind went back to the wrong you'd done to her all those years ago. The suffering you'd caused. The damage. That's why you waited until the boat returned so you could put it into the painting. It was your attempt – subconscious, perhaps – to acknowledge your connection to Lizzie. But as the *Marlow Belle* passed in front of you, there was no sign of Lizzie on the back of the boat. There was just Oliver in the cabin at the front asking Lance to speed up because he'd seen you painting on the riverbank.

'As the boat went around the corner and disappeared from view, did you see Lizzie and Oliver come onto the back of the boat? Did you even see her shoot him? Or was the first time you knew something was up when you heard two gunshots and then saw a body being swept towards you on the current? I can't imagine Oliver was in good shape with a bullet in his side. Maybe he even saw you in the gloom and headed towards you, thinking you'd save him? That would make sense. But then we come to the crisis point. One way or another, Oliver came ashore – in terrible pain I imagine, and terrified – but he'd have had a single purpose, which would have been to tell the first person he saw that Lizzie had just tried to murder him, had dumped him for dead in the river, and that her fingerprints were all over the gun in his hand. He had to make sure she'd go to prison for attempted murder.

'But Oliver didn't know how you'd spent the last few months torturing yourself for the wrong you'd done Lizzie all those years ago. And in this moment, as Oliver stood in front of you, I think you thought that this was fate finally offering you a chance at redemption. If you'd destroyed Lizzie's life in the past, this was your chance to save it in the present. Whether Oliver gave you the gun for safekeeping, or whether you ripped it from his hands, I don't know, but you took a couple of steps back, raised it and fired it – the bullet going straight into his heart.

'This was the third shot that was fired that night, but only the second that went into Oliver's body. And no one was around to hear it apart from you and Oliver. It was the last sound he heard.'

Judith saw tears in Rebecca's eyes, but she had to remind herself that it didn't matter what the circumstances were, wrong was wrong. It's why she still wore her wedding ring after all these years. She knew you carry the decisions you make for the rest of your life.

As Judith had been talking, Becks had come to the front of the auditorium and now stepped into Rebecca's eyeline.

'I'm so sorry,' Rebecca said, seeing Becks.

'You know you'll have to make a confession,' Becks said. 'Because if you don't, Lizzie will go to prison for a crime she didn't commit. You'll have wronged her a second time.'

The doors at the back of the auditorium burst open and Suzie ran in holding some old ledgers in her hands. The audience gasped at the interruption, but were soon clucking with excitement when they saw who it was. Joshua followed a little more calmly behind her.

'We've got them,' Suzie said, trying to catch her breath as she handed the ledgers up to Judith on the stage. 'Joshua's got all the old records from the Marlow Youth Club. These cover the 1980s and 1990s – all the kids who were signed in and out, and the youth leaders who were present each time.'

'Do we even need to look?' Judith asked Rebecca.

'No,' Rebecca said in a barely audible whisper. 'My name will be there. With Lizzie Jenkins'. It's true. Everything you've said. It's what happened. When Oliver came out of the river, it felt like divine intervention. I could right a wrong I'd committed in the past. All I had to do was pull the trigger . . .'

Tanika approached.

'Rebecca Lewis?' she said.

Rebecca looked at Tanika and nodded her head. She understood what had to happen next.

'Will you come quietly?'

Rebecca started sobbing. Tanika put her arm around her shoulders and helped her out of the auditorium. The entire audience watched her go, rapt.

Once she'd gone, no one knew how to break the silence. No one, that is, apart from one person.

'Can we *please* finish my scene now?' Mrs Eddingham asked.

Chapter 37

To the consternation of Mrs Eddingham, the audience burst into excited chatter, Duncan turned the house lights on, and the performance was abandoned. As for Judith, piecing together the story of what had happened on the day Oliver was murdered had left her feeling utterly exhausted.

'I don't know how you do it,' Suzie said, proud as a mother hen, as Judith joined her friends in the auditorium a few minutes later.

'It was just a matter of following the logic of the situation through.'

'Poor Rebecca Lewis,' Becks said.

'Poor Oliver Beresford,' Judith said, to remind her friend where the guilt in the case lay.

'No, of course.'

Verity came over, a little unsure.

'Thank you,' she said to Judith. 'He really planned the whole thing like that?'

'He really planned the whole thing like that.'

'And it ended with him getting killed by someone he'd never met before – and a retired teacher at that. The story – and headlines – will all be about how Rebecca Lewis killed him for Lizzie Jenkins' sake, won't they? Oliver's just a bit player.'

As she spoke, it was hard to tell whether or not Verity was pleased with this state of affairs, but Judith reminded herself what a good actor she was, and guessed that Verity was secretly thrilled that Oliver had been thwarted at the last minute.

Duncan came over and nodded in appreciation.

'Good work,' he said, like a king bestowing praise on a favoured courtier.

'I think you can do better than that,' Judith said.

'All right,' he said with a reluctant smile. 'That was pretty impressive.'

Duncan turned to go, but Becks said, 'Are you going to be OK?'

'You mean . . . my health?'

'As time goes on, if there's anything I can do to help, just ask. There's a whole support network available to you through the church if you want it.'

Duncan nodded in thanks and turned and left.

Judith saw Toby being mobbed by half a dozen women, none of them under the age of seventy. His performance as the Reverend Chasuble had clearly delighted them, but he caught Judith's eye and gave her a warm smile. He then held her gaze for a short while longer before turning back to his adoring fans. In those few seconds, Judith saw an acceptance in Toby that he would only ever be an amateur dramatic performer, and he was going to be happy with that. She was pleased for him.

Judith was surprised to see Suzie frowning.

'What's the problem?'

'I was wrong, wasn't I?' Suzie said. 'I was convinced your life was in danger, but it wasn't, was it?'

'More than that,' Becks said, 'Lizzie wasn't the killer after all.'

'Meaning you promised you'd not talk about tarot cards ever again,' Judith said.

'That's what I don't understand,' Suzie said. 'They've never let me down before. There's always a moment when you realise the cards were telling the truth all along. But with Rebecca arrested, it's over, and there never was any real threat you had to face.'

'So you agree the cards weren't telling the future?'

Suzie sighed.

'Very well,' she said. 'I admit it. The cards didn't tell the future. There never was any kind of threat to your life.'

★

As the crowd drifted off, Judith knew that she should go to the Maidenhead Police Station. She'd no doubt have to give a statement. But her heart wasn't quite in it. She just wanted to go home, crawl into bed and turn off the lights. Tomorrow could wait until tomorrow as far as she was concerned.

So she bade goodnight to Becks and Suzie, got on her bike and cycled through the late-night streets of Marlow. It had rained while she'd been in the theatre and the streets were washed clean in the moonlight, a few people spilling out of the Butcher's Tap as she passed. As she whizzed across the bridge, she had a good look at the roaring weir and decided that life was pretty good. By the time she'd turned onto Ferry Lane and cycled the remaining distance to her house, she was feeling almost upbeat. She would make herself a nice cup of Horlicks and take it to bed. Even the thought of the drink made her smile as she got off her bike. It was a favourite of her great-aunt, the woman who'd originally owned her house, and it always reminded Judith of the summers she'd spent with her.

Even so, Judith closed the front door behind herself and made sure she locked it carefully. She couldn't tell if her tiredness was making her anxious, but she had an instinct that she needed to be safe inside her house.

As she hung up her coat next to her grey cape, Judith smiled. She was almost getting as paranoid as Suzie. She'd start believing in tarot next.

She went into her sitting room and got on her knees in front of the fireplace. Blowing on the ash, she saw there were still glowing embers from the afternoon's fire, so she threw on a few more logs, knowing they'd catch soon enough. She then went through to the kitchen and clicked her kettle on. As she waited for it to boil, she got out two slices of bread, buttered them and then slathered on some jam. She got down her jar of Horlicks and put two heaped teaspoons in a mug.

A few minutes later, Judith was sitting in her favourite wingback by the fire, warming Horlicks inside her, her bread and butter to the side and that day's *Times* cryptic crossword in her lap.

Yes, she told herself, it was all very well larking about the place catching killers, but this was where she was at her happiest. When she was at home, and safe, enjoying her own company.

She was studying at the first clue when there was a loud banging at the door.

Judith tutted to herself. Who could be calling at this hour?

The knocking at her door started up again, even more insistently.

Judith put the paper to one side and got up with a huff of irritation. Whoever it was had better have a good reason for interrupting her evening.

She went through to the hallway only for the knocking to get even louder.

'Hold on, I'm coming,' she called out as she slid the bolts open at the top and bottom.

She swung the door open to find a tall woman standing outside. She was about fifty years old, was wearing a long, black coat, had glossy dark hair that fell to her shoulders, and her tanned skin and heavy eyebrows gave her a Mediterranean look.

Judith had never seen the woman before in her life.

'Can I help you?' Judith asked.

The woman tilted her head back, her eyes staring directly at Judith.

'You're Judith Potts,' she said in an accent that Judith immediately recognised was Greek.

'What of it?'

'You're my step-mother,' the woman said, fire in her eyes. 'And you murdered my father.'

Fear punched into Judith's stomach as she realised who the woman was and her world collapsed.

Acknowledgements

I came up with the idea for this book at the Marlow Town Regatta in 2023 while talking to a fabulous local artist, Bee Skelton. (As further thanks, she gets a name check in the book during the Marlow Art Trail chapter, which is a wonderful event that's held every year here in Marlow.) Bee suggested it would be fun to use a painting as evidence of a crime rather than a more typical photo or video. And this gave me the start I needed.

But I soon realised that the murder I was looking for was going to need a flamboyant murder victim, and that's how I hit upon the idea of putting the local amateur dramatic society at the heart of the story. And here I had a dilemma. I live in Marlow. And when you set murder mysteries in the town where you live, you can either do lots of research and risk upsetting the people who so generously shared their lives with you only for you to say that they're potential killers, or you can choose to do no research at all. As I'd done lots of amateur dramatics at university, and have always been wildly in love with theatre and theatre people, I chose to do no specific research into the Marlow amateur dramatic scene.

So imagine my surprise, as I was finishing the second draft of this book, when I saw that the Marlow Players were putting on *The Importance Of Being Earnest* as their spring show this year. What were the chances? I'd been looking for a 2024 production of the play to see so I could help sharpen my memory of it, and here it was, only a short walk from my house. My wife Katie and I went to see it and it was an absolute joy from start to finish – with brilliant acting, some proper scene stealing from both the major and minor characters, and a full house laughing their socks off. I almost felt bad that I'd just written a book that suggested the Marlow theatre scene contained so many suspected murderers. Almost.

As ever, I need to thank my amazing editor, Manpreet Grewal, and literary agent, Ed Wilson, for all of their help with shaping this book. But my biggest thanks goes to my wife, Katie, and our two children, Charlie and James. Although this book is dedicated to Katie's mother, who very sadly died a few weeks ago, everything I write or have ever written is really for the three of you. Thank you.

Robert Thorogood
Marlow, August 2024

Turn the page for an exclusive extract
from the third instalment of the
Marlow Murder Club Mysteries

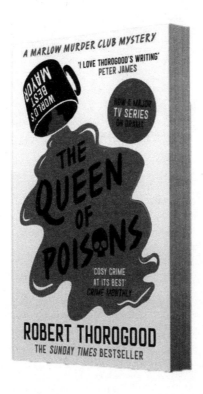

THE QUEEN OF POISONS!

Chapter 1

Suzie Harris was on a mission.

She wasn't sure she'd be able to see it through. In fact, she knew the chance of failure was high, but she was going to give it her best shot. She was going to try to sit through a Marlow town council planning meeting.

Suzie hated meetings, and the idea of a planning meeting seemed even more impossibly boring, but she'd recently come up with a ruse to make a financial killing, and she figured she'd need allies on the planning committee. So she'd decided to attend one of their meetings to discover who the key personalities were, how they made their decisions, and – most importantly – if any of them could be bullied into looking favourably on any application she later submitted.

The meeting was being held in the town council, a pretty Georgian house that overlooked the River Thames by Higginson Park. The entrance was a highly polished black door that wouldn't have looked out of place in Downing Street, and while most of the two-storey building was set aside as office space, it also contained an old debating chamber that was still used for formal meetings. Entering it, any visitor found themselves standing on a viewing gallery for spectators with a few steps that led down to a large room that contained half a dozen desks, filing cabinets along the walls, and a serving hatch that opened onto a little kitchenette. On the far wall, the town's coat of arms of a swan captured in chains was carved into a wooden shield that looked down on proceedings. Like the town of Marlow itself, the debating chamber managed to be both grand and pocket-sized at the same time.

On this occasion, a screen and projector had been set up beneath the coat of arms so the committee could better inspect the planning applications as they worked through the agenda. Suzie, having arrived nice and early, was sitting in the little gallery with a notebook and pen ready to write thumbnail sketches of the council members, detailing their strengths and – more importantly – any potential weaknesses she could exploit.

The first person to arrive was a man in his fifties who was wearing a pinstriped suit, blue shirt and a sky-blue silk tie with pink dots on it. He was broad-shouldered, had plenty of swagger about him, and his smile was so natural and effortless that Suzie found her heart gave a little skip.

'You here for the planning meeting?' he asked.

'That's right,' Suzie said, before reminding herself that she wasn't in fact a schoolgirl who found men attractive just because they had a sharp jawline. As he squeezed past her and trotted down the stairs to the chamber below, he lifted his elbows to show how very fit he was, before striding over to a desk where there was a pile of printouts already waiting.

'Are you here for a particular application?' he asked.

It was only at that moment that Suzie realised she hadn't worked out a cover story for her presence.

'Yup,' she said, if only to buy herself time.

'Which one?'

'I'm sorry?'

'If you've got interest in a particular case, it's important we hear what you have to say. What application are you connected to?'

'You know,' Suzie said, desperately extemporising, 'the one . . . on the . . . the main road. The big house – I mean, it's not all that big at the moment, but the owners want it to be . . . you know, bigger.'

Even ever-optimistic Suzie could see that her cack-handed explanation had confused the man, but before he could ask any follow-up questions, the door opened and a woman entered. She was about sixty years old, and whereas the man seemed to radiate goodwill, this new arrival, Suzie thought, seemed to suck the joy out of the air as she looked about herself. Her manner reminded Suzie of all of the many dry-as-dust teachers who'd been disappointed with her at school.

'"But soft,"' the man called up from the chamber below, '"what light from yonder window breaks?"'

'Don't be facetious,' the woman snapped, before wrinkling her nose as she squeezed past Suzie. 'Sorry, do you mind?' she said.

'Not at all,' Suzie said, already deciding that she didn't like the woman. She struck her as the sort of person who knew the cost of everything and the value of nothing – and the cost would always be 'too much'.

'Good evening, Marcus,' the woman said as she sat down at the desk. 'Have you any conflicts of interest you need to declare this time?'

'That's for the chairman to know,' Marcus said with a wink as he headed over to the serving hatch at the side of the room.

Suzie could see that there was a man in the kitchenette, bringing cups and saucers to the counter of the hatch. He was wearing blue polythene catering gloves as he put down a wooden caddy of teabags, and she found herself thinking that it really was health and safety gone mad that catering staff had to wear protective gloves to serve tea.

'Cup of tea, Debbie?' Marcus asked the woman as he took a cup and saucer over to a metal samovar that was sitting on the counter in the hatch by a Nespresso coffee machine that had a dispenser of capsules next to it.

'No thank you,' Debbie replied.

'Suit yourself.'

Marcus returned to the table with his cup of tea.

The main door opened again and a man entered, although he stopped when he saw Suzie blocking his way.

'Well hello,' he said with a nasal voice that managed to be amused, patronising and superior all at once. Looking at him, Suzie saw that he had thinning hair that he combed over his otherwise balding pate, and a long, pallid face that made Suzie think of a soap-on-a-rope that was nearing the end of its life. The man had about the same amount of charisma as well, she thought.

'Do you want to get past?' she asked.

'Don't mind if I do,' the man said, believing himself to be quite the wit, and then he pushed past Suzie and headed down the steps to the main chamber.

'Hail fellow, well met,' he said by way of greeting to Marcus. 'Debbie,' he added, and Suzie once again noted the superior tone to the man's voice.

'Tea, Jeremy?' Marcus asked.

'None for me, thank you,' Jeremy said as he sat at the table. 'Not unless and until the council supply us with the biscuits they promised at the last main committee council meeting. In their absence, I won't be taking any caffeinated libations,' he added, and then reached for a copy of the briefing notes.

'Well, if it isn't Suzie Harris!' a mellifluous voice announced from the doorway as Geoffrey Lushington, the Mayor of Marlow, entered the chamber. He was about seventy years old and he was quite short and plump, with a thick shock of unkempt white hair that surrounded a perfectly circular bald patch on the very top of his head. Suzie always thought he looked a bit like a gnome. A jolly gnome with an impish sense of humour. Everyone in the town liked him.

After the first time Suzie and her friends Judith and Becks had helped the police solve a series of murders in the town, Geoffrey had insisted on throwing a drinks reception in honour of the women. He'd said at the time that all local success should be championed, and no one had been more successful than Suzie, Judith and Becks. Suzie had liked him instantly.

'So what's your interest in the planning committee tonight?' he asked as he passed Suzie and trotted down the stairs.

'Oh, nothing much, Geoffrey,' Suzie said, realising she had to modify her cover story since her calamity with Marcus.

'Is that so?' Geoffrey said, heading over to the window of the kitchenette, sliding out the next coffee capsule from the dispenser and slipping it into the Nespresso machine. As he did so, the man in the kitchen turned away from the hatch, opened a little fire door at the back of the kitchen and left through it, letting the door close behind him with a clunk.

'Just exercising my democratic right to witness the committee in action,' Suzie said to Geoffrey, playing what she hoped was an ace card.

'Quite so, quite so,' Geoffrey agreed, as the machine poured coffee into a cup he'd put under the spout. 'Although you've not attended a council meeting before.'

'Haven't wanted to before now.'

'Fair enough,' he said, taking his coffee over to the table.

'Actually,' Debbie said, standing up, 'I think I will have a coffee after all.'

As she went over to the Nespresso machine, Marcus offered a glass jar of sugar cubes to Geoffrey.

'Sugar?' he asked.

'Thank you,' Geoffrey said as he plucked out a cube. He plopped it into his coffee, gave it a stir, and said to Suzie, 'Although, I can't help noticing that the last time I passed your house, you'd finished your building work.'

It was true. After having been left in the lurch by a cowboy builder some years before, Suzie had finally managed to get the extension to her house finished by signing up to a reality TV programme. As part of the show, the TV company completed the building work that had been left unfinished, but they also tried to confront the original builder who'd done a runner. In Suzie's case, all they'd been able to discover was that he'd wound up his company and retired to Spain. When the episode finally aired, Suzie had been a little disappointed when it didn't make more of a splash, but she'd perhaps over-estimated how much the general public cared about daytime home makeover television shows.

Nonetheless, the whole experience had had a happy epilogue. It was because of the conversations she'd had with the TV show's architect that she was currently attending the planning meeting. Not that she was going to tell anyone on the committee this fact.

'You're not wrong there,' Suzie said to Geoffrey. 'The building work's finished.'

'Wasn't there a TV programme or something?'

Suzie tried not to be offended by Geoffrey's lack of engagement with her television career.

'Anyway,' Geoffrey continued, turning to face the other members of the committee, 'anyone know where Sophia is?'

'She didn't say anything to me about being late,' Debbie said.

Geoffrey looked up at the clock on the wall. It was a few minutes past seven thirty.

'Well, I'm sure she'll turn up in due course. How about we get started?'

'Point of order,' Jeremy said, raising a hand.

'You're not doing this again,' Debbie said.

'We can't start the meeting without Sophia. We're not quorate.'

'Then you can't raise a point of order,' Marcus said as he stirred his tea.

'What's that?'

'If we're not quorate, the meeting hasn't been convened, so there can't be any points of order just yet.'

Marcus tapped his teaspoon on the side of his cup and placed it in his saucer with a smile.

'No, good point,' Jeremy agreed, trying to save face. 'Good point.'

'So how about we convene the meeting,' Geoffrey said, 'rattle through the applications as speedily as possible, and I'll get the first round in at the George and Dragon.'

'Not until Sophia arrives,' Jeremy said.

'I'm sure we can be quorate as long as more than fifty per cent of us are present,' Marcus said.

'That's not what the standing orders say. Debbie, you're secretary, are you minuting this?'

Debbie seemed to wake up from a reverie.

'What's that?'

'I said, are you minuting this?'

'Of course not,' she said. 'The meeting's not started.'

'So I call the meeting to order,' Geoffrey said. 'Item 1, the proposed addition of dormer windows to the first floor of 13 Henley Road.'

Debbie opened a notebook and picked up her pen ready to start taking notes.

'This meeting isn't legal,' Jeremy whined.

'Of course it is,' Marcus said.

'Jeremy, don't you remember what happened last time?' Geoffrey said.

'And there it is!' Jeremy said. 'Always patronising me.'

'I'm not,' Geoffrey said.

'He's really not,' Debbie added.

'And there you go, taking sides!'

'I'm not,' Debbie said, irritated. 'Chairman, please can you speak to Jeremy.'

'He's not the chairman!' Jeremy said.

'I think you'll find he is,' Marcus said, enjoying the bust-up tremendously.

'He isn't.'

'No, really, he is.'

'He isn't,' Jeremy said, banging his fist hard on the table. 'Authority is only invested in the chair once the meeting's convened, and *we're not quorate!*' he added with a fury that startled everyone in the room, including himself.

No one wanted to break the silence that followed.

'Sorry,' Jeremy eventually said. 'I've been under a bit of pressure. Don't know where that came from,' he added, hoping it could mend the fences he'd just smashed.

'I'm so sorry I'm late,' a breathy voice announced from the door.

Suzie looked over and saw a tall woman in her fifties standing in the doorway. She had rosy cheeks, straight blonde hair down to her shoulders, and dark eyeliner that accentuated her eyes dramatically. The woman radiated good health, and perhaps, even more so, wealth. Her hooped silver earrings, exquisitely cut summer dress and polished brown brogues made Suzie tug at the blue Aertex shirt she was wearing under her dog-walking coat.

'Hello,' the woman said to Suzie with the interest of someone inspecting an exotic animal in a zoo.

Suzie realised she didn't know what to say to someone so radiant, and the woman sashayed past her leaving the fragrant notes of what Suzie guessed was a very expensive perfume.

'Sorry I'm late,' the woman said to the others as she headed down the stairs to the chamber below.

'*Now* we're quorate,' Jeremy said in a voice that suggested he finally felt vindicated.

'Ah,' Sophia said, 'has there been a procedural issue in my absence?'

'Nothing we couldn't handle,' Marcus said. 'Now, can we start the meeting?'

'How are you, Sophia?' Geoffrey asked.

Suzie couldn't be sure, but did Sophia's smile falter before she answered?

'I'm well, thank you, Geoffrey,' Sophia said as she sat down at the table.

'A cup of tea?'

'No thank you.'

'Or coffee?'

'I think we should just get this meeting over and done with, don't you?' Sophia said with a smile, but once again, Suzie picked up what she thought was an odd vibe. In her notebook, she wrote 'Tension between Sophia and Geoffrey?'

As the meeting got under way, Suzie settled into her chair. This was her chance to discover who she should approach about her own planning application.

Sophia, she guessed, was far too posh and self-regarding to be someone she could ever influence. In Suzie's experience, people like Sophia didn't pay much attention to people like Suzie.

Marcus seemed perhaps a better prospect. She'd certainly enjoy getting to know him, she knew. But, again, there was a patrician air to him that put Suzie slightly on guard. He was perhaps too well-dressed, too pleased with himself – too much of a peacock. And she was pretty sure she'd have been far more capable of influencing him if she were a man rather than a woman. Or younger and prettier.

As for Debbie, she seemed such a negative person that Suzie knew she'd never be able to convince her to do anything as daring as her suggested planning proposal.

This left only Jeremy and Geoffrey. From Jeremy's outburst about correct procedure, Suzie guessed she'd never manage to influence him, so what about Geoffrey? The more she considered him, the more she thought he could be just what she was looking for. After all, he'd thrown a drinks reception for her, so he was already predisposed to like her. And he was also so obviously a positive soul. It also helped that he was chair of the committee. If she could get him onside, she was sure he'd be able to convince the others to go along with her plans. Yes, she thought to herself, things were looking up for her, they were looking up indeed.

As Suzie allowed herself to start thinking about a future of untold riches, she saw Geoffrey take a sip of his coffee, cough once, then choke quite badly – and then cough much more violently – and then he fell off his chair and dropped to the floor, where he lay entirely motionless.

Sophia was the first to react, crying out 'Geoffrey!' as she dropped to his side. Marcus, Debbie and Jeremy rose from their chairs in horror.

Sophia called out to the room, 'Someone phone for an ambulance!'

Debbie was finally stung into action, and she pulled out her phone, jabbing at the screen in panic. As she did so, Suzie started to head down the stairs to help, but Jeremy stepped across to block her path.

'You can't come down here, it's for council officers only.'

Suzie had the briefest impulse to push Jeremy to the side, but she could see that Debbie was already talking to the emergency services, and she realised her time could be used more profitably elsewhere. She headed back up the steps, pulling out her mobile and pressing speed dial as she went. It started ringing as she pushed through the door that led into the little corridor outside the debating chamber.

'Judith,' she said as the call was answered, 'it's me, Suzie.'

'Hello,' Judith said from the other end of the line. 'How are you?'

'Oh, good, thanks for asking. Much better than the Mayor of Marlow.'

'What makes you say that?'

'Well, there's no easy way to say this, but he's just died. I think it's possible he's been murdered.'

Discover the gripping and funny Marlow Murder Club Mysteries from the *Sunday Times* bestselling author. Now a major TV series!

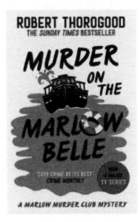

The Marlow Murder Club are on the case . . .

From serial killers to dead mayors and deadly drama clubs, the Marlow Murder Club are there to succeed where the police fail. So, join Judith, Suzie and Becks as they investigate crime throughout Marlow and come face-to-face with some of their most challenging cases yet.

ONE PLACE. MANY STORIES

Bold, innovative and
empowering publishing.

FOLLOW US ON:

@HQStories